THE ODYSSEY OF KATINOU KALOKOVICH

a novel

by

Natalie L.M. Petesch

© 1974 by Natalie L.M. Petesch
All Rights Reserved

ISBN: 0-934238-01-4

Published by

Motheroot Publications
214 Dewey Street
Pittsburgh, Pa. 15218

For information on ordering
contact Motheroot Publications

Originally published by

United Sisters

First Motheroot Edition, Sept. 1979

Cover: Virginia Tan
Typeset: Kathryn King
Editor: Mary Allison Rylands

Price per single copy $5.00
Mail orders add $1.00 for handling

...Life piled on life

Were all too little ...

Tennyson's *Ulysses*

... a man cannot tie himself or not with bonds that cannot
be undone. .... There is no way of making himself immune
to the different person that may come to life in him at any
moment ....

Doris Lessing's
Briefing for a Descent into Hell

TO MY MOTHER

Who
never owned
a washing machine
a dishwasher
a Hoover cleaner
or a fur coat.
Who
never drove an automobile
nor once left Detroit
after arriving there
from Russia.
Who
died there
At the age of 35
Without learning to read or write.

PART ONE

1

What she always remembered about her own girlhood was that her brother had entered into it as an infant. It was on that day her own childhood had ended. She was a tall, thin girl with eyes, they said, as green as a lizard; and already the pits which were to erode her cheekbones like antholes in the desert had left their mark on her face. Already that energy which characterized her, frightened other people. But she had stood then, herself motionless, frightened by that howling apparition, her brother Yasha. Weight nine pounds—a bomb of flesh tearing through her mother, Channa, in cataracts of blood and water (she had seen it all at home before the shrieing ambulance had carried Channa away). Kate had pressed her face against the glass in the maternity ward: fourteen babies lying in a row, each one swaddled in blue or pink blankets, like Easter eggs. They lay in their cribs separated from the world by glass: like so many potatoes, cabbages, apples in a grocer's window. Most were crying, their mouths watermelon pink; others looked lifeless, white as boiled egg. Still others had cheeks that seemed polished to a high cherry-wood finish, as though the womb had sucked their cheeks to this cordial-colored beauty before ejecting them into the world of artificial light. A few babies were black or brown tinged with coral, as if the strange new air of this world were already causing them to decompose before her eyes.

Yasha's dark hair was already curling on his brow; he scowled (at her, it seemed) as though the helpless cries of the others angered him. And she was always to remember him in this first rage, his small handsome face wreathing suddenly into savage wrinkles, like a perfectly mirrored reflection onto which a stone has been cast. Why was he angry? she had wondered. Was it because he would be a man and they had cut him into mortality? Altogether, Kate had decided, the gift of life was an astonishingly bloody one, both for the gift and the giver. She had thought she was glad she was not a boy till she realized with envious disillusion that Yasha's suffering, his trauma of circumcision was also a form of idolatry: for Yasha at once inherited their household.

In spite of their poverty (a subject on which her father, Jacob K., never tired of expatiating: his lamentations were Jacob's only reward for the terrible self-denials he taxed himself with, such as walking from the trolley stop instead of transferring, to save two cents), and in spite of Channa's trembling legs after a delivery which had taken forty hours

1

(*What a big head he has*, their aunts had exclaimed, as if even this source of Channa's torment were an added achievement on Yasha's part)—in spite of these things, a *briss* was held. A *briss* was held at which Jacob K., still young enough to be proud of what God had wrought in his name, spent nearly a year's income. True, everyone said things were getting better: hard times were really over. Nobody had thought that prosperity loomed in the form of a new war: but apparently any kind of prosperity was better than none at all, and so they celebrated: unto us a son is born. The wine was poured; uncles and aunts came from Chicago and New York. Channa had worn a black dress with an exquisite rope of pearls falling to her lap like a basket of heavenly fruit. Kate had wondered, even then, upon seeing the pearls, whether they were real—and if they were real, were they costly, and if they were costly, were they really "poor"? It was to be her first inkling that thinking alone, apart from action, could carry you far into certain kinds of knowledge. She thought about the *briss* and about the pearls for years after Yasha was born, and came to the conclusion (shortly before entering high school) that the reason she had worn Mama's old black dress to her one and only party was that they had not cared. By "they" she meant Channa and Jacob K.—her parents. It was a bitter admission, but too plain for her to avoid the evidence. They did not care. Therefore, they did not love her; therefore, they would not spend a cent on her—either for clothes or education. Nobody told her this. She grasped it, as it were, from the dawn of comprehension, from the cumulative impact of that moment when she stood outside the maternity ward, looking at Yasha's face flushed with what had seemed to her even then a wholly understandable and intelligent rage: who would want to be born?

Jacob K. tapped on the glass, waved peremptorily to the nurse; he was suddenly changed. The years of economic struggle lifted from him as a great weight. That boy was *his*, his commandeering forefinger seemed to say to the nurse, as though it was by the singular power of his hand that the boy was identified, not the flimsy piece of tape wound around the baby's wrist, small, smooth, thick as a plum, on which they had labeled him: Yasha Kalokovich, M(ale). The hospital had misspelled the name, but that hadn't mattered: Americans could never spell Jewish names. Jacob K. and Mama had actually considered changing their name at this time. Yasha would be a doctor (of course), or a lawyer. How could he go through life with the burden of a misspelled name? Jacob K. had suggested Kalokovich be changed to Brown, Miller, Jones, Smith: whatever people, by dint of hard repetition had learned to spell. But Channa rebelled. She had painstakingly learned to carve out the letters of her own name in pen and ink, sucking

2

on the nib of the pen as though she were drawing blood from her new literacy. And she absolutely refused any substitutes, feeling, she said, it might be bad luck—throwing God's gifts into His teeth, as it were. The image had wrought in Kate's mind a portrait of a god with great teeth, like a huge hare: He stood poised on a cloud, and as Yasha came sailing through the heavens, flung in His teeth, He seized the infant and put him back into a hat . . . . Kate later drew this scene for her second grade art teacher, calling it God, the Jack Rabbit; but her teacher refused to let the other children in the class even look at it. It was sacrilegious.

"Ah, he's a fine boy," Papa murmured as he pressed both palms against the glass in his urgent desire to get closer to the new Kalokovich. "He's a fine boy. You have a fine brother, Kate," he added to Kate, as if his earlier eulogy had been private and he conferred on her a now official caste. She was grateful, at least for the *Kate*. She had struggled long enough for the right to her own preference in names. Her parents had always called her *Anna*, insisting on ignoring her middle name, Katinou. The Katinou derived from a Greek friend who had saved Kate's precarious life by delivering her, apparently, on the floor of the Kalokovich bathroom. In enormous gratitude Channa had overcome her religious scruples at taking a *goyische* name and had allowed her middle name (to have a middle name at all was, apparently, allowed only in cases where the child seemed in danger of dying) to be—not Bashe, after somebody's dead great-grandmother—but the name of the Greek friend who had actually saved Kate's life, blowing air into her lungs like a blacksmith with bellows (Kate had always carried this image of herself, and once she had even dreamed of it, over a blacksmith's forge. In the dream, Alexandra Katinou-as-blacksmith stood holding her namesake, Kate, between giant tongs while fires blazed and life-giving oxygen was seared into her lungs). Her skin, too, was incidentally seared, cauterized into flawlessness by the flames.

"He's small," Kate said disparagingly of her brother.

"Small? He's *big*," Jacob K. contradicted her at once, affronted. "You should see some of those boys . . . They're so small, they can't even breathe. They have to put them in incubators."

"What's that?"

"It's so they can breathe. When they're *small*, they're just like monkeys. They're wrinkled; they can't see nothing. They're too weak to eat . . . . *He* eats already, like a horse. Two ounces, they weighed him after. Look, your brother, how handsome . . . . A skin like a peach," he added as if in apology, while avoiding her gaze: "But naturally all babies are born with skin like a peach. Peaches and cream, you could eat them . . . ."

3

"You mean, when I was born I was like *it*? I had a skin like *that*? He turned troubled eyes toward her obliquely. "What do you mean? Who said anything about it? You were born on the floor of the bathroom. You fell out, you rolled like a ball. She—the Greek, what's her name?—she picked you up. You were like dead . . . ."

She stared at him, sensing his evasion. It was one of those moments of insight in which all the previous knowledge one has been holding back comes crashing against the breakwater; floods of truth inundate one's consciousness. She knew then what had shaped her father more than having been born a Jew, more than having fled from Russia, more than having been poor and despised in this Land-of-Gold-in-the-Streets, even more than the brief bouts of tuberculosis which had come at regular intervals the way the rich take cruises abroad now and then, was the inalterable fact of his skin: that his face was a mass of scar tissue and holes like a sieve. He had survived smallpox but he had, so to speak, died of it. And his loathing for himself was at this very moment so intense as his hand ran along his closely shaven face that he dropped his offended palm and placed it back on the smooth glass.

"A picture, he is. With roses. Like myself. You've seen my picture?" He turned toward Kate, his gaze landing lightly like a *flèche* just above her brow; and the lightness of that gaze pierced her. She sensed that in his self-loathing he must find her own face unbearable.

Of course she must have always known that she had not been born this way. The change came when she was three years old. She remembered the day because it was early October, shortly after Yom Kippur, and she had been wearing the new patent leather shoes, so shiny she could almost see her reflection in them. But she didn't need to. She knew she was a beautiful child. Aunts, uncles, cousins, envied her her auburn hair, her milk-white teeth, her cheeks like fresh strawberries. Altogether an edible delight, what every Jewish mother believes in her heart she deserves: if not a boy-child to rule over her in her old age while she wilted with pride (my son, my son) then at least this apotheosis of eternal youth, a flesh and blood kewpie doll with a white ruffle at her throat, curls to her shoulders, and a mouth like a kiss. Even now Channa kept Kate's picture in a framed oval where it would be the first things guests would see, as if to say to them, See first, how her baby had been, then they would be obliged to understand that Anna Katinou as she presently appeared in the living room was Channa's misfortune, a misfortune from God.

Because it was also a Friday evening she had been allowed to wear her organdy dress and patent leather shoes, although the High Holiday was over. Besides, she was growing so fast, Channa said, let her wear it: she'll outgrow it soon enough and then who will wear it? (Her mother

4

had the idea she would never be pregnant again; because she had *not* breast-fed Kate, and nevertheless had not yet become pregnant—breastfeeding was considered a specific against pregnancy—her mother believed herself to have been cursed by early sterility: to have an only child was proof that the fault was yours, not God's). So Kate was allowed to wear the shoes. Because the streets were dusty, Channa had instructed her take a bit of vaseline and polish them till they shone (in retrospect Kate realized that this occupation was also to have kept her rooted to the spot till sundown). So Kate had sat down in the front yard. Even then she had been aware of some enormous beauty swaying across her consciousness, something special which loomed larger than herself all around her, a carpet of dandelions. There were not yet so many cars on the wide street which was later to become an expressway that it was unsafe for a child to sit near the curb. And Kate, bending to inspect the tip of her patent leather shoes became aware of a radiance, like yellow stars, glancing off the black surfaces. Not dancing shoes, but shoes dancing, she remembered thinking, and had laughed at the reflected spectacle of the dandelions in her shoes. She had then carefully created a lariat of dandelions and worn it on her head as a crown. The Indian summer breeze had blown around her, her holiday frock had glowed with a summer transparency, the organdy filtered the light like the wings of dragon flies, and the soft yellow flowers moved toward her, nuzzling her elbow. Years later, when she had painted innumerable canvases hoping to find somewhere just such a pure distillation of dandelions, she was forced to admit that it was something more than visual, that it had been a sense of union with these particular dandelions. Then *she* had been as perfect, natural, brilliantly-colored and incorruptible as these.

The crisis of joy turned out, however, to be the precursor of fever. That night she began babbling over her milk like a little tippler. ("What did you give her, Channa? Wine, maybe? She's drunk as a Cossack.") and by early morning she was dreaming or thought she was dreaming that on the black kitchen stove ricocheting hailstones of steam fell and hissed. They carried her (in this dream) to the back room where the potatoes were kept cool all winter, and there they slipped her, straight and stiff and two-dimensional as a piece of plywood, between bedclothes smooth and cool as butcher's paper.

And, of course, it had been no dream at all; it had happened, every bit of it, they assured her afterwards, astonished at her memory which had taken on these imprints, like an ineffaceable dye. Nothing serious, everyone said afterwards. All kids have these childhood diseases. But on Kate's strawberry cheeks, like a gratuitous curse from the angry gods had remained these harrowed pits, these slashes, like a fall of scimitars.

5

For a year after her illness she was quiet, withdrawn, slow to pick up new words. Pale and dreamy, she paid little or no attention to the relatives who came to see Jacob K. and Channa. Jacob K. began to refer to her (in Yiddish, of course, so that she would not understand: but she had long ago understood everything they said in Yiddish) as "the blighted one." He explained it to his brother, Moishe, by the fact that she had literally fallen on her head at birth: "She rolled out on the bathroom floor like a coconut. A dead one, she looked. Banging her head: that was it." One summer evening Jacob K. thought he had reason to decide that Anna Katinou was not merely stupid but positively not right in the head. He had instructed her to keep watch for the ice-cone vendor and to call him, Jacob K., downstairs when his tinkling bicycle came to their street. Anna Katinou would then have the ice-cone of her choice: strawberry, lime, banana, apricot .... All evening Anna Katinou played on the back porch of their tenement; from time to time she would run down to the street to see if the vendor were coming. When darkness fell and the street lights came on and still the ice-cone man had not come, she wept. Checking with neighbors who testified that the vendor had come just before sundown, Papa said she was *a stupid*: the man had been and gone long ago. It had been her responsibility, he said, to watch for the ice-cone man on his route. If she couldn't even do that, what good was she? Besides, the guy was a *goniff*, he sold them scrapings of ice with nothing but colored syrup over it and charged them a dime: here Jacob K. pocketed the dime. Anna Katinou screamed at him that he was a liar, no vendor had passed, therefore he *owed* her the ice-cone, and if not the ice-cone, then the dime, it was her dime . . . she would buy one tomorrow. But Papa insisted the ice-vendor had actually come, she had failed to carry out what he had instructed her to do, she was to be punished with no ice-cone at all . . . Upon which Kate became hysterical and screamed at him that he was a liar and a cheat: quick as a scorpion's tail Papa's hand had lashed across her lacerated cheek—only once, as though the cheeks were burning hot and he scarcely dared to touch them. Kate was sent to her room to howl with rage and to think over her crimes.

Soon after that, when she reached kindergarten age, Jacob K. automatically registered her for the Special Class. Their tenement was in a black ghetto where it never occurred to anyone to doubt the white Jewish parent's estimate of his own child: she had fallen on her head.

She had been left scarred and stupid from her illness. What could a father do? He shrugged, turned his own face away from the strong sunlight in the kindergarten and left Kate to the company of the epileptics, the stammerers, the mutes, the cerebrally-impaired—all herded together under the anonymous grouping: Special. (The word "Special" was used

6

to avoid the stigma of being retarded—though it was one of the ironies of *That Place*, as Kate was always thereafter to refer to it—that no one was so retarded as not to know that they were in that class because they were supposed to be dumb.) It was not until the second month in That Place, that Kate drew the attention of her teacher.

On this particular day Kate had noticed that The Twin Brothers (both of them afflicted with some sort of congenital albinism) were engaged in bitter fighting. The twins were usually listless, kept under mild sedation for being "trouble-makers," but on this day someone had forgotten to give them their tranquilizer, so they were now trying to tear each other's hair out. Both had very fine, thick heads of hair, and in spite of their albinism were rather handsome; but their vision was poor, they shambled when they walked, and their lips were thick and wet as bull dogs. They aroused in Kate a mixture of pity and horror. On this day they seemed determined to kill each other; the teacher was busy showing a bright-eyed and eager-looking boy how to use an abacus, as if she had forgotten, momentarily, that they were all supposed to be stupid in That Place. "You mustn't do that!" Kate had remonstrated sharply. "Dippy! Put down that stick!" she cried out, hating to use his name, but the cruelty of the times forced her to it. The boys were called Dippy and Dopey, as if like dwarves, they had no other name. Everybody pretended they were decent enough nicknames, like Dicky and Ricky . . . . When the boys refused to stop, Kate thrust herself between them, gave them both a resounding slap (something, at least, she had learned from Jacob K.), so that they turned away sheepishly. "What would your mother say if she saw you two killing each other like that?" she said, lecturing them harshly, her hands on her hips the way she had noted grown-ups stood when they wanted to give you a particularly impressive tongue-lashing. The boys may not have understood her words, but they looked at her hands on her hips and must have assumed she was someone with authority, for they cringed away in silence. Behind her, the teacher had been calling for several minutes, "Anna Katinou Kalokovich, what *are* you doing?" But fortunately, Kate had not heard her, and she had settled the thing before the teacher could reach the three of them. To Kate's surprise the teacher was surprised. Somewhat diffidently she came and touched Kate's hair. "Why, you're not. . . stupid," she murmured. "You're not stupid at all." What should have been obvious to anyone had been miraculously overlooked. Kate was totally deaf in one ear. However, due to the red tape of the system, she was obliged to finish off the half-year with the "Specials." By that time Kate had already learned to read at home, she never knew how she did it, which she thought was a pity because she would have loved to have shown all those bored Specials how it was done. The school quick-

7

ly skipped her to 2B when the new principal came and the whole thing was hushed up. Even Kate understood that it was not anything to talk about: there were people who were not above having second thoughts about you even when you were acquitted.

The scars on her face, however, could not so easily be skipped. "Nothing at all. She'll outgrow them. They'll fade. They're hardly noticeable already," they assured her mother. But later this incantation changed to, "Who will care? She'll find a husband anyway. Don't worry. Sooner or later they all do. With those eyes she could talk the Devil into braiding his tail ...."

So that, at least, was hers. She pored over her eyes, knowing they were beautiful. People said they were green, but she knew they were not. It amazed her that the whole world was more or less color-blind. Her eyes had more than five colors in them, but on her identification papers, as well as (much later) her passport, they were recorded as green. It was by this inability people showed at perceiving the differences in color that she became aware that her eyes were not only "beautiful" but that they took in most of what others left out. Other people judged their world simply by what they were used to seeing or by what was rumored—by primary colors, primary qualities (good and evil). But she was still too young to understand, however, that there were wide gaps between her insights and experience. The things she thought she knew were like those picture puzzles drawn by numbers; she had no dark outline of experience to link all these insights together into a meaningful picture: dog, five-pointed star, father, mother, brother.

What Kate did not understand for years, for instance, was that they were afraid of her. That the sheer intensity of her green gaze, her shaking rage when they questioned her "rights" ("Where does a Jewish girl get such ideas? Not bad enough she looks like a witch, she has these *ideas*?") frightened them. What were these ideas? They did not know, fortunately, where she got them, else they would have burned her books. How lucky one is to have illiterate parents, she thought, when after the *briss* she went to the library to find out about circumcision and discovered along the way, a whole school of thought arguing that she, Anna Katinou Kalokovich, was doomed to be motivated all her life by her desire to possess a penis. Although it seemed a weighty burden to have to carry, it never occurred to Kate to deny it, since she was at an age when anything in print held more validity than even the most empirical experience. If someone in a book had claimed that dandelions were black, she would have held her convictions in abeyance, waiting till she saw a few more dandelions. She was naturally not sophisticated enough to understand that when great men erred they erred

8

greatly. But at least she was lucky her parents could not read English. Jacob K., it was true, was fairly adept at *The Detroit Times* and *The Daily Forward*, but was never to carry his ambitions any further.

Thus she was able to read anything with perfect immunity, so long as she did not read at the dinner table where they could see her.

"Put away your book, Katie. It's not nice to read at the table," said Channa.

"You should help your mother set the table," said Jacob K., anxious to derive from the moment an inexorable rule of conduct for the future. Conversation with her father was always thus extremely practical, bearing upon her future behavior or reminding her of past failures: it was a kind of system of debit and gain, keeping moral book in a world of anarchy.

"What's the name of the book, you haven't put it down since you got home?" Not that her mother would have recognized the title; it was merely Channa's way of avoiding a heightened conflict between Jacob and their daughter. There was never any way of knowing what might be Kate's reply. A simple amenity could suddenly become explosive; her daughter, alas, was full of notions which Channa explained away as "typical *Americanische* ideas." How far she, Kate, was from the typical American girl her mother imagined she was, Kate could not have told her. She was only dimly aware of it herself, her first year in high school. But the myth of her Americanization was a myth she herself fostered, because it tempered the shock Channa continuously suffered in this country in which, apparently, she understood nothing, nothing, nothing: all was changed from "Home." While Channa was dreaming of finding a husband for her in a few years (if only they had more money, if only they could move to an all-Jewish neighborhood, if only Jacob would go to the synagogue regularly and get to know the young men praying at night), while her mother was dreaming of ancient rituals and wedding canopies Kate was already in a very real hurry because she had recently come across an old issue of an art magazine devoted entirely to Van Gogh and she had realized that, of course, the world already had all the yellow flowers it would ever need. So what would *she* Kate Kalokovich, do? She had discovered this special issue of the art magazine at Moe's Newsstand, which sold secondhand paperback books for a dime as well as old magazines and what were grandly called "Art Supplies." It was here that Kate secretly purchased her art supplies every week—a few colored pencils, chalks and tubes of oil paints. What she longed to buy was a really professional easel and a palette into which she could press her thumb with pride. But she dared not spend that much money; it would be immediately noticed. And the source of it would at once be suspected: every week she allowed

9

herself to steal fifty cents from Jacob K.—no more, no less. With the passion of inexperience she had decided that this bare minimum must suffice. She did not believe in stealing. She had been brought up to believe that certainly any man who took what was not his was a thief. She had never doubted the justice of Jacob K. who fired one black boy after another for pocketing empty beer bottles or slipping packages of cigarettes into his zippered-up jacket. Jacob K. had a dozen traps which brought these thieves to exposure sooner or later; and he never forgave them, never overlooked a "first time." Because, he said, if you let them get away with it, they'll steal you blind. It was the inexorable law of the establishment: catch a black boy with bulging pockets, and the next week there would be another black boy—preferably one without pockets.

It was therefore with many misgivings—not to say absolute terror—that she had decided, with the bright luminosity of youth which imagines its virtues ought for some reason to be rewarded—that she must have fifty cents every week for oil paints or die. She had many times specifically asked Jacob K. for this amount, using a word she had read and which she had understood to be a basic idiom with Americans if not their birthright—"allowance." But he had laughed in her face. Who had ever heard of such a thing—paying one's own children? Didn't he give her food and lodging and, during the school year, twelve cents a day for lunch? (It was this same twelve cents which had been going on alternate days for paints.) Hopelessly, Kate had realized there was nothing for her to do but become a common criminal. She would steal fifty cents every week. It was fairly easy to do, in spite of Jacob K's vigilance, even during the winter months when she was not going regularly to Eastern Market to shop for the store. She would simply impalm the piece of silver in one hand while she gave the customer's change in the other; then she would bend over quickly and slip the coin in her shoe. One per week. It was a silver-clad rule which allowed her to rationalize that she was no thief but an honest employee making out his own paycheck every week: or at worst, an unemployed artist receiving dole.

On the day that she had discovered there wasn't any hurry after all, that Van Gogh had already done it long ago, she had taken two of her purloined coins and gone off to Moe's Newsstand. In spite of her chagrin over those sunflowers which had stared up at her like some ghost from the past, she had felt buoyant, even joyous. She would hurry anyway, she had decided. There was, after all, the obvious danger that there were other things, things she had not yet even thought of promising herself to do, which might already have been done. She bought two tubes of plain zinc white, one of ochre, and one of black; and, after a

10

long struggle with herself, a sable brush with a fine stippling edge. Her weeks of hoarding were over and she had rushed back to the tenement house, her treasure concealed in a folded newspaper.

Fortunately, no one had been home. She had made at least three trips up the galley-like stairs to the roof. To her dismay she noticed that by the time she was ready to work her sneakers were black from the softened tar and her hands were coated with soot. She realized her main problem up there was going to be how to keep the soot and tar from saturating everything in a rainstorm of black dirt. On the roof she had found a torn and abandoned piece of tarpaulin which she set up as a canopy, tying it with clothesline across two smokestacks. It was a marvelous tent, with the added advantage that it was so shabby nobody would want it: it was not even leak-proof. She thumbtacked the butcher's paper (looted from Jacob K.'s store) to keep it from sliding, and with a great sigh of accomplishment looked around her.

Fear and trembling and sickness unto death. What was there to paint? Her joy in her preparations faded as she looked around her. Stringy clotheslines graying in the powdery air like the shrinking heads of old women. Smokestacks—round, black, extending for miles throughout the glack ghetto. Tar dripping like sorghum on the roof which was pitted with gravel, so that one wouldn't, like Tarbaby, get stuck forever on that melting roof. And red chimneys—an entire city of them—the bricks sutured together with a thick black mortar of dust, all rising into the sky like a vision of some strange and uninhabited planet. She had bought two tubes of white, but that day all she had used was the running blood-red of carnelian, and the near-bruise purpling black. When she had finished, her despair over the view from the roof had turned to delight. She had not at that time realized the importance of the alchemy that had taken place.

But her recollection, now, of that triumph caused her to smile warmly at her mother. "It's *The Interpretation of Dreams*," she said, knowing that the title would be meaningless. But she was grateful for Channa's intention, which was to distract Jacob K. from The Harangue. Like Humpty-Dumpty, The Harangue sat at the edge of her father's personality, ready at any second to fall and smash into rage.

"Dreams?" To her surprise her father laughed tolerantly. It was always surprising when he laughed. For then it was that his burnt-out skin became transparently pink as the blood rose to the surface; and the glow of geniality made him look pleasant and boyish: one could imagine someone loving him, dancing with him, anticipating his caress.

"Freud? It's a Jewish name?" her mother said, searching Kate's face, as if to say, of course it couldn't be a German name: she had faith in her daughter, and Kate might be "wild," but not yet so far lost to them as to read books by Germans.

11

"Ah no. Who needs them?" said Kate, feeding her parents' ethnic pride. Since she rejected most of what they intended for her, she felt that her, at least, it was a kind of compassionate honesty to give credit where it was due. "Freud, Marx and Darwin. Two out of three of the greatest minds of the nineteenth century: Jewish."

"Marx?" said her father suspiciously. He had not stayed to see the Revolution when he had fled from Russia; but he had been old enough to grasp the names of people who had destroyed the tyrannies of Russia —without, he believed, having substituted any better ones. He had learned from radio broadcasts that the country was in such chaos that it was not safe for him to return: they would seize him and either arrest him or put him into the army, he frequently informed Channa, frightening her as if his arrest were imminent: "You don't read Karl Marx do you, Anna? What do you understand about Karl Marx?"

In all honesty Kate was able to assure Jacob K. that she understood nothing at all. Last summer her attempt to swallow the nineteenth century trinity in a single volume had forced her to reevaluate herself. She had found them—all three—too difficult, and Marx totally incomprehensible. She had been led by her history teacher, Mr. Ardley, to believe that one could understand anything, merely by trying. He was a great believer in *free will*, was Paul Ardley, and he described to her how he had forced himself to read four hours a day according to the advice of someone named Johnson (she had thought at the time that this Johnson was a friend of his), and he, Paul Ardley, had managed to become a history teacher at their high school in spite of "the following facts." These facts were (he counted them off in an emotionless voice as if he were explaining to her the five causes of World War One): that he had had polio when he was ten years old, leaving him "as you see me," he added stonily, holding her eyes in his so that she would not look down at the heavy braces which bound his legs, but would see, rather, only his eyes; that his father had died two years later, leaving him and his mother to survive on Aid to Dependent Children; that before he was out of grade school he was already earning twenty-five cents an hour at Neisner's (which was on strike) as a scab supersalesman of onion slicers; that when he had graduated to a full-time job as a ticket-seller at the Fox Theatre at the rate of ten dollars a week, working from five to midnight, he had begun studying history at Wayne State . . . . His voice had seemed to her tremulous with some sort of pride or shame or hope, she did not know which; and she could not understand how it was he appeared so moved in spite of the fact that he told this story of himself as if it were only a mere footnote to somebody else's life—with an irony and comic despair that made it all seem as if it had never happened at all. "So . . . ." Mr. Ardley had concluded, if he

12

could read and understand Marx at her age, why so could she, "Anna Katinou Kalokovich," he said, plucking at her name as if it were some sort of instrument which he was, cautiously, putting in tune.

But Kate declared herself ignorant. She could not read Marx, she said. She found the language frozen, the concepts so vast and apocalyptic that they were totally beyond her comprehension. The only idea which seemed plain to her was that things were bad and would get a lot worse. In fact, they were to get so much worse that someday people would kill each other in their struggle for power. The idea of people in faded overalls killing others in wrinkled business suits made her wince, and it was, as it were, in consciousness of her failure to fulfill Mr. Ardley's image of her that she one evening picked up a book at the library about Sweden. After that she and Mr. Ardley got into terrible arguments. She declared herself a social democrat, and he said she was terribly naive and, besides that, a fool: Sweden was an underpopulated area of blond, blue-eyed Caucasians. What did it have to do with The World? He seemed to be in despair. He seemed to feel he had failed her as a teacher, exclaiming with frightening irascibility as he erased the pattern of Hegelian synthesis from the blackboard: "Not being able to understand is no reason for not being able to believe!" And this had seemed so ludicrous even to him that the tears of frustration which had begun to gather in his eyes began, instead, to shine with laughter. He stood in front of the blackboard leaning on his crutches; his face turned livid with silent laughter. "Mr. Ardley, are you all right?" she had asked timidly, putting her hand to his shoulder—fearful of touching him where he stood, for fear she might upset the perilous balance upon which he was poised, his crutches wavering as though the axis of his world were beginning to falter. He crushed her hand to his lips, holding the fingers with an intensity which hurt her, yet she accepted that intensity and was pleased with it. "Paul," she had murmured to her surprise: she had not even realized she knew his first name.

In fact, she had had no idea she was in love with Mr. Ardley. Mainly she had concentrated her adolescent daydreams on the boys in her class who were her own age; she would never have aspired after a man she thought of as a man old enough to be—not, of course, her father— but at least a youngish kind of uncle, like Jacob K.'s younger brother, Moishe.

Pale with fear, Kate now picked up the crutch which had fallen and handed it to Paul. He took it from her in bitter silence; a light glistened on his lashes.

"Damn . . ." he said. "Damn. Damn. Damn."

"Paul," she repeated.

They embraced awkwardly, his lips dry and hot. "Let's get the hell out of here," he said. She followed him out of the school building as meekly as if he had summoned her to write some historical sequence on the blackboard. As they entered the narrow gravel path leading to the parking lot, he motioned her ahead, single file. She could hear the crunch of his crutches upon the pebbles, the soft, regulated grunt of breath as he heaved himself behind her, the rubber-tipped ends of the crutches narrowly missing her heels at every step. She accelerated her step. "You don't have to hurry," he said quickly. "If you're ahead of me, I can pace myself . . . ." He swung the crutches rhythmically; there were seconds of silence when his legs did not touch the ground at all. It seemed an act of perpetual daring; like a man on the flying trapeze, he hung suspended in space for seconds; then, with a heavy swing he landed on the immovable fulcrum which bore the weight of his body. Kate listened intently between swings, waiting in the moments of silence for the slight expulsion of breath which signified that he had accomplished still again that tremendous act which she took for granted like breathing.

At the door of the car she stood, wanting him to tell her: should she herself open the door? But he insisted on doing it for her, one inert knee propped up with a kind of coltish, awkward grace against the rear door as he manipulated his keys. "Get in," he commanded softly. She leaped in, suddenly extremely conscious of her body; she found herself repressing an instinct to seem less agile than she was.

They drove in silence, watching the road as if at any moment tender fleeing animals might leap up and fling themselves onto the front of the car. She wanted Paul to make love to her, but it was something she could not say. She wanted to assure him that it would be all right, that she had every confidence in him, that it would be a simple act, one falsely exaggerated by centuries of myth into a mysterious ritual; she wanted above all to say that she did not believe in the artificial categories of vestals and scarlet women: but fear and a certain delicacy kept her silent.

Instead, they both accepted as a kind of necessary interlude the constraint and fever of kissing, the long drives through the northwest section of the city, the exhaustion without fulfillment. They were oddly patient with each other, as if they had known each other a long time ago, and now there were gaps, the explanations of reunion. Many evenings they were guilty of a kind of innocence which kept them sitting side by side while fantasies of love-making ran through their heads —when all that was needed was a decisive act such as picking up a phone, dialing a number, heading straight to the nearest motel room. But neither of them was capable of that. They separated every evening

14

—feverish and irritable with each other. Kate began to believe that Paul would finally reject her on the basis of her virginity: it had happened to her once before. One evening several months ago, after an unforgettable evening, a young musician whom she had met at the high school dance (she was not attending but merely watching), upon realizing that she was a virgin had dropped her as if she were a dangerous toy. The experience had left her with the conviction that virginity was a handicap which falsely differentiated her from men: by limiting her experience it limited her humanity; it therefore must ultimately limit her as an artist: she wished to be a part of all that she had met, not an innocent girl in a pretty frock, ignorant of life.

"What kind of a Marxist *are* you anyway?" she had challenged Paul one evening when they were about to separate again, their bodies exhausted, their minds empty of every thought but their singular obsession. "A fine intellectual," she chided. For some reason her words struck him in a way she could not have foreseen; he promised at once that the next time she could get away from the watchful eye of Jacob K. they would go straight to his house.

Kate stared around her in surprise at Paul's living room. She had not anticipated this immense space. Later, she was to understand that the wide floors were not a luxury but an absolute necessity—an extension to his cage . . . . Books lined the walls, that was what she had expected. What she had not expected was that the entire room was kept as tidy as building blocks. Everything was arranged with painstaking, almost geometric neatness, as though layer upon layer of existence—joy, sorrow, sickness, death—were carefully arranged in geological strata. The whole had the global neatness of a spider whose entire universe was inside this web; if he slipped and fell into its solitude, he would tear his house down with him. She was eager to ask him about the reproductions on the walls, but she did not want to use these powerful paintings as a Conversation-piece. Moreover, they had come to make love: there could be no other end to their absolute privacy. She managed to limit her curiosity to one or two questions, heard the names Daumier, Jack Levine . . . . The people in the paintings were hideous, yet at the same time she understood that they were beautiful. It was her first grasp of the principle of esthetic distortion as a deliberate technique.

Paul stood near the record player, his back turned toward her. "What . . . is there something you'd especially like to hear?" He bent with exaggerated attention to adjust the needle.

"No. *Don't!*" Kate said, almost angry with him.

He turned toward her in confusion, his face pale.

She scarcely knew what it was she was fighting against: some

15

parody of an idyll perhaps, which would reduce their intentions to the skill of a well-played sonata. "I mean, if you *want* music, soft light . . . *enchantment*," she added harshly in a voice so torn by the desire to do away with all fakery and phoniness that she sounded positively cruel.

He nodded grimly. He cast a helpless look around the room in which they stood, as if he were wondering whether it would suit their needs. In a final plea for sanity, in a wish to help her rescue herself, his voice ending on a laugh as if to show her he was only joking, that he knew she would not use the escape offered her, he asked: "How about something to eat? The kitchen? . . . ." He shrugged toward a large bright room in which Kate could see an assortment of aluminum pans hung from nails. Clumsily nailed, the plaster ran in cracks, like a runnel of sweat down the walls.

"Why don't you show me . . . ." She paused in terror. In spite of every effort to control her face her glance rested on his legs. Her voice dropped to a whisper. ". . . the rest of the house?"

She knew she was expected to precede him; she had learned that that was the way to avoid a sudden collision which might throw him totally off balance. He indicated with a glance the direction in which she was to go; she almost ran ahead of him into the bedroom.

Its barrenness was startling. The bed itself was unusually high. There were solid platforms bearing its weight up on four sides. The headboard was composed of a series of ascending slats, ladderlike; the footboard was the same, with heavy sculptured newels on either end, used, she understood at once, for support as well as for hanging clothes. There were long casement windows which opened onto a fire escape, but which seemed rarely, if ever, opened or washed. Sickle-shaped layers of dust made the glass seem laminated; a single cord hung from the curtain rod. From this window came the only natural light in the room. Kate's senses demanded light; she wanted to see everything; above all, she wanted to be able to see Paul's face. But her psyche whispered that he would prefer darkness. Without waiting for a word from him, with the daring and terror of a parachutist pulling at a ripcord, she yanked at the curtain.

"You don't like our view." he murmured ironically.

"All courtyards are alike," she said. "They're either square or rectangular: and opposite one's window are other people's windows, looking in."

He persisted in the same tone: "You don't want them to look at us? . . ."

She laughed. "I want the freedom to look at *them*. But they're not to look at *us*. Unless we decide we want them to." She stood gazing at him. He seemed to grasp her challenge, her avowal; slowly, with-

16

out a word he set his crutches against the wall.

He sat upon the bed. "Come here," he said, and then he said what she had been waiting for: "Help me," he ordered. She knew he was perfectly capable of undressing by himself; but it was his gift to her—that he would let her help him.

She watched as he loosened his belt. "Pull," he directed, and she pulled. She knew he was watching her face in the dim light, and she knew that in her determination to show nothing but tenderness and trust that all emotion had been removed from her stiffened face. He smiled sadly and unexpectedly caught her with his right arm. "Katie," he said. "Katie." His kisses fell on her in an awkward, oblique angle, on her ear, her hair, her cheek. The use of her name stirred her. She murmured a helpless cry: her ignorance was hurting them.

He dropped his head down on the pillow. "Kate," he instructed, his voice shaking. "Would . . . put those damned things on the floor?" She picked up the braces—shocked, not at their hideousness but their weight: that he carried these anchors of legs around all day long positively stunned her, so that for a moment all passion abandoned her. She turned to him in wonder; he was gazing at her with satisfaction: she had passed the ordeal.

She looked at his body, freed now from its metal prison. Slowly she began removing her own clothes while he put out his hand to ease her of her blouse, her brassiere. When she too was naked she sat beside him. Her hands lay on his body as though she were about to sculpture him from these rare new materials. Later she was to reflect upon how she had gazed upon him, her first lover. She remembered mainly her visual delight in his torso: the tremendous shoulders and arms, their muscles developed to carry not only his body, but his braces, his books, his crutches: his arms were the twin pillars which kept the temple from caving in. To balance herself Kate placed one hand on his thigh. At once the lifeless bone struck her palm like metal. She felt his abdomen shudder as though she had struck him a blow. She looked up; he held her eyes for long seconds with his. Kate waited, having faith in those tremendous arms.

For some reason, on that first occasion, he did not make any attempt to arouse in her what reference books refer to as excitement. It was as if they both understood that what they must perform was a delicate act which might be painful, but because of their concern for each other, both would survive.

"Caress me," he said.

She caressed him. What she must not do, she told herself, is cry. She had read somewhere that women always cry the first time, even when they were relieved to be rid of their stupendous ignorance. Instinctively she drew closer to him so that the shape and warmth of her body would let him know that she was not afraid. Suddenly his powerful arms, their muscles moving like rope, wove around her entire body; he lifted her, he smiled at her with delight. She smiled as if from a great height; then slowly he set her down. He stopped when she gasped with pain. Perspiration stood upon his brow. Again their eyes held. His hands tightened in a vise around her, resisting his instinct to press her like a butterfly on a pin.

"It's up to you," he said finally. "I'm afraid of hurting you." At the thought he closed his eyes, she could feel him shrink from her. She discovered tears of pain were running down her cheeks. She thrust herself forward. He held her to him with such intensity that her arms bruised under his touch. As she rested on him, her lips still trembling, she could taste the salt of his sweat.

"Poor Katie," he murmured. He seemed to feel very guilty.

Kate wanted to explain that it was she who, out of her intense need for freedom, had insisted upon this: that this necessary, even austere act of their coming together had liberated her forever from simpering hypocrisies.

"Did it hurt much?" he asked, caressing her back.

She lifted her face to his. "Yes. It hurt a lot."

She saw his relief at the simple truth. "One couldn't exactly expect it not to," she added lucidly.

He smiled. "You did well," he said, as if she had answered all the questions correctly at the blackboard.

She felt an immense pride in herself: she had wanted to do well. She considered it one of those things in life, like painting, which should be done well. It did not occur to her to wonder whether Paul was the one to judge such things: it was sufficient that in this *rite de passage* she had been given a high rating.

18

2

She roused herself from sleep. "I can't stay," she said ruefully. "They'll kill me." In the weeks she and Paul had been seeing each other, he had not yet become accustomed to the idea that she was accountable to Jacob K. for every hour.

He pondered a moment as if wondering who "they" were. "Your parents, you mean?" he asked tentatively.

Kate laughed at his innocence. "Do you think perhaps they'd approve? Maybe you should come and ask for my hand," she added lightly. But she was sorry she had said it. The subject of marriage was taboo, it hurt him too much to think of it. He had been in love once, while still in college, with a lovely Irish girl barely out of the convent, but the girl's parents had refused him on every ground except the real one: that they did not want their daughter to spend the rest of her life with a man who would never walk without crutches. Like Kate's parents, they perhaps dreamed of an ideal man for their daughter—someone with a prosperous business or respectable profession that would not keep him too busy, allowing them, the grandparents, to visit their daughter and her children regularly; a son-in-law who would be more than willing, on the holidays, to take the old folks for a drive through the park or around Grosse Pointe in his new automobile. (For Kate's father the configuration *son-in-law* always held in the background that which no poor man would have dreamed of in his Russian village, a shining black automobile, freshly delivered from the Ford factory where Jacob K. had once worked a seven-day week.)

"Why, what would they say, your father and mother, if they knew about us?" The phrase, *your father and mother*, struck her as peculiarly Gentile. She herself never thought of them in such biblical language: thou shalt honor thy father and thy mother. As for what they would *say*, the thought of Jacob K's reaction made her laugh bitterly. Paul sat leaning against the headboard, watching her with a worried frown.

"Oh, oh, oh," murmured Kate in mock terror, which was only partly simulated, at what Jacob K. would say if he knew they were together. Because she loved Paul she wanted to explain herself to him; she needed him to understand the kind of freedom she wanted, the sort of life she wished to escape from—a life so delimiting for a woman that nearly any act of independence violated some law. And above all, the Jewish law of her father's fathers, so fierce in its sexual code for women. Even a breach of propriety could bring the wrath of Jacob K.

19

down upon her head: a daughter of Zion, like Caesar's wife, must be above suspicion.

In her desire to express all this to Paul, she found herself explaining how a few months ago she had met a young man who was the only person (except for Paul, of course, she added, hastily touching his hand), with whom she had for a few hours experienced a sense of herself as a real person. This brief episode, a single evening, had at once precipitated a violent confrontation with her father. "This'll give you an idea,' she added, "of what *they* would say . . . Oh God! what they would *say* if they knew about us . . . ." She leaped up suddenly to sit at the opposite end of the bed so as to be able to look at him while she spoke. The soles of his feet, strangely no narrower than hers, touched hers, as though the oval space they thus created were a sacred ring they guarded with a barricade of their own bodies.

It was the evening of the high school dance. She had not really "attended" the dance: she had never been held in a boy's arms while dancing in her life. At home, however, as if in preparation for some unknown experience, she would often turn on the radio and dance by herself. She was too ignorant to think of dancing as sensual; she knew only that the music set her toes and shoulder to moving, that she invented entire choreographies as she slipped and glided and flowed, a slim bodiless girl falling away from herself. She did not ask herself what kind of music it was as she blended into it—waltzes, partitas, rondeaux, improvisations, her whole body spinning, falling, rising—it was a gift she had never suspected in herself; she had always thought of her body as being somehow like her face: flawed, awkward, unchangeable. And now here was this girl, fluid as a scarf, whose image flowed in and out of the mirror like water.

Her father, Jacob K., would often pass through the front room where she was dancing on his way to the kitchen where the light was better for shaving: his smallpox scars made shaving a daily operation as skillful as surgery. On one occasion Jacob K. stopped to watch her; a worried frown tightened his face. *"Meshuggah,"* he announced. "American girls are all *meshuggah."* But he continued watching. It was a May evening, she had left the windows open, the window shades up. Outdoors the branches of a sycamore scratched rhythmically against the trees. She had been thinking how she would like to paint a pair of green bears on a copper background: two dancing bears, embracing each other with awe and delight.

Jacob K. scowled, watching her now with a new suspicion. "Is that what they teach you at school?" he demanded. "To jump about like a lunatic?"

Kate had stopped short in the midst of a long ripening leap across

20

the floor. Her face colored in shame. She was wearing shorts and a bare-backed halter. She had never yet worn a brassiere and she felt suddenly that her nakedness was a disgrace. She sensed at once that Jacob K. had been as offended by her nudity as by her dance.

He added in disgust. "Is that the way a respectable girl goes around the house, half-naked, with the windows up so all the neighbors should see?" With a single angry lunge, Jacob K. had crossed the room, yanked down the shades, shutting out the green bears .... "What are you, a *knafke*, that you have no shame?"

Her cheeks burned. It was the first time she had heard the word *whore* applied to herself. She had worked side by side with Jacob K. in their store in the black ghetto since she was tall enough to reach the counter and she could not fail to understand that such an epithet was Jacob K.'s worst insult, a word he used for white prostitutes who slept with black men (even among prostitutes Jacob K. maintained a hierarchy of judgment). Kate stood in the middle of the room, trembling helplessly; her eyes filled with tears of shame she could not conquer. When, at last, with a hot look of dismissal, Jacob K. left the living room, she ran to her sanctuary on the tenement roof and wept for hours. She did not understand at that time that Jacob K. was protecting himself against an invasion of lovers: she had sensed only Jacob K.'s fear, she had not understood his jealousy.

She spent the rest of the evening on the tenement roof, refusing to come down: neither Jacob K. nor her mother ever followed her there because the ascent was difficult, even dangerous. She reached the roof by a series of metal ladders, the first of which projected from her own bedroom window as part of the fire escape. Once outside, she climbed the rusted, tilting rungs to the roof, a drawstring bag of drawing pencils and paper slung over her shoulder. Here on the rooftop, in the past year she had done over a hundred drawings in black and white, sketches which she did not keep at home but in her locker at school (she kept only books and drawings in her locker; winters, she lugged her heavy coat around to class all day). Recently Kate had begun to work again with colors—rich reds and yellows. She now began sketching Jacob K. as a tiger, devouring her. Of course it did not look like Jacob K., it was a tiger: but she knew who it was all the same. And there was herself, backed up against the wall, there too was the fire in the background, yet here was this foolish tiger, whose flame-colored body merged with the flame-colored forest, blocking off his own last retreat from the forest in order to take time to eat up this innocent girl. She smiled lovingly at herself as she drew a stick-like raggedy-Ann doll with taffy hair and a face smooth as a well-baked muffin: the muffin was about to be swallowed. That was all right, because in the very next moment the apocalyptic fires were obviously about to consume the jungle. Kate smiled to herself at the retributive aspect of these drawings; but they had an intensity which crackled with the throaty voice of a real fire.

The following evening, which was a Friday, Kate went to her school locker to store away *The Tiger* where Jacob K. might never find it (who knew what capacity for self-recognition tigers had?). She began gathering up her heavy books from which, over the week-end, she hoped to grasp that elusive St. Elmo's fire, Freedom-through-Education: *Geometry II, Literature for the Ages,* Xenophon's *Anabasis,* Caesar's *Gallic Wars,* and *Economics Made Easy* (she was on the "college track" though Jacob K. had made it clear there was no money for her to go to college). The combined weight of all these books was such that she felt she must be developing curvature of the spine from carrying them back and forth to school. There were times when the sheer bulk was demoralizing, she wanted to cry with physical frustration. She knew there were people who did not walk a mile or more to and from high school every day, but the idea of asking Jacob K. for money for transportation was so remote, that years later, she did not even remember having thought of it. It was while she was piling these books on her arms like a hod-carrier, that she heard the dance music and remembered that the seniors were giving a dance.

Kate had never heard a live band and the impact was astonishingly personal. The song they were playing was sentimental, but there was a direct appeal in the music: it said, *let's have a good cry and then love one another.* Kate understood that part of it. What she did not recognize was that the particular wooing softness, as of some small wild animal outside her door, was a muted trumpet. She did not even know such wooing effects were deliberate—she thought herself personally, and foolishly, vulnerable—in fact, just such an unpredictable girl as Jacob K. had always said she was.

Kate did not need anyone to tell her that Jacob K. would be strongly against what she was about to do, even as she did not need to be told that "good" girls did not smoke or drink or have babies before they were married. These concepts had never been taught her; they had simply permeated the atmosphere, learned from the harsh judgments pronounced upon those women who fell by the wayside: such women were never again regarded as anything but Women of Easy Virtue, upon whom there was perpetual open season by Men of Quality (that is, men who were engaged to "good" girls who technically preserved their virginity, whatever other liberties they allowed). But this certainty of Jacob K.'s disapproval only intensified Kate's impression, as she glanced into the gymnasium as a child might look upon a carousel at a carnival,

22

that she was gazing upon the happiest people in the world. They were dancing: clinging to each other's bodies as if they were the only buoys in a dissolving world. Couples were spinning, sweeping, diving, in the most fantastic shapes and combinations, their eyes raised to the ceiling as if all this greatness had nothing to do with them. Kate clung to her books as though tied to a masthead; she could barely refrain from hopping up and down to the beat of the drums. She scarcely knew what seized her rapt attention most: the brightly-lit gynmasium decorated with streamers, the look of concentrated joy on the faces of the dancers, or the embattled good humor on the faces of the musicians who joked and laughed and from time to time yelled out encouragement to each other and to the dancers.

"Go!" the saxophone player would yell to the piano man (he was actually a boy of about sixteen), and the notes began running like broken packets of nickels—quick and silvery, rolling, jingling, flowing among the dancers' feet. And the dancers bobbed and writhed and bent as if to gather up the music flowing around their feet; then with a jack-knifing movement of their backs, like divers swimming for coins at the bottom of a transparent sea, they flipped themselves away from their own feet, stretched their arms out to seize some unseen chord in the air . . . and began the whole process again.

Kate had forgotten herself in the enjoyment of this ballet; but now she was ashamed: she had never danced with a boy, whereas these girls were so cool, graceful, harmonious, so absorbed in the rhythm of the dance, they seemed scarcely to know or care with whom they danced. Marveling at their calm, Kate turned her attention to the boys.

They seemed very tall to her—fully grown seniors, graduating into Real Life. All appeared to her remarkably handsome. Some were blue-eyed, their cheeks flushed with a heightened sense of life. Others were pale, austere, dark-eyed, dancing with an introspective look as if they were listening to the rhythm of their own blood. Some were fat, but oddly graceful, using their weight as a kind of fulcrum around which they moved themselves. One or two looked thin and mean as hail-stones, glancing around with a tight little smirk as if to say: *this piece is mine.* And yet there was not one among them who at that moment was not a hero to Kate: because without a male partner she could not go out on the dance floor . . . She was at once consumed with envy of those careless girls on the floor who carried their bodies with a swing and a sensuality meant to reveal the secret they wished to reveal. There were moments, Kate saw now, when the bodies of the couples touched, when the imagined aplomb of both partners vanished: then a chemical redistribution followed, a constraint seized them, their dancing became for a moment awkward. Then the couple would move together as if in mutual understanding and sit for a while on the benches which lined the wall—the boy's arm flung across the girl's shoulder, the girl's breast just touching the boy's shirt. Kate watched as one couple dropped to the sidelines. The boy sat fanning himself with a dramatic self-conscious movement; the girl laughed, flattered, as if everything he did were a compliment to herself.

But now suddenly it was becoming painful to remain there, stupidly watching a spectacle from which she was as totally excluded as though she did not exist, could not exist, would never exist. The brightly colored dresses first blurred before her eyes, and then as if her effort not to cry had caused the spectacle to arrest itself, the dresses fluttered to a stop, drooped like flags. The musicians suddenly shot a crescendo into the air, a kind of lurching and self-mocking sob; and the set was over. The leader called out a break. The musicians began reaching for a smoke; the drummer knicked at his cigarette with his thumb and forefinger, as though it were a hangnail he were picking at; but did not light it. The trumpet player set his horn down on top of his carrying case and took a long-legged step down from the small stage.

"Not a bad gig," he said to the others. "Better 'n Memphis. And cooler here than L.A."

Kate was dazzled. She attributed the "superiority" of these musicians to the fact that they were not local, but had been brought from what seemed to her an immense distance (the band had started in Los Angeles and was systematically booked Eastward and back). Kate stared at the trumpet player, trying to imagine the life he led, which must be so different from her days spent at school, her evenings spent at Jacob K.'s store, helping him accumulate enough Savings Bonds for his old age, "the best security," her father always said . . . . Something of her wonder must have been in her eyes. The trumpet player stopped to look her over curiously. His hands wandered over his body, searching for a match or a cigarette.

"Say, Green-eyes, you got a match?"

She shook her head, numb with surprise.

His gaze wandered over her, as if appraising her books, her shoes, her face . . . . Kate raised her head defiantly, making no claims for herself. She was like a penniless shopper, with nothing to offer in exchange for attention received.

"Say kid, what's a pretty girl like you doing not dancing?"

She felt his intentions in the *pretty girl* were friendly and not mocking, as they might have been in a boy her own age, so she replied: "It's not *my* dance." She tried hard to force her voice to register disdain, but felt that her whole body must reveal her longing to dance. "It's for seniors."

"Seniors, hell. Dancing's the only democratic institution we got left in this here country. Put down those things, those *books*." He waved the delicate ash of his cigarette over the books like some sort of wizard, exorcising spirits. "Slick-man, play me a tune," he called to the piano player.

"But man," protested the piano player. "It's my break-time and I got to take a leak. Besides, what you doing there, Shaddy? That's jail-bait if ever I saw one."

"Shut up! Am I going to bed with the kid? Am I?" Shaddy demanded angrily. "I'm just going to dance her around a bit." And with a slightly self-conscious flourish, he put his arms around Kate.

He was a head taller than Kate, so that her forehead came just to his mouth. Kate turned her head slightly so as to be able to see his lips; they were two rounded seams; the upper lip was swollen, flushed from the mouth of the trumpet: they were the lips of a horn blower. It was hot in the gym and patches of sweat glowed from his soft cotton shirt. He wore no tie, but over the shirt he wore a kind of sleeveless green velvet poncho, wrinkled and not very clean, but still retaining the softness of velvet. As he drew her closer to him, she was astonished at the sheer physical daring of dancing: she had not realized, for instance, that dancers could literally feel each other breathe.

Because of the intermission the gymnasium floor was empty except for a few couples who took advantage of this extra piano time to float soundlessly together across the polished floor. She could hear behind her the slow *swish, swish*, of somebody's gown, like the lapping sound of waves.

Almost immediately Shaddy's body became taut with lust; she pretended not to notice it, but to her surprise she felt no embarrassment, only a kind of primitive pride and interest in having prompted so mysterious an impulse. Shaddy murmured appreciatively, "You're quite a little dancer: who taught you that?"

She felt guilty about the *that*; she wasn't certain he meant the slow dance step she was following with the docility of a blindered horse.

"Say, I could go for you," he said. He held her body so close that if Jacob K. had seen them, she would have been treated to the full clangor of his rhetoric on "bad" women. Kate was discovering that, in spite of Shaddy's clichés and the commonplaceness of their situation, she was flattered. Even Shaddy's language seemed properly vulgar, as though Nature had necessarily simplified Boy-meets-Girl to these bare elements: but they did not seem wicked.

"Can I drive you home, Green-eyes? What's your name?"

"Katinou Kalokovich," she answered promptly.

He studied her a moment, as if her name were something like one's

25

hair which had to be smoothed down in place from time to time.

"Can you wait for me, till after the dance?"

She shook her head. The break was over, the other musicians were calling, "Hey, Shaddy. Break it up! Back to the salt mines!"

Shaddy waved one hand behind her, holding her closer with the other. "Shut up, you bastards. Don't you know a nice girl when you see one?" She and Shaddy continued to dance. It was something expressly forbidden, she could see that by the looks of the other musicians. They danced one entire number while the band leader scowled down on their heads, swinging his baton slowly and deliberately over them. Finally he dropped his baton and leaned from the bandstand: "Hey, Shaddy, cut it out. Give the kid a break, will you, and get back on the horn, eh? For Chrissake . . . ." he added with disgust, and turned his back on them.

"Wait for me," Shaddy whispered. "Don't go way." "But I can't,' she said, terrified. "My father will kill me."

. She saw that he thought it merely an exaggeration, an evasion. "Aw, come on, don't kid me. What's your Daddy got to do with it?"

She had decided to wait for him; or rather there had been no decision. The logic of his question: "What's your Daddy got to do with it?' had stirred answers to other questions she had not yet asked herself. So she had waited, enchanted by the music, by the colors, by the wooing bodies of the couples whose mood by midnight had reached a new intensity: they now leaped away from each other like nervous insects, or leaned upon each other for support, unable to dance and waiting openly for the final tinkle of the piano to be released from the dance floor into erotic bliss.

At last the final set was played, Shaddy's muted trumpet played *Goodnight, Sweetheart* with such sweetness that Kate wondered if what she felt were "love." Then quickly, with what might have seemed an angry gesture, Shaddy locked his instrument into place.

"See you at the Metro, you guys," Kate heard him say, while they all grinned at him in a congratulatory way, as if what he were doing redounded to their collective glory.

"Right, boss," they retorted and the drummer gave a caterwauling whistle.

"Cool it, Shorty," snapped Shaddy to the tall, lanky drummer who rolled his sticks on the drum like a growing thunderstorm.

Shaddy stood before Kate a moment in mock astonishment: "Holy Jesus, you still got those books? Baby, you not gonna do *no* reading tonight." Then at her look of alarm: "Let's go put some food in our bellies. You like barbecued ribs?"

She looked at him uncertainly. "You mean spare ribs? Pork?"

She had never tasted them.

He doubled over with laughter.

"Well, I see you're about to *learn* something," he said, placing his arm around her waist so that his hand rested on her breast. She knew that she was supposed to turn her body away so as to resist this invasion (while gracefully inviting it), but after waiting for him all evening, such a gesture would have seemed to her hypocritical. So his arm still around her, they hurried toward the garage where he had parked his car. Here, he stopped to kiss her. It was a quick friendly kiss, almost brotherly; it was as if they already knew each other too well for public passion. He helped her into the other side of the car, carefully tucking her skirt in after her, so as not to get it caught in the door. His touch around her legs was light and protective.

The car seemed enormous to Kate. He appeared a little unfamiliar with it and flooded the engine. He explained that whenever they were booked anywhere for a week or two at a time, he rented a car. He added that a guy couldn't expect a girl to ride the trolley, could he? Kate was astonished. It had never occurred to her that a "date" might positively demand the comfort and elegance of a car. She herself would have been happy to ride the street cars with Shaddy. "What would your old man say, for instance, if I came up to your house with an umbrella and a brown paper sack and I said, 'Listen, do you mind if your daughter and me ride three buses and a trolley: I'm taking her on a picnic.' Wouldn't he kick me out the door fast, don't you think? 'A cheap sonofabitch,' he'd say. 'Get lost,' he'd say."

This was so far from what Jacob K. would say that Kate shivered with nervous laughter. She began to laugh hysterically, the tears filling her eyes. Again he tried the engine: "Say, I like the way you laugh," he said; and bending over, he kissed her again on the cheek this time, but still in that comradely way. "Easy to laugh, easy to love," he said, and clicked his teeth as if to a horse. "Come on you crappy old Buick 8, fluid drive, automatic transmission, with air-conditioner and heater included absolutely free: get hot or go home!"

The Buick seemed to clear its throat gracefully, "got hot" as directed, and within fifteen minutes they were at the Y'all Come Back Bar B Q—which was as astonishingly crowded as though all the banquets in Detroit had been postponed till after midnight.

Kate recognized the piano player and the drummer sitting together, their faces oddly dreamy and glazed, their mouths awash with red barbecue sauce, as if they had quite forgotten they were members of a well-known dance band and had reverted to being children. They threw pellets of bread at each other, sang out for the waitress, fought over the bottles of hot sauce and threw coins into the juke box like millionaires.

Shaddy steered her clear of their booth, saying loudly, "They're barbarians. Slick's from Boston, that's what's the matter with *him*, and Hubert—only don't ever let him hear you calling him Hubert—*Shorty*, I mean, he's a Mormon from Utah: they get that way once you let 'em out. Just pretend you don't see 'em. I'd take you to a *decent* place, but this one's open all night. And the food . . . ." Shaddy licked the tips of his fingers lightly in a way that made Kate laugh without knowing why.

But at the same time the phrase *all night* was a chilling reminder. What was Jacob K. doing by this time? Calling the police? Rousing the neighbors from their beds to tell them his daughter had not yet come home? The thought that at any moment Jacob K., followed by local guardians of public morality, might appear in the restaurant, might pull her from the booth, might rail insults upon her and Shaddy and literally drag her home by the hair—this sudden hallucination made her cold and silent with fear. She sat hunched over the menu without seeing it, her arms folded to her bosom. She did not leap up and run; but she was momentarily too frightened to speak.

Shaddy must have sensed this. He put his arm around her, spoke soothingly. Then slowly he read the long menu to her as though it were a mysterious litany. It had a calming effect; she even managed to smile somewhat at his absurd pronunciation, enjoying it.

"There's a girl," he said.

The truth was she had never before seen a menu from which people actually ordered and ate the incredible things she had seen her father sell to black people in the store: spare ribs and hog maws and chitterlings in metal pails. She had been told such food was inedible, fit only for "niggers." Now, having run through the menu Shaddy ordered for them both, two platters of ribs.

When the waitress brought them their food, Kate was amazed at her reaction. The smell of the freshly barbecued pork evoked such voluptuous hunger in her (she had eaten nothing since serving Jacob K. his usual Friday night supper at sundown), that she felt faint. Her mouth began to water embarrassingly. "Oh my goodness," she exclaimed inadequately, feeling it impossible to express what was happening to her. She scarcely knew how to eat such food—looked helplessly at her knife and fork. So she watched first as Shaddy set his teeth into the meat: the delicately cooked flesh yielded at once to his bite as though each rib were an ancient instrument on which the full savage mouth would create music. Kate then followed his example, making small humming sounds of pleasure in her throat as he ate. She was happy: she ate and gazed, ate and gazed, as though life were solely a matter of this great grotesque Art Museum to which one had brought a hot lunch. Everywhere there was the odor of food, heavy as incense; music from the juke box played intricate jazz patterns she did not understand on instruments she did not recognize; and in every corner of the restaurant were people, dressed as colorfully as if this were to be the last night of their lives.

Guiltlessly she stared at the people who inhabited Shaddy's world: women called to each other across the booths, they seemed to know each other well. They wore the most vivid clothes Kate had ever seen, vying with each other in an open competition of color. Even their hair glowed with colors Kate had never seen before—silver fox, bronze shades the colors of Indian corn, and plump purple lacquered to a high iridescence like pigeon feathers.

Kate had never before seen women guiltlessly laughing and talking together in the early hours of the morning, women who were not afraid or ashamed of being in an all-night restaurant patronized by blacks and numbers runners and night club owners and taxi drivers and prostitutes. Most of the women, she gathered from their conversation, worked at a nightclub nearby, were singers or dancers who had finished their "set" and were enjoying the nighttime equivalent of their lunch hour. "Come on, Kate, you're not eating," urged Shaddy. His eyes followed hers, and he laughed as if he were reading her mind. "It's a great life. See their nightclub tan. Pale as the Mojave desert. In the morning they look like the bottom of a Bromo-seltzer glass. Sleep all day, up all night. Me, I try to live regular even when I'm on the road. I go to the gym, work out, swim, lift weights, use the barbells." He showed her his arm which did not seem to her the arm of a weightlifter at all; there was still something childishly undeveloped about it. "Gee, kid," he added irrelevantly, "it sure was nice of you to wait all that time. I didn't hardly expect you to be there when I got through."

She blushed, feeling that perhaps she had been too open, too unassuming. She had waited by instinct, to please herself—not him: she had not understood that he too might be unsure of himself. She began listening to him now as she would to music whose rhythms were at once pleasant and predictable. Like a samba, she thought, Shaddy's Samba.

"Now eat," he said. "You look like you could use it. How much you weigh?" Then, without waiting for a reply: "You should take care of your body, your body takes care of you. The way I see it, we live on borrowed time."

She sat, somehow amazed at the resounding clichés. No, not a samba. More like those old-fashioned but high-scoring horseshoe rings the kids in her neighborhood use to play with. Shaddy would sit looking at her in contemplative silence while he arrived at some philosophical conclusion, then rrr-ing, right around the neck of a problem: "Bet

29

you never ate spare ribs before, that right? I can tell you don't know a thing about them. Here: let me show you." He seized a rib from her plate and with an agile feint, he began gnawing and growling at it like a puppy. The sheer impulsiveness of his comedy made Kate laugh, she had never seen anyone so spontaneous. The tears ran down her cheeks: was she laughing or crying, she wondered? Shaddy took her handkerchief and wiped her cheeks. "I'm gonna make you laugh, baby," he said. "I'm gonna make you laugh all over . . . ."

Although the food was delicious, she was too excited to eat much of it. People kept coming up to their booth. A black man yelled, "Hey, man, where you been?" to Shaddy, and Shaddy leaped up to cross the room and shake hands with him. From their brief words of exchange Kate understood that he, too, was a musician. Shaddy gripped the black musician by the neck with one arm and pretended to punch him with the other. "Why you sonofagun," Shaddy repeated. "Who let *you* out?" But he did not invite the black musician or anyone else to join them at their booth.

Suddenly Shaddy said roughly: "You want anything else? Some pie, maybe?" She shook her head, the idea of eating pie at two o'clock in the morning sounded to her like drinking champagne from a slipper or swallowing live goldfish.

Shaddy seemed irritable as they left the Y'all Come Back. Although, with a glance at the big clock, he had hurried her from the restaurant he now seemed reined in, uncertain. He glanced at her from time to time out of the corner of his eye, but Kate did not know how to respond. He took a toothpick out of his shirt pocket and idly put it in his mouth, then nervously, he threw it away. He put his arm around her again as he strolled toward the car. With great lazy movements he started the car, this time without trouble—scarcely looking at her. He did not ask her where she lived; instead, he drove out from the restaurant parking lot and drove idly around the block, his face a study. The street they were on was well-lit; a couple of black policemen strolled by, swinging their clubs rhythmically. Shaddy frowned and turned a corner. He pulled up behind a broken-down red truck which said on the back: Second-Hand Furniture. A-1 Condition. Clean Mattresses. Ice Boxes, Kerosene Stoves, Curling Irons. Like New.

When Shaddy had switched off the engine, he sat in silence, one arm flung back over the front seat. "Guess nobody'll bother us," he said in an assessment of the street. Behind them was an alleyway and a fire hydrant stationed near a vacant corner. She understood that the truck in front of them gave them privacy on one side and that the fire hydrant would keep drivers away on the other. She did not need to ask what this privacy was for, she understood that part of it very well.

What she did not understand was that after their first long embrace—her teeth set solidly against Shaddy's moist, open mouth, her hands set across her lap like a board—what she did not understand was that Shaddy knew from this more about her than she knew herself. He leaned back in disgust. "I *thought* so! Holy Jesus, you don't know a damned thing about . . . kissing!" The euphemism was in deference to her obvious ignorance. Ten minutes later he was gripping her as if he would like to break her in two for having led him on in this stupid way: Christ, what was he supposed to do with a virgin, and his first night in Detroit too? His ethics were simple: he would sleep with any girl, but he wouldn't take on a virgin. No, he refused to have that on his conscience. He shook his head ruefully. She sure put one over on him. He didn't know there were any goddam virgins left anymore.

His respect, awe, deference, were amazing to Kate. She would not have believed it was the same man she had met several hours before who now began to question her with great calm and seriousness about her life, her school, her plans, her age.

"Oh, baby," he groaned, "you too young for me!" He glanced nervously at his watch. "When's your birthday?" Kate burst out laughing; it was as if he were wondering whether he had time to wait around till she grew old enough to take to his hotel room. "What I want to know is, what were you doing at that dance anyway?"

"But I already told you. I came back to get my books . . . . I heard the music——"

"But I thought you were jivin' me."

She looked haughty. "Why would I do that?"

He thought a moment. "I don't know. Why would you? Why do girls do it?" he asked as if rhetorically. "Girls always jive you. They want to be persuaded, that's all."

"Persuaded?"

He saw that she could not grasp it. "Well, it's like this. They got to *look* like they don't want it, see? They got to *look* as if they don't know anything about it . . . . Then me, I come along. I act like I believe their jive. I act like I'm with it. All the time I'm slipping my hand under their skirts . . . ."

She felt depressed. "Is that what you were doing? I mean: pretending that you believe me?"

He agitated his arms, torn between a sense of the preposterous and genuine exasperation; he wanted to go to bed with somebody, he explained. But she was a *virgin*. So that was that. No hard feelings. Well, he'd pick up a girl on his way back to the hotel.

She sat stunned. "You mean . . . ."

He touched the back of his hand to his mouth. "Look, between

31

here and the Metro Hotel I can pick up ten chicks who'll give me anything I want for a five-spot, a Round-the-world if I want . . . ."

She was learning things every minute. She wished he would go on talking; the intensity of her desire for information, no matter how garbled (she felt that she could later unravel the sad truth from the comic exaggeration) overcame her fear of what would happen to her—the humiliations she would have to undergo when she arrived home (she was painfully aware of the lateness of the hour). Nevertheless, she would have stayed there in the car all night, asking questions: she had discovered in this man a fountain of Realism.

"What is that? A 'round the world'?" She asked it politely, as she would have asked her Latin teacher to explain the Ablative Absolute.

He explained. She sat quietly in the car, her mind attempting to cope with it all: there were women who would service a man with whatever devices he needed to lance the boil of his lust. Kate tried to imagine it, but it was beyond her: it was like trying to imagine a concentration camp, there was a point at which one's vision blurred.

"They do all that for five dollars? To anybody who wants her to?" She wondered for a momen if Shaddy were not some sort of compulsive liar. He assured her that women did—and sometimes for less money than that. The younger ones always charged a bit more, he added lucidly.

Kate stared. "Why?" she demanded, sounding very much like her brother, Yasha, who had recently become curious about sex. "Why are they willing to do all that . . . *work* for five dollars?"

He looked surprised. "Damned if I know!" He kissed her again, his full lips had become dry and hot. Then he pulled himself away with a self-conscious gesture which reminded her of one of Channa's friends who drank tea with their little finger out. "I'll take you home. You're sure one hell of a disappointment to me." But he did not say it as if she were a disappointment. He sounded like Jacob K. on Sunday morning, when he had flicked open the register to see how much the morning's take ran to, and it was surprisingly high. "Look I'll be coming back this way from Boston. We got gigs to do down-Maine a-way, and all along the Cape this summer. Then we head back. Depending on how long it takes, we should hit Detroit again about the last part of August, first part of September. You give me your address. I'll drop you a line when I know about when we're heading back this way."

"You can't. You can't drop me a line," she said. "I don't know where I'll be."

"What do you mean? What are you saying? Don't you like me, Kate? You can trust me, you know. I respect you, you know. I'm not the kind of guy . . . ."

32

"I don't know where I'll be by September," she explained, with a pride whose source she could not have explained. "I'm going to summer school. So I can hurry up and graduate. I've got to get a job . . . ."

He did not seem to understand the enormous repercussions of this. It seemed to him, apparently, a natural thing for a girl to do: she did not explain to him that in her culture everyone who could possibly afford it went to college, they did not "get jobs." She felt at that moment it would have been impossible to describe to him Jacob K.'s petty tyranny or her desire to be an artist—partly because she did not know herself how to explain what an artist "did." She suspected there was a paradox somewhere which she could not explain to Shaddy: she had said that she needed a job. That was simple enough, but how to explain that she needed to be an artist—which probably would have nothing to do at all with her getting a job? She was beginning to feel rather foolish when Shaddy showed that practical side of his nature which she was to learn later to respect: "Well. Go to the post office. Get yourself a P.O. box," he said. "That'll be sort of permanent, I guess?" he glanced at her interrogatively, but Kate only shrugged her confusion: such devices were altogether new to her. "O.K. then. Send me the P.O. number, care of this address." He scribbled his forwarding address on a card, flicking on the dashboard lights so that he could see. With a guilty glance at her he observed that it was nearly four o'clock . . . . Kate nodded her terror, begged to be taken home at once. Shaddy agreed: the unexpected turn of events appeared to have exhausted him, for he groaned as he twisted himself awkwardly back to the steering wheel. He began moving the car away from the curb at the exact moment the two black policemen they had seen over an hour ago turned the corner onto their street.

"Holy Jesus!" exclaimed Shaddy, pretending to mop his brow. "Good thing they didn't catch us a while back, else we'd *both* of us been booked!"

At the thought they both laughed, as if something delightfully dangerous had just managed not to happen.

She had not realized as she described her evening with Shaddy that Paul had been leaning forward from the headboard, resting his weight on his palms. He looked impatient, as if he had been waiting for some time for her to get her story over and done with; Kate flushed at her own egocentrism. She had not meant to lavish so much detail on her meeting with Shaddy, but she meant, or thought she had meant, to cast light on what it meant to be a daughter of Jacob Kalokovich. Something had gone wrong; she could see that Paul was angry, hurt.

He asked stiffly: "And what happened when you got home?" Something in his voice suggested that he asked only out of politeness, that it was not her suffering at the hands of Jacob K. which chiefly concerned him.

"Happened? I was beaten."

His eyes narrowed incredulously. "Beaten? How, beaten?"

"Beaten with a belt. An ordinary man's belt, with a buckle. That's where the goddam term comes from, *belted* . . . ." She had wanted to sound light-hearted, as if it had all happened long ago and she could now afford to be facetious about it; but her throat was tight with remembered humiliation; her words sounded choked.

But Paul did not seem to notice. Instead, he sat with a preoccupied air, straightening the disordered bedclothes as if he had just noticed them. There was a stain on the sheet which he covered with a pillow before resting his arm on it. Then from a bag hanging from a newel at his bedside, he took two rubber balls which he used for isometric exercises. He stared down at the balls, clasping and unclasping his fists at regular intervals; he knew the rhythm so well he did not need to count. Finally he looked at Kate, sighing heavily: "Well, was it worth it?" he asked. At her look of confusion he repeated: "Was it worth it? The punishment you took?"

The question annoyed her. She sensed what answer he would have liked to have heard, but she refused to indulge him. Why should she lie about that? Lying was one of the things she had meant to free herself from when they had begun this affair. So she replied, trying to sound neutral—neither defiant nor humble: "Yes. It was worth it. I'd do it again in an instant. *I experienced something I had never experienced before* . . . ." She was unaware of her emphasis.

"Aah! So that's what's important . . . . And in spite of everything, you'd want to . . . be willing to . . . be *beaten* for the pleasure of . . . ." He seemed appalled at her depths.

She tried to understand. " 'In spite of everything'?" . . . she repeated, breathing heavily, as if there were a mist screening his words which she could clear away by breathing on it.

"*Me*," he said sharply, as if reminding her.

"Oh." She tried to understand how she had got herself into this particular corner, but could offer no word of defense.

"You wouldn't have the least trouble going to bed with that guy now," he continued. "No petty conventions in your way . . . . Or should I say his? I've cleared the path for him," he added brutally. "He'll be back, that one. Did you get that damned post office box?" he demanded.

She admitted that she had. Months ago. As Shaddy had instructed her.

"Well?" He turned his back toward her as he carefully replaced the rubber balls in their drawstring bag. She saw that the muscles of his back were jumping nervously.

"Well, *what*?" For the first time since meeting Paul she was totally baffled: she was unprepared for this reaction to what she had thought was an honest picture of herself, of her life before she had met him.

"*And have you heard from him*?" he asked with such heavy sarcasm it was clear he thought her echoing question 'Well, *what*?' a mere evasion.

Kate was beginning to understand now of what she was being accused. She found herself trying to conceal the disappointment in her voice as she admitted that no, she hadn't heard from Shaddy.

"Tell me something," he said harshly, and his sternness frightened her. "Why are you here? With me? This very minute. Why are you in bed with a *cripple*?"

"Stop that!" she cried. "You understand perfectly well—" She could not bring herself to utter the word "love," It seemed too sentimental a word to express what they had experienced together. It cheapened their . . . friendship. Sorrowfully she dressed and sat in an armchair.

She had never seen Paul dress so quickly; he was in a positive fury to get back into his clothes, to put on his braces, to be as mobile as he could. As he tightened his belt around his waist, he turned toward her with controlled rage: "Now tell me: why did you *tell* me all that?"

"I don't know. I mean, *now* I don't know. I thought it was . . . . I thought it would explain to you about . . . how I feel . . . how I think . . . ."

"—and how you dance!" he gasped with outrage. "You wanted to show me . . . what *we* could never have together—the music, the dancing . . . ." He moved his crutches backward with a stomping gesture.

"Ah! . . ." she murmured, understanding at last.

"—and added to that, the sheer *commonness*, the unconscious display of . . . this cheap little musician's bodily charms . . . the whole sickening bit about the *dancing* . . ." he uttered the word as if it were obscene.

He was so convincing Kate found herself wondering if in fact his reaction was perhaps justified. Then she realized that whether it was true or not was unimportant: it was how Paul felt about it that mattered. She decided she should apologize. She had hurt him and she was sorry: she had failed to understand that a story tells as much about the listener as about the person who tells it. Even as she begged his pardon, kissing him, pressing her cheek to his chest, bringing him back to "reason" as people called it, she imagined a painting, calling it "Story-telling": two talismanic shapes on wood, like twin totems painted in white on white, so when the sun struck it, the white wood would reflect into space its dazzling highlights of the Imagination. "Let's not quarrel," she said. "Let's drive out to the country. Before the last leaves fall. I'll pack a lunch, what do you say? So much . . . healthier. *You* know all the answers to your own questions anyway."

"Yes," he said bitterly. "I know the answers. But I haven't begun to ask all the questions yet . . . ."

Kate pretended not to hear him. Instead, she began preparing a picnic as if this act of good will could heal the breach which had sprung up between them. Paul stood in the kitchen door watching her. Since his illness Paul had become a vegetarian, and he reminded her now to boil some eggs for their picnic. He would sometimes lecture her on the evils of putting flesh into one's diet. Meat, he explained to her now, was always at some stage of decomposition: the dying cells were there, only one couldn't see them, though sometimes one could smell them. . . He attributed the tremendous strength of his upper body to the discipline with which he regulated his exercise and eating habits. Over these, at least, he had absolute control. It was as if he harbored a secret delusion that his paralysis was a bad dream. Like "the State," it would eventually wither away and in its place would be the real Paul, made whole again by beige-colored soybeans and green leafy vegetables and the bright-yellow methionine of egg yolks. While Kate thoughtfully assembled tomatoes and prickly pear and scallions and cheese and black bread and olives, Paul observed that she was putting together a Renoir picnic, and he reminded her that *he*, at least, was not a golden-haired girl with silken tresses, and that he did not intend to *eat* that prickly pear, no matter how pretty it would look on the yellow tablecloth in the green grass.

"Who'd put *you* in a Renoir anyway, you idiot?" she laughed, relieved to see that he was no longer angry with her. "Just you wait and see what I really think about you, you Robespierre the Incorruptible." Turning to the blackboard they kept on the kitchen wall for grocery lists, she began sketching in chalk a cartoon of Paul-as-Marxist-Hero: Paul breaking forth from the oval of egg (labeled Thesis) into another—boiled—egg (labeled Antithesis), and rolling head first into a Superegg (labeled Synthesis): only to roll off the wall—humpty-dumpty—in the end.

Paul looked at it smilingly. He admitted it had a flair, an eclat, and she had done it so quickly too . . . . But he added solemnly that she ought not to waste her time doing cartoons, they were not her *real work*. . . . "Besides, it's all too serious to be joked about."

In silence Kate looked down at the boiling eggs: it was another one of those revelations they make when they tell you about yourself, she thought.

They drove to the beach in silence. Kate noticed that Paul was having trouble with the ignition and she began imagining a crisis in Paul's life which soon took on the clarity of precognition: Paul is driving through strange territory; it is night. He is surrounded on either side by long limbs of pine trees which seem to be holding the lonely stretch of highway together. Paul stands in the road, leaning on his crutches. There is not a gas station for miles; no houses visible. Only a long stretch of narrow road separated by a white line which reads every now and then: NO PASSING. There are a few bright stars ahead, but there is no traffic on the road. Paul begins to walk, to heave his huge torso forward, the crutches swinging. He is like a man walking into the desert with two pails of water swinging from the yoke on his back; when the water is gone there will be nothing for him to do but lie down in the sand, in a narcotic sleep. This image of Paul, hiking through the desert with a yoke on his back gripped her with such intensity that Kate began to regret that the whole day was to be spent in an outing—to wish instead that she were back on the roof, inhaling the cindery acrid air of the coal-burning ghetto furnaces: only to be painting this vanishing vision of Paul which had the strength of divination. What a strange thing, Kate could not help observing about herself: to be headed for a picnic—sun and air and clean water to swim in—and to be wishing oneself instead back into a kind of physical damnation, all for the pleasure of painting a little canvas before the intensity of the image faded. It was like cramming oneself into a telephone booth on a hot summer day to talk to someone you loved, someone far away whom you could never really get to talk to except while you were in the telephone booth.

"Looks like a good spot," Paul was saying, and she realized that the problem with the car had been a simple one. Paul had merely flooded the engine while trying to back into a narrow little road not far from the beach. She knew that Paul had been offended by her long silence, because he now seized their lunch basket and hooked it over one arm, allowing it to bump against his crutch in a way she knew he hated while he inched his way along the uneven path toward the water. It was only about five hundred yards, but the day was sultry, the sun seemed to boil the sky up into heavy cast iron clouds which stood clouted into space—rigid, insoluble. The sweat was running down Paul's back in two solid curves which meshed like interlocked gears at the base of his spine; there, the shirt greyed to a solid block of moisture. Still, he dragged himself on, too proud, even, to allow himself to gasp,

37

though she could see the quick rise and fall of his enormous chest. He left her behind, as far behind as possible—something he had never done before. Kate took it all as a personal rejection and found it hard to revive their carefree, picnicking spirit when they had finally reached the riverside and Paul commanded: "Just put the blanket down. It's too hot to eat."

They had hardly arranged themselves comfortably on the blanket when other picnickers found their spot. Slowly their small island of privacy was invaded: first by a grandmother washing off a little girl who apparently had been eating in their car and was now sticky with fruit juice and cookies, then a boy and girl, barely teenagers, dressed in bathing suits and loaded with fishing gear. The boy stood in the boat, balancing it with a leg on each side to keep it from rocking as the girl threw in their gear, their lunch boxes, and a couple of life preservers. Then the boy jumped from the rowboat, landing in the sand like a high jumper; he dragged the anchor toward the stern of the boat and gave it a powerful shove with his shoulder and knee. "Anchors aweigh!" he shouted with triumph, and leaped back into the boat before it could glide away from him.

Kate watched them with pleasure. Their joy was like a vibration in the atmosphere. They were so young, their skin was incandescent with heat; the girl's hair, sun-bleached, was light as zinnias, the boy's hair glowed black and iridescent. Kate turned to smile at Paul, as if to say how good it was to be alive and have the sun burning down upon and through them, as though some sun-god lusted after their mortal flesh. But Paul was not looking, either at the young couple or at her. He was busily setting up their little transistor radio so that it would stand upright without being overturned in the sand. He fenced in the radio with a tiny barricade of pebbles. When he looked up she was surprised to see that he had understood at once her sigh of dismay, for he said, "I never look at them any more."

"At . . . them?" Involuntarily she turned in the direction of the lovers who had gone off in the boat. Behind Paul, scrambling up the hillside was a group of children, pulling up beach grass and throwing it at each other.

"People at beaches. The damned fools who're always kicking sand in your face. They can't stay put. They've got to be running through your picnic, knocking over your stuff. This radio—I've had it fixed twice this summer. Sand's bad for radios, just like a watch. And these kids, they never watch where they're going." His voice faltered at what he must have seen in Kate's face. She felt as if he had taken her afternoon's joy, tied it to a stone and dropped it into the river.

Paul seemed to want to explain. As he spoke he gripped his left

38

bicep with his right hand in a fierce, rhythmic gesture, clutching his own arm so tightly as to leave fingermarks on it. Each time he did this the flesh of his arm quivered, horselike, then restored itself, powerful, printless. "This isn't as bad as the Boston beaches, of course. There you have the ocean. Like at Revere Beach. You have these big pebbles lying around. Seems nobody can resist a pebble. First thing you know people are throwing them around like tennis balls."

She was somehow surprised. "You spent a lot of time near the ocean?"

"We lived there. That is, *we* lived there. All year. Tourists and summer people came when it was warm," he added with contempt. "They turned us out of our own house every year. We doubled up with an aunt in the summer, rented our own house to strangers. The summers were always the worst."

Kate could feel the surge of energy in him. It resembled hatred in its intensity, but it was not hatred, it was desire, a longing so intense that it was in danger of congealing his blood, like the transfusion of the wrong blood type. Still, she struggled against understanding: "You didn't like your aunt?"

"Who? My aunt?" He looked dazed, surprised as if he no longer remembered having mentioned his aunt. "Oh, she was all right. But her house was a mile from the beaches. A mile to the beach, a mile back. By the time I got there, my armpits were sore. Like bedsores, you know? It was the friction. The salt water was good for me though. Even the walking, the doctor recommended it. 'Builds up the shoulders,' he said. So I'd go every day, and pretty soon the long walk to the beach became bearable because at the end of it I knew a special spot was sort of reserved for me, a spot of my own where I could be cool, quiet, *private* the rest of the day. It was right alongside this huge rock. Every day I'd spread out my blanket alongside that rock, in the same spot. I *loved* that rock. It was like a private room in a hotel to me—a private room in the middle of the beach. It was big enough to give you shade, I didn't even have to carry a pillow, the rock was smooth enough to lean against. It even had a kind of fissure where I could put things—a book, my sunglasses, you know? *My* rock."

He had arrived one morning to find his rock had been appropriated—by a pair of lovers, no less—"not too different from those guys out there." Paul waved his arm in contempt at the boy and girl who were no longer in sight. It had been a pretty cool morning, so he had decided to wait a while, to see how things turned out: lovers did not usually arrive so early in the morning. The bathing suits of these new arrivals were half-covered with parkas and there was a big sleeping bag

39

in *his*, Paul's, fissure, so Paul concluded they must have been there all night. Pretty soon, he calculated, they would scurry off to get breakfast, or to play tennis, or roam around the shops in the village—or whatever it was which took up so much of these people's time that they could, apparently, spend their entire summer on the beach without lifting a hand to do any mortal work.

So Paul had settled himself on his blanket about thirty feet away, determined to wait out the lovers and establish his right to the rock, once and for all. They must realize that on all this long beach that was *his* rock. He had slowly, theatrically, straightened out his blanket, laying his crutches down as weights on either end of the blanket to hold it down in the light morning wind. He had then taken out a book to read, prepared to stay . . . . There was a dead silence from the sprawled lovers; he saw them exchange glances, as though he had invaded *their* rock, instead of the other way round. From behind his sun glasses—which were surfaced with mirrors so that they could not see his eyes, but he was able to stare right into the glare of their faces, as it were—he watched their every movement, trying to assess his chances. They lay together entwined, the white and brown of their tanned legs resembling the laminated whorl of a sea shell; the sand clung to their thighs like sugar. The boy now began murmuring to the girl and Paul observed how the girl rolled her head at him. In recognition of his right to be there? Or was it merely an appeal? Anyway, it was clear they wanted him to go, he thought disdainfully, and as if in challenge, he arranged his heavy legs in front of him. In the clean morning silence he could hear his own straining as he breathed heavily over his braces; he was not at that time strong enough to lift his legs with one hand while supporting himself in the sand with the other: it was partly for this reason he had cherished the rock. It was always there at his back, strong, incorruptible, pointing skyward like a Rodin hand. There was even a concave place in his rock upon which the small of his back rested itself perfectly. Now and then water would lap close enough to him so that he could dabble his hands in it and moisten the sunburnt flesh of his upper body. He never removed his braces on the beach, but if he wanted to, he could turn his body around and cool the overheated metal in the fissure which was always shaded, always slightly damp.

He continued to sit on the blanket, staring at the lovers as from a hilltop; the morning silence was so penetrating, the few yards which separated him from the lovers brought their voices up toward him as from a valley. He heard the boy's voice express his anger with Paul: ". . . with the whole damned beach to himself!" *But that is not the point, not the point at all*, Paul thought, turning his sunglasses like a search beam upon the lovers. It was precisely that "the whole damned beach" was not his at all, only the rock was his. It was as if a part of him had slowly grown into it; during his life, as time passed before him like the endless waves which drenched the beach, he would eventually pass utterly into the rock: it was a memorial to himself, his cenotaph. All this was so clear in his mind that he felt it must reverberate like a horn through the scallop of sand which separated him from the lovers. He even tried thought-waves: perhaps if his waves were intense enough, they would get the signal and vanish: *"Go!Go!Go!"* he hissed at them silently, with such intensity it seemed impossible they could not hear. Perhaps there was not enough hate in his waves. "I hate you. You. Both of you. Go. I hate you. *Hate. Hate. Hate. Hate.*" This time, his passion or virulence or perhaps something about the set of his head with the sun glancing off his glasses with small metallic explosions, like radioactive rays, attracted their attention.

"Let's take our stuff . . . ." whispered the girl. Paul held his breath in triumph. He instinctively reached for his crutches, ready to move to his rock. He would smile at them, thank them: they had understood.

They had indeed understood; but their use of this knowledge was quite another matter. Instead of rising to go, as one might expect, with an apology and a rueful smile, the boy, with unexpected perversity, whispered loudly: ". . . give the fuckin' bastard what he's lookin' for . . . ."

For a moment Paul was apprehensive the boy would attack him. Paul was nearly twice the boy's weight, and he could, when necessary, wield a crutch with the concentrated, propelled power of a hammer— but still, the boy was young and wiry, with hard muscles at the stomach like a strong swimmer. And besides there was the inalterable fact of which he was only too keenly aware: that in a real fight, he was like a beetle. Once down he would not be able to kick his way up to a crawl- ing position on the crumbling sand. The weight of his braces could keep him pinned down to the sand for hours.

But the boy's vengeance had apparently taken on another form. If Paul would not remove himself from their sight, then the sight of them was to be shoved down his throat with a violence: Paul was to be treated as if he were in fact a mere insect crawling in the sand, who might irritate them, but not stop them.

". . . a fuckin' *voyeur*," spat the boy angrily. Paul noticed now a slightly foreign intonation, as though the boy's English had been learned abroad. Somehow this made the boy more formidable, as if there might be mysteries and moralities of which Paul were unaware; they did things differently where that voice came from. The harsh na- sality of the vowels ground like metal plates in the hot sand.

What followed struck Paul like a blow; they utterly ignored him.

41

Slowly they began to make love, removing their parkas and bathing suits as if in a dream, Paul's dream. The boy undressed the girl with a sensuous deliberation as if challenging Paul to do anything about it, as if to say silently, "Look at this and this and this, you'll never have anything like it, you crawling iron-plated scavenger." Then he turned his body slowly, pointing his erect sex at Paul as if in deliberate, flagrant insult. Paul sat watching, hypnotized by the spectacle, understanding also that it was an expression, not so much of their passion for each other but of their contempt for him: as though they said, he had bargained for this, and in their hate they were determined to wound him to the soul by darting these poisoned visions into his very eyes. The boy suddenly began to rock, moving briskly, his eyes on the girl. The girl moaned as if Paul were not only not on the beach but as if he, Paul, had never existed, could never exist; as if, if there were such a thing as Karma, reincarnation and lives to come, their eroticism nullified any possibility that Paul would ever have another form, could ever redeem himself into a new life: their moaning pulled universes around him, obliterating him utterly. In his shame and humiliation Paul could have beaten them to death—for their impudence, their prurience, their lewdness, and especially for their indifference, as vast and voluptuous as the rolling sea.

When they had finished (still without so much as looking his way), a mutual understanding permeated their silence. They walked together, their thighs seemed joined as if in a single motion, down to the beach. In the water, dipping and springing and diving like dolphins, it seemed they had actually, truly forgotten him.

Their laughter leaped into the morning light as though laughter too had a color, blue as the sky. The blue sky and their light blue laughter merged into a vast vault filling up the universe. In his rage, scarcely knowing what his intention might be, Paul pulled himself slowly to his feet (usually he used the rock) and made his way over to where the couple's belongings were strewn: their parkas and sleeping bag, a few clothes, a beach towel and an open beach bag, its contents shamelessly revealed to the world. He could see an opened spiral notebook and from where he stood could read in huge red capital letters the word, *WOW!* Several packages of contraceptives lay in the sand, their red and yellow tinfoil shining like fool's gold.

Using his crutch as a stick, Paul easily flicked the box of contraceptives away from the couple's belongings. Then, cautiously, his eyes on the lovers, he continued to flip the box toward his own blanket, using his crutch as a lever with each swinging motion of his body. Methodically he pushed the box of contraceptives to the outer edge of the rock, then with a single masterful stroke tossed the box like a piece of flotsam or seaweed onto his blanket. Then he eased himself down, grunting with the effort. Quickly, with short spadelike movements, he scooped out a deep hole, a spot which the rim of the tide might moisten but where the high tides rarely reached: he did not want the box washed away. To insure their destruction, he first emptied the box of contraceptives, shaking them into the hole like matchsticks. When he was done, he discovered to his pleasure that he had built a small mound of sand, like a child's castle. Calmly he took up his book and continued to read.

He remained there, audaciously, until the lovers came out of the water; then he folded up his blanket like a carpet bag and tied it to the rung of his crutch. Within an hour he had returned to his aunt's house.

That night he dreamed of the lovers, their bodies struggling together like Laocoon. They struggled so desperately that the very flailing of their flesh on the beach scooped out a small trench in the sand. Then when their erotic torments were over they lay motionless together as if in a shallow grave. In his dream Paul stumbled upon the motionless bodies and with a great thrust of his shoulder, like Sisyphus pushing a rock of sand, he covered them and fled.

In the morning he rose especially early, shoved a neat little sandwich and a pear into his beach jacket and make the trip to his rock. He knew he must arrive at his rock before the lovers: it was as if a second day of usurpation would give the lovers a certain claim to his rock. He had to break the continuity of that kind of claim.

To his relief he was the first one on the beach. His little burial mound was somewhat flattened out, the waves had washed around it peacefully. The sky was as clear and blue as a great intelligent eye. The sunlight lay gently on his shoulders. Into the fissure of his rock he placed his lunch, his beach jacket, his crutches and his book. Then he leaned back against the smooth shoulder of his rock, too peaceful even to read. He felt happy, triumphant. There was no vindictiveness in him toward the couple. He had been victorious, he had recovered his rock. In the warm sunlight he dozed.

When he awoke he was hungry. He estimated that he had slept a good healthful sleep of about two hours. What awakened him, as usual, was the gradually increasing volume of human voices on the beach. First there would be one or two cries, full of loneliness and delight. These would be the voices of the Daring-of-the-World for whom being the first to plunge into the icy whitecaps was a matter of personal pride. These were solitary souls, fiercely healthy, whose own company provided them with all the competition they needed. After these Loners came the mothers with small children who, having breakfasted their toddlers, found it easier to submit to the tyranny of beach-watching than to sit beside their cottages, babysitting. The mothers would bring buckets of plastic toys for the children; they would establish an imaginary circle out of whose boundary the toddlers were not allowed to wander; then they would sit till lunch time, leaning back on their hands, content to call time after time, "Come back here! Come back here this minute!" Last to appear on the beach were the lovers and honeymooners who usually slept late: *his* couple had been a notable exception.

What had awakened Paul was a mother calling sharply to her son: "Don't bother that man. He's sleeping." Paul opened his eyes to find a kid about three or four years old watching him. The boy was dressed in a neat little sailor's outfit with a jaunty French navy beret and he was staring unabashedly at Paul's braces as if he thought Paul were some kind of cowboy who had lost his horse or a space man whose activities would all be explained to him in a moment. The child would look at the braces, then glance out to sea as if he expected a boat or a plane or a space ship to appear to carry Paul away.

"Timmy. Come here!" his mother called sharply. But Timmy evidently knew that his mother, once she was settled down on the beach, would not get up to fetch him. She was hugely pregnant and must have found walking around on the beach tiring; she sat, not looking at Paul but busying herself with arranging a beach towel, a gallon-sized thermos, her large straw hat, and repeating as though hypnotic repetition would bring the child back. "Timmy, what did I tell you? Oh for Christ sake," she murmured plaintively, "*where* did I put that goddammed film?" She began emptying her beach bag of everything in it, finally flinging out onto the sand a yellow box of film which looked astonishingly like the box which Paul had buried not far from where she sat. Involuntarily Paul glanced at the burial spot, but he could not identify the exact area; it was now quite flattened out by trodding feet. The woman was rapidly shoving film into the camera as if her whole purpose in coming out that morning were to take pictures of her son. "Don't get any sand on yourself, Timmy. We want to send this one to Daddy."

Maybe, Paul thought, if he gave the kid part of his lunch, a cookie or something, he'd go back to his mother and stop staring at Paul as if he were an animal in a zoo and he had to stay and watch to see what the keepers would do to him next. Paul leaned over toward his rock and felt around inside the fissure for his beach jacket. He'd stuffed a few oreos in one of the pockets, just in case: he didn't like oreos himself, but he had discovered he could rid himself of Prodders and Sniffers (Dobermans and Poodles) by throwing a cookie as far away from himself as possible. He couldn't *throw* the cookie now, of course, but perhaps it would work with the kid anyway.

But his hand searching for his beach jacket touched nothing; it seemed, rather, to fall into space as one would fall into the shapelessness of an elevator shaft. Paul reached as far as he could, slowly, painstakingly—not yet so frightened as to roll on his side and peer inside the fissure: he believed he knew the size of his "storage space" to the millimeter. He now glared angrily at the boy, Timmy, who seemed somehow mixed up with the emptiness of his rock. "Move out of the way, kid. Move away will you? Get away from my . . . rock," he snapped, clenching his teeth as he rolled over on his side to get a full view of his space in the rock. He could now feel fear, outrage, humiliation, flow from his flesh in cold sweat. It was only by an act of will that he managed to control the terror that gripped his kidneys: they had stolen everything. He knew at once who had done it. No other persons could have wrought so cruel, so *knowledgeable* a vengeance. The sonsofbitches had waited till he slept; then, doubtless from the other side of the crack in the rock had soundlessly stolen his things: his beach coat, his lunch, his crutches. Robbed him in coldblooded, vindictive revenge.

It was a while before he realized that he was still rolled over to one side, his body still curled up as though in some terrible prenatal confusion. "Turn this way, Timmy!" the mother was still calling, her voice rising shrilly. Timmy shrugged his refusal, his eyes fixed on Paul, as though he were some giant from the fairy-tale world he knew so well, a giant with feet of iron who was about to crush the rock with his furious strength. "The bastards!" Paul cursed aloud, pummeling the sand till holes like eyesockets appeared beneath his pounding fists. "They took everything. Everything. Damn. Damn. Damn." Gripping the rough edge of the rock he managed to raise himself to a standing position. He stood there for seconds, reeling like some blinded Samson, his steel legs forming an immovable pivot above which his body trembled. Then he realized that the stupid woman opposite him was clicking her camera, was choosing precisely that particular moment to seize her son's transfixed expression of terror in those fleeting seconds before the iron-legged giant toppled face forward into the sand . . . .

"My aunt came later with her car," Paul explained, as if this were what chiefly concerned her. "I never went back to the beach."

But Kate was not concerned with how he had survived on that day. She was thinking: earlier she had believed she was describing her father's tyranny, when in fact she had been revealing her own sensuality, her passion for dancing, her attraction to Shaddy and to his way of life. Her story had worked like a mirror in which Paul saw her clearly, but she had remained invisible to herself: the mirror worked only for

45

listeners. Now, with an attention to detail most unusual for Paul, he had tried to "explain" to her his indifference to other people; yet what he had explained was not indifference at all: what he had revealed was an unremitting and covetous attention to other people's joy.

With a sense of exhaustion, as if she had learned more than she wanted to today, both about herself and Paul, she lay down beside him in the sand, so close she could feel against her lips his measured pulse. They lay in silence, breathing in the sunlight.

3

Because she was employed by her father, Kate was not covered by any of the labor laws she had read about: she had no social security number although she had worked since she was tall enough to see over the counter. During the summer she would come to the store with Jacob K. when it opened at eight and work till it closed at ten or eleven. Winters, they would tear themselves from their beds every Saturday and Sunday and walk while it was still dark—breakfastless—in absolute silence, the two miles to the store, their eyes fixed on the grey snow crusted with cinders which the tenants of Black Bottom had collected from their coal stoves. Some mornings they wore so many layers of clothing that they walked like robots, the half-frozen steel joints of their arms jutting out stiffly from their coat pockets. When they arrived at the main street of the black ghetto, an area which years later was to be torn down into an expressway, Papa would abruptly turn into the Greek restaurant owned by the husband of the woman who had delivered Kate into the world: Philo Katinou. Papa would buy a cup of coffee and a single doughnut.

Kate was allowed either pie and coffee or pancakes and coffee: never any variation—this was an unspoken but unbreakable rule. Although with her whole mind and body she hungered for the spicy sausages and eggs and corn bread and home-fried potatoes she saw heaped up on the platters for the black workers sitting beside her at the counter, her father always regarded their food with such invincible disgust that Kate believed there was something inherently bad about Philo's food. Only later did she understand why Jacob K. would not allow her to eat the meat in Philo's Restaurant. It was Jacob himself who supplied Philo with sausage, and Kate had once seen how it was made: after the green mold was carefully scraped from scraps of meat that were no longer visibly fit to be sold over the counter, the mixture was saturated with salt, pepper and sage, sprinkled with paprika and dyed with food coloring, then soldered together with pork suet, stale cracklings and whatever else was available. So her father's revulsion was based on sound principles of hygiene. It had not been the first time her father was proven correct on grounds which only he was aware of: like his indictment of certain widows as being "out for your money," or of the black prostitutes in the ghetto who "would let you do anything for a basket of okra." (Why okra? Kate used to wonder, till later she learned that most of the prostitutes were black women up from the

47

South.)

Although the winters were bad, the summers were worse; then the long days were interminable. On Saturdays, Kate would begin that bitter siege at the door to her father's heart which might or might not lead to freedom: she never knew in advance. There was no recipe for success, only Jacob's arbitrary whim, or the boredom of his old age. When he finally let her leave the store it was always as if he were not allowing her anything, but rather punishing her, it was so against his nature to let her have what she wanted. Anything she asked for, even if only the rare chance to go swimming was instantly suspect: *why* did she want to go? What profit or joy could come from leaping into the water with a bunch of kids? So on those infrequent Sunday afternoons when she was not so much set free from the store as dismissed for reasons she was somehow to understand were not to her credit, it was because she had begun begging, pleading, plotting, even weeping from early Saturday until mid-afternoon Sunday (which was the quietest part of the day). On those rare Sunday afternoons when she was finally freed to go, Kate would slowly (*slowly,* because it never did to reveal to Jacob K. how happy she was to get away), pack a brown paper bag full of cookies, taking only the broken ones which were hard to sell. Then she would drink a pint of milk. Papa was always generous with milk, because he believed that tuberculosis was their family's personal and eternal foe, a constant threat to their survival. He often reminded them that he himself had been "cured" of tuberculosis by consuming enormous quantities of milk on his brother's farm: milk, therefore, was the miracle drug of their family. Like poor Papa's other terrors—of bankruptcy, of imminent arrest, of deportation—his fear of ill health was not paranoid, but based on the bitterest experience: Kate's mother was now back in the sanatorium with "another touch of t.b." Whether it was that Channa's lungs were congenitally weak, or whether she had not drunk enough milk (he himself still drank at least a quart a day, into which he beat two raw eggs), he simply could not understand Channa's recurring illnesses, it was a mystery. But he never failed to remind them of his fear of dread bacillus, more powerful than the Czars of Russia, snuffing out peace, prosperity, whole peoples, with its silent breath.

There was one technique for putting Jacob K. into a good humor which Kate had discovered worked with a high rate of frequency, provided factors over which she had no control did not intervene. Unfortunately, it was her inescapable ignorance of these other factors which often forced her hand too early or caused her to affect a saucy, coquettish manner when she should have pretended to be abject and cringing before his show of power (her intuitions depended entirely on what she thought she read in Jacob K.'s face). This technique was most often successful because it was based on Jacob K.'s needs, not her own. He needed her to go to the Eastern Market early Saturday mornings to buy produce from the farmers, which he would then retail to the ghetto blacks (he had a few white customers, but they also shopped at the Eastern Market for perishable produce and did not patronize Jacob's Market). Since her mother's first confinement at the sanatorium years before, the responsibility for this Saturday morning shopping had fallen to Kate.

On this particular Saturday, because Kate wanted desperately to be with Paul the following afternoon, she had decided it would be best to begin the struggle for freedom early. She looked around the store with an air of super-efficiency, as of one who is irreplaceable and knows her worth (actually she despised the whole business and believed—mistakenly—that any idiot could be taught to haggle with the farmers for their bushels of potatoes wrenched from the cold Michigan ground).

"You're all out of eggs," she announced. "Those are the last few dozen I brought out of the refrigerator."

"So buy eggs," Papa conceded, as if it were really stupid of her to go through this inventory. But she knew he admired her skill. So she displayed her ability as though her cleverness were a kind of strong drink she must get him drunk with before she could get what she wanted.

"And lemons. But they were still too much last week. Thirty-five a dozen. You'll have to get a nickel apiece for each one. And you know how *they* are: they always want you to say, 'Six-for-a-quarter . . .' I'll get the smaller ones, they'll go faster."

A slow smile of involuntary admiration touched her father's cheeks without softening them.

"And what about potatoes?" She knew all about the potatoes, but she wanted him to see that she knew: it was all in the game leading to tomorrow's freedom. "Why don't I get a bushel? I'll get some of those little ones, you can mix them up with the Idahoes . . . . Or I can bag them up for you ahead of time, five pounds for a quarter."

"It's too heavy for you. How can you carry a bushel of potatoes?" He pretended to scoff at the idea, but she knew he wanted the potatoes. He wanted her to bring back the potatoes: but he wanted, also, to be absolved from the responsibility of having asked a young girl, his daughter, to lug potatoes through the streets of Detroit, "like a nigger." He even said it, as she expected (she thought to herself that things were going well: tomorrow she would be with Paul): "You want people to say now your Mama's in the hospital, your father lets you carry potatoes through the streets like a nigger?"

"I'll take Dizzy with me," she said, as if this would cancel out all

49

her own exertions. Dizzy was their black "boy." They called him Dizzy because of his admiration for Dizzy Gillespie, the trumpet player. "So you like Dizzy," Papa had said, without knowing who Dizzy was. "Maybe you're dizzy yourself," he had said and winked at the boy, as if this were a joke between them—an odd role demanded of Dizzy in which he was required at once to be the butt of the joke and the chief appreciator of it.

"We'll take the wagon," she went on to explain, as if for the first time—though she could not calculate how many times she had made this trip in the past five years. "Dizzy will lift the bushel onto the wagon for me. Then he can pull it for me. I'll just keep behind it. So people won't steal." Actually, whenever they came to a curbing, she and Dizzy would struggle together like a pair of mules to get the wagon, one wheel at a time, up on the sidewalk. Sometimes they simply risked the Saturday traffic and walked most of the way in the street. But she would never have said that to Jacob K.

After this sort of interchange with Jacob K., Kate would list four or five more items in season and then she would start out alone to Eastern Market. The arrangement would be to have Dizzy meet her later at a prearranged spot, so that he could remain working at the store till he was needed at the Market. By the time Dizzy arrived, the wagon would be full. A look of complicity would join them on their way back to Jacob's store—the black boy of sixteen, soon to be swallowed up by the army and sent to Georgia, and the high school girl who carried Shaw's *Intelligent Woman's Guide to Socialism* hidden at the bottom of the empty burlap sacks. She would sometimes be a half hour late and Dizzy would know then that she had spent this time leaning against the women's toilet, reading. In fact, Kate had a system for stealing reading-time, calibrated, she believed, to the exact minute, to be within Jacob K.'s credibility limits. This theft of time from Jacob K. was hardly calculated, it was an instinct.

Jacob K. now gave her ten dollars. She knew if she spent it shrewdly, accounting for every cent and every egg, as it were, he would be pleased. This was precisely the moment to add, "By the way, I saw Bessie Halpern at the Market. She asked me to go swimming with her tomorrow afternoon. Her brother's going too," she added, lying ruthlessly, for she knew that while Bernie Halpern was no prize, Jacob K. would be relieved if she married him because he was a Jew. Bernie's father owned a dry goods store on the same street and Jacob K. had known the family a long time: undistinguished, but "respectable."

"Swimming." Papa mouthed the word with distaste. "A big girl like you running around with your *tsitzkas* showing. Kicking your bare legs like a baby. You should be thinking about other things. How

50

long since you've been to see your mother at the hospital, she sacrificed her life to you?"

While Jacob K. said this, she had been making out the shopping list, using the only kind of paper Jacob K. permitted—a piece of butcher's paper which Kate tore from a roll like paper toweling. They kept fancy stationery in the store but whenever she wanted to use any, he would complain: "For one piece of paper, you're going to waste a whole box?" She had finally understood that it was a question of the lifetime value of the butcher's paper as compared to the lifetime value of fine paper. Calculated over, say, fifty years, the use of expensive paper was an extravagance, it could lead to bankruptcy or penury in one's old age. As she leaned over the piece of butcher's paper, blending her Gothic script with its surrealistic watermarks, she discovered that Jacob K.'s remarks about her mother had caused her hand to tremble. She had long learned to laugh, if painfully, like a clown or nigger, at Jacob K.'s idea of what a girl in America should learn to do: but when he impugned her loyalty toward her mother, she wanted to turn on him like a baited animal and bite him till he bled. To calm herself, she raised her eyes from the butcher's sheet and rested her eyes on the calendar—as if the number of days which remained to her before graduation would help her control her rage. But her eye was caught instead by the huge black lettering: WAYNE COUNTY FUNERAL HOME. ESTIMATES FREE. How much does it cost to die in this city? she had found herself wondering, and decided she would call up for a free estimate: perhaps she could afford one.

This grim reflection helped her through the moment. She was able to hang on to her wrath just long enough to remind herself, like a litany, that tomorrow she would see Paul. She and Paul needed desperately this opportunity to be alone. Since their last trip to the beach, a kind of cool discretion had settled upon Paul. It was as if he distrusted himself, fearing he had said too much, and refusing to speak freely to her again. Although it seemed to her that it was he who had changed since that trip to the beach, he accused her of not being the same. He would break away from her in the middle of a caress and say she was not thinking of him. "Of whom am I thinking?" she had demanded at once, with curiosity. For she had not been thinking of anything at all—only of Paul's head and shoulders, like a great psychedelic poster aglow with colors: his suffering blue eyes, the tortoise-shell flush of his skin. When he had accused her of thinking of somebody else, she had promptly begun thinking of somebody else. And since Shaddy Fierhazzi had been the only new person in her life in years, she had begun thinking about Shaddy. She had gone to her post office box twice a week to see if the promised letter would arrive. Once she had

51

received a card written in Shaddy's winsome mouthful of clichés: *Swing is king, baby. I'm raking in the chips. How's by you?* But no promise of returning to Detroit, unless this proof of his existence was to be interpreted as a guarantee, a sign, that he would return. Harmless as this postcard had been, however, it had driven a further wedge of silence between her and Paul.

But now her father was suggesting that the only possible pretext for relieving her from her duties at the store was so that she could fulfill her duty to her mother. With a twinge of guilt (or was it that Jacob K.'s artful methods were overcoming her resistance?) she admitted that during this entire summer she had not once been able to force herself out to The State-San, as in their wretched expertise they referred to that place which over the years had become as familiar to them as the Community Center was to local blacks. The State-San was bad enough to visit in winter, when the snow piled everywhere rose like a white barricade encircling the hospital and the winds howled from a scrawny wooded area not yet destroyed by the encroaching megalopolis. But to visit that death-house on a bright summer day was like willfully wrapping your head in a shroud, shutting out the sunlight and bliss of youth forever.

"Not tomorrow," she said hastily to Jacob K. "Tomorrow I've already promised Bessie Halpern I'll meet her at Belle Isle. I'll be home early," she added in desperation (he had clearly weakened her whole effort by his reference to Mama; she had not meant to offer to cut short any moment of that hard-won time).

But he nailed her to it, sensing his advantage. "What time? What time is early? You come home midnight these days, like somebody walking the streets. What kind of girl isn't in her own home before twelve o'clock? What will the neighbors say, they hear you coming in when the house is dark? They'll say now that she has no mother, she runs in the streets . . ."

"Oh for God's sake, Papa, you don't give a *shit* what the neighbors say and you know it!"

The fury her outburst evoked was more frightening because he made a visible effort to control it. Jacob's face reddened; a pulse, blue and bruised as a weal moved across his temples.

"Go!" he yelled, in a voice oddly low and hoarse. "Get out of here! Get out of here and do your work before I crack you with this hand, you'll remember it till your dying day!"

She fled, not daring to utter another word. Her hands trembled— it's not fear, it's rage, she told herself—as she unlocked the big wooden wagon which Dizzy had built especially for carting bushels of produce. Apparently some neighborhood kid had been sawing away at the chain;

one of the links was broken but whoever had tried to steal it had not managed to wrench it free   Too bad: it wasn't worth much, but it would have made some kid a fine toy. She imagined the wagon as it might look if she were to paint it all colors of the rainbow. On one side of it she would draw a black boy, hurling down cone-shaped hurricanes into a center of light. Then, inside the wagon, their faces showing above the rim, she would paint kids of all colors: brown, black, amber, rose: it would make a good poster, she thought critically, and managed to forget Papa as she began to worry again about whether her talent for posters meant she had less talent for Great Art: had Michelangelo ever done posters?

Although the wagon was empty, it was still difficult to get it up over the sidewalk curbing. She had been told never to ask strangers for help, they might misunderstand. Until recently she had not known what it was they might misunderstand. Her fear of the ghetto had never meant fear of the people who lived in it. Although the ghetto abounded in drunks and prostitutes, it was at that time still a relatively "safe" place. The drunks who sank to the streets in their own vomit, and wet their pants as they slept were more pathetic than intimidating. The female prostitutes often fought among themselves, but she had never seen them approach a white child in the streets, not even to talk to—as if their instinct was to protect the young from some sort of contagion ...

What Kate feared on these trips was not Darkness as such, but only a certain alley which, if she wanted to save time, she was obliged to pass through in order to avoid walking many blocks around a public housing project. Ever since that first time when she had discovered she was terrified—of the dim light, of the stench of rotting garbage, of the well-fed rats who nosed like domestic pigs in the piles of refuse—she had forced herself to take this shorter route. She never learned to understand her fear. Finally she simply relegated it to a vague concept which she called *natural* fear. But whatever kind of fear it was, she learned from it that by an act of will she could walk through the alley. She would do it each time, murmuring in a talismanic chant: *I am scared. I know I am scared. But I am doing it.* In this way she had discovered that it was possible to go on doing a thing even when it no longer made any sense at all: but that, nevertheless, some sort of energy or fragrance was created, as from a slowly burning wick.

This time, perhaps because Jacob K. had succeeded, by his psychological assault, in forcing her to think about her mother, she failed to go through her ritual-to-purge-fear. She did not want to think about her mother. Kate had found in the past that she could confront her father's contempt: that she could muster up against his will-to-power (over others) an equal will-to-contempt, thinking: *The son of a bitch is mistaken. He is mistaken about me. I am a real person and I will get out of this muck.* But her sense of identification with her mother was so intense, it was like being sucked into the sea; it left her powerless to resist Jacob K.'s allegations of neglect. Her mother had been a brave woman of unusual intelligence who, like hundreds of thousands fleeing Russia, had come alone to a city teeming with strangers. The courage of that effort made Kate think of some trapped animal who gnaws off its own leg to escape. Yet her mother had not escaped; her marriage to Jacob K. now seemed to Kate the ultimate entrapment, and convicted Channa (in her daughter's view), of some genetic fault against which she, Kate, must be eternally vigilant: Kate saw it in herself, for instance, in the way she held her coffee cup. Just like Channa. In the way her eyes narrowed with rage. Just like Channa. In the way, when she was nervous, she plucked gingerly at a torn hangnail till it bled. The fault was there: if she were not careful, it would surely get her.

On Sunday afternoon the struggle for freedom continued. They had a record-breaking business that morning. The store seemed to be prospering as never before. Black people from the neighborhood, and knowledgeable whites from the other side of the city knew that stores were open in the black ghetto seven days a week. They streamed in to buy items Jacob K. could never rid himself of during the week: it was as if a famine broke out in the city every Sunday morning. On this Sunday morning Kate had dressed more than thirty small chickens. From where she stood in the back room, dipping the chickens into boiling water, flaying them of their feathers with two deft swoops, she could hear Jacob K. joking with his customers. He always joked, something she had never understood. It was as if he had a *persona* which he wore for his black customers; but as soon as it was no longer necessary to play his role, he dropped his mask and allowed himself to be overcome by his hard life—the eighteen-hour workday spent exiled into the company of people he despised but whom he was obliged to cajole, cozen and even, sometimes, to caress, in order to persuade them that they too deserved to buy the Good Life. Once the store was closed, however, an archetypal bitterness would seize him and his conversation would fall at once into its familiar mode, heaped with scorn, anger, contempt for the blacks he lived by.

Now by three o'clock the usual lull had descended upon the store; summer flies buzzed over the bacon rinds. Jacob K. picked up Saturday's newspaper (he did not buy a Sunday paper because he did not think it was worth the extra money). There was a pay telephone next door in Philo's Restaurant; but instead of asking outright whether she was free to go swimming with Bessie Halpern, Kate now announced in a low, neutral tone, as if she did not want to disturb Papa at his newspaper, that she was about to go and telephone Bessie Halpern. This would be interpreted as a signal. At this moment if Jacob K. had already decided she was not to be allowed to leave the store, then it would be his choice to grumble: "Where are you going? You're running off to chatter with your friends on the telephone. There's plenty of time to chatter all week long. Pretty soon people will come. There'll be another rush for supper." If, however, he nodded as if he were indifferent (Kate knew that he was never indifferent to the loss of "help" in the store), then it was understood that she might take another step toward freedom. She might now hook her swim suit under an index finger and with a great show of *expecting* to be liberated (to show the least shadow of doubt was to sacrifice all previous effort) she would force herself to slowly sip a half-pint of milk while her throat constricted with anguish at the possibility that a half-dozen customers might suddenly come in . . . . At this crucial point, she was still far from free: it was still Jacob K.'s prerogative to look surprised at the entire dumb show, as if he had not seen any of it, and with a look of reproach would command her to put away that foolish swim suit and "all her other notions along with it—they were going to have a really busy afternoon . . . ."

This afternoon, fortunately, no one came in. The flies continued to buzz. Jacob K., absorbed or pretending to be absorbed in his newspaper, might scarcely raise his head as she tried airily to dismiss herself: "Well. Bye . . . See you tonight."

"*Tonight?*" An unfortunate choice of words. She cursed her glib and thoughtless tongue. Her fate now hung on their definition of time.

"Well. Evening then. Later. Whatever you want to call it." She tried, in spite of her fear, to laugh. "You know this crazy language. How can anyone tell time by it?" *Success.* She saw his small mouth pucker with satisfaction. It was a crazy language, but he had mastered it. People were always commenting on the fact that although he had never been to school, he could read newspapers and could calculate a whole year's profit and loss in his head.

"O.K. Evening by you is Late-at-night by me. What time are you coming home? Now your mother's not home, don't think you can tramp around Belle Isle till all hours . . . ."

Her answer, casual as it must seem, required the flattery of a courtier and the cunning of a courtesan. "Oh, say, suppertime. We're not bothering to take a picnic. The Halperns are too stingy to let Bessie carry anything away from home. You know how they are . . . . So, I'll be back in time to fix us a nice snack before you go to bed . . . . Do you have plenty of herring in the fridge?" She pretended to check the supply of marinated herring, her heart beating fast with an anxious desire for freedom, for Paul, for something better than this jolting punch-and-judy theater of tyrannies with real puppets.

"*Nu*, get started. You talk so much you'll never catch the bus. And tomorrow early, don't forget. You should visit your mother, you haven't been in three months . . . ."

Victory. What better proof of her absolute devotion than to have been thinking specifically of his, Jacob K.'s, delights at the moment before embarking on one of her useless adolescent pleasures? The bit about Mama, Kate understood, was a mere broom, sweeping her expertly out the door with a final fall of dirt on her conscience: so that, after all, the final victory would be his.

Ridiculous and petty as these scenes with her father always were, they taught her early something about the nature of power which she was never to forget. She was often, later, to hear among her intellectual friends, thoughtful and provocative variations of the theme that Power Corrupts. But from Jacob K. she learned that powerlessness too corrupts. Having no authority over any peons, being only one man with one vote and with very little money compared to the robber barons of the world, Kalokovich exerted a power over his family as absolute as that of a Czar, a power made more fierce and repressive because he knew that its reign was due to be overthrown by adolescent revolution.

4

It was a long ride out to Paul's house and by the time she arrived she was thoroughly tired—hot and thirsty. The temperature had been near ninety all day.

The air was still clean and relatively cool in Paul's section of the city; there was even a proliferation of weeds on untended lots which gave the neighborhood an air of spaciousness. Paul's house was surprisingly well cared-for. It struck her that that neat little lawn and the trimmed hedges must be paid for regularly. This realization reminded her also, as if it were something new which had to be dealt with but which she refused to face up to, that Paul had to hire someone for nearly every service of his life: stoke the furnace, wash the windows, varnish the floors, care for his car. Now he was thinking of buying the home in which he had been living; he explained that he could then nail things up or tear things down to his taste. He was also thinking, he had said, of buying the two properties across the street from him. Without meaning to they had got into a quarrel about property and heirs which had bordered on a personal crisis. Paul refused to see any contradiction between being a landlord in the capitalist system and being a Marxist. When Kate had remained silent at what had seemed to her a rationalization—she had no argument against Paul's clear need for as much economic security as he could get—he had become excited and rhetorical and insisted that it was only the inheritance of property which should be done away with.

"Well what about your heirs? Don't you want your children to have . . . these houses?" She waved her hand vaguely in the direction of the properties.

"I don't plan to have children. Ever," he had replied at once. It was not something Kate was accustomed to hearing from people, and when she had looked at him in surprise, he had added: "For God's sake, Kate, what would I do with kids to support? Haven't I got enough trouble?"

At the time she had wanted to talk more about it, but she was afraid that such talk would lead to a discussion of marriage—something they both avoided. The thought of being bound up in husband, home and children did not attract her (she thought perhaps she was too young); and as for Paul, he was in his own way so shackled by his physical handicap that any discussion of taking on further responsibilities could only humiliate him. So there was a tacit agreement between

57

them that marriage was a subject for the conventional middle class—or for sentimental teenagers; but that for them to discuss their love affair in terms of the future would be idle and hypocritical. They trusted each other, they learned from each other, they needed each other, she thought. For the moment that would have to be enough.

Paul was already standing in the doorway of his house staring at her as if he could not believe she had actually arrived. "I've been waiting for you for hours . . . ." he said at once.

Her eyes widened with surprise. "But you know how he is . . . ."

"He? I suppose you mean your father . . . . That sonofabitch. Do you really think he believes you when you tell him you're with Bessie Halpern?"

She sighed. "I don't know what he believes. Like most people I guess he believes whatever he wants to . . . Are you going to let me in?" she added with a tired smile. The sun was on her back and she suddenly felt the weariness of her morning's struggle to get away from Jacob K.

He moved away from the doorway so that she was, at least, out of the heat into the cool living room. "What do you mean? You think people believe whatever they *want* to believe? Are you suggesting there're no standards for *any*thing? Just a subjective kind of moral relativism?"

"I'm not sure what I'm suggesting. I'm just tired." She wished he would offer her something cold to drink instead of . . . just standing there carrying on what seemed to her a useless semantic argument, his eyes narrow with thought, his fingers clasping and unclasping the bars of his crutches. "I'm just too hot to think," she added with as much patience as she could muster (no need to be irritable with him: it was Jacob K. who had worn her to this frazzle). "Is there anything cold to drink?"

"Just beer . . . Well, what you're really saying is that it's possible for a person to have no moral convictions at all. I mean, if he can believe anything he wants to believe, obviously he doesn't believe anything . . . ."

It struck her that he used words like *conviction, beliefs, ethical principles, moral values,* as if they were parts of the body: everybody had them, only in some people they were deformed.

"God, how do I know what I mean? I've been working since eight this morning. It's eighty-nine degrees out there and *I'd like a drink of water.*" She realized with shame that what she was saying was: why can't you wait on *me* for a change? She was virtually so tired that what she wanted was a miracle, no less: she wanted Paul to throw away his crutches and skip into the kitchen and pour her a glass of freshly-squeezed lemonade. Then to pick her up in his arms and carry her into the bedroom: like in the movies, she thought sourly. The hopelessness of this dream made her want to cry; and she did not want to cry today. She had managed all morning not to shed a single tear in spite of Jacob K.'s senseless caprice: what she wanted now was joy, not tragedy.

"What I'm saying," she articulated slowly, hoping her despair would vanish if she managed to appear cheerful, "is that each of us survives on delusion. When people threaten those delusions, we have to . . . well, we have to decide those people aren't clever enough to know about such things. That they're stupid, selfish . . . even insane. Otherwise . . . ." She shrugged, feeling her point was painfully clear. Her immense physical weariness was a trap into which she could catch herself telling unwelcome truths.

"And one of those delusions," he said drily, "is that *any*body can play amateur psychiatrist if she wants to."

"I don't have to be a psychiatrist, even an amateur one, to know when somebody's kidding himself. Or herself." Paul had not moved to get her the glass of water. Her lips felt parched with heat: should she ask him again or should she just go to the refrigerator and fix herself a cold drink? She looked intently into his face to see if she could find the answer to his rudeness there; but unlike Papa, whose face she could read like a topographical map, Paul's face was enigmatic. The very lines creased into his forehead by physical pain were deceptive; they drew the eye's attention and one failed to notice the growth of tension like shadows around his eyes where the real pain lay.

"Well, yes. And of course—love," he said firmly. His voice was a challenge.

She jerked her head to attention. "What do you mean 'of course, *love*' like that—as though you were reading something from a menu?"

"I mean: to follow your premise, if people can deceive themselves about anything, they can *of course* be deceiving themselves about love.'

Was he deliberately beginning a quarrel in order to send her away?

She sensed something brewing; fear seized her and she remarked with sudden irrelevance: "I'm thirsty. I'm dying of thirst."

Her manner seemed to startle him. He had obviously scarcely heard her previous request for something to drink. A look of annoyance and shame crossed his face. Of another man, Kate could not help thinking, one would say at this point, *he leaped to his feet, he sprang to get her a glass of water, he stood up, flushing guiltily*. Of course, none of these things happened; he merely stared at her sternly, as if he were seeing her for the first time and was overcome by what he saw. Then he shaded his eyes with his hands. "Katydid, Katydidn't . . . Katydid, didn't . . . ," he murmured incomprehensibly.

59

She sat appalled. "For God's sake. What's the matter with you? You've been treating me . . . you've acted as if I were your worst enemy since I came in here."

He glared at her challengingly. His face was a rash of pink and white. His lips were dry. "Well, are you; *Are* you?"

To cover her real fear (he seemed so angry she thought him capable of striking her), she walked awkwardly toward the kitchen (as if she were ashamed of being able to propel herself there on her own two feet, she thought). She opened the refrigerator door, discovered they were out of ice. For some reason that affected her more than all the frustrating events of the day: "Oh God, Paul," she whimpered wearily. "Couldn't you have filled the ice trays? On a hot day like today?"

His voice was bitter, ruminative: "What you really mean is, couldn't I *at least* have filled the goddamn ice trays?"

She stared at him, torn between honesty and compassion: it was what she had meant.

He suddenly opened up a direct attack: "Do you still have that post office box?"

"Post office box? What post office box?"

"Whaat post office box? What post office box?" he mimicked. She had never before realized how degrading it was to adults when they imitated the chanting tricks of children in order to humiliate each other. "I mean the fucking post office box that you rented so that you could keep on writing to that sonofabitch. Well, *tell* me," he said, choking for breath. "Do you still have that post office box?"

"Of course I have it . . . ."

He slumped somewhat, whether in victory or defeat it would have been hard to say. "Well, at least she didn't lie to me," he muttered.

"O.K. Now you listen to me." He thrust his chin downward and indicated with a contemptuous gesture that she was to stay exactly where she was. She felt pinioned against the refrigerator. She thought wildly of some way of escape. Why, he is perfectly capable of . . . .

"He telephoned here for you today. *Twice*. A guy with a weird accent. What a hell of a nerve, trying to get in touch with you here. Here! Of all places. Obviously a guy who's used to getting what he wants . . ."

"Shaddy called *here?*" She tried to keep the edge of pleasure from her voice.

"So that *is* his name. That's what he said. That's really his name then. He gave me his real name. Obviously a man of truth and honor, your Shaddy. We had quite a talk."

"A talk? For God's sake. Talk about what?"

"About you? Who else? Your Shaddy says—in his own crude way

—that you're his girl. He figures he's got a prior claim. He wants to know what you're doing out *here*? . . . ."

Her heart lifted in spite of herself. She did not speak.

"Where did he get that idea?"

She believed she could honestly say she did not know.

"All right. I believe you. That you and he—that you didn't have something going before I even met you?" His voice ended, pleadingly on a question. But the suggestion that what was right with him would have been wrong with Shaddy provoked her into saying: "Wait. I didn't say there was nothing between us. There *was* . . . But how shall I say?—it wasn't merely sex . . . ."

"Oh 'merely sex' is it now? You were hot enough for it at one time."

She felt herself flush, not with shame but anger. Paul's intention of degrading her by such language was so obvious she was left speechless.

"Anyway, the sonofabitch is coming here. So you can explain it all to him."

"Here? But why would he? I mean, why would he do that?" She wondered with involuntary admiration if all this were not some clever invention on Paul's part to test her . . . . She leaned back against the refrigerator. It was poorly insulated and she could feel its coolness enter her tired body. She had forgotten her thirst.

"Oh, he'll be here," Paul said cuttingly, moving away from the refrigerator. With a tone of dismissal he added: "Now get yourself a fucking drink."

She heard Paul go into the bedroom where he dialed the phone. She could not hear what he said. He did not come out again but lay on the bed looking at the ceiling like a man plotting a jailbreak.

Shaddy's arrival startled her. In fact she was surprised to realize, when the doorbell struck the silence, that she was still sitting at the kitchen table. He rang the bell with an insistent, peremptory sound as if he had no patience for the excuses one might make for locking a door. Kate continued to sit at the kitchen table—uncertain what she should do and at the same time vaguely angry that these two men felt they had a right to force this confrontation on her. It would not have been the way she herself would have come to a decision. There was something barbarous, something primitive in their combined determination, arrived at without her knowledge, to force her as it were to choose between them.

When Shaddy actually walked into the house his appearance was something of a surprise. Kate had almost expected him to walk in with a breezy air, calling "Hi, baby!" to her in the kitchen and perhaps vanishing again when he saw that she and Paul were virtually living together. But instead he appeared grave, somber, weighed down with a new dignity. He flashed a quick look around the living room: his eyes widened then darkened when he saw Paul standing like a colossus between his crutches.

She heard him say, "Kate here? I'm Shaddy."

"Yes. Kate's here. Come in," Paul added after a silence. Shaddy was already in.

"I want to talk to Kate," Shaddy said. Then, involuntarily, with a penetrating look at Paul from head to foot: "If you don't mind."

"I do mind," retorted Paul. "I mind a hell of a lot. I think you've got a hell of a nerve coming here like this. If Katie wanted to see you, she'd have written you . . . ." He stopped.

Shaddy took a sharp breath; he moistened his mouth with soft kneading movements of his wide lips.

"Look—I'm sorry, but I don't even know your name, it's not like we've been introduced—" here he could not resist a sardonic grin; but Paul had turned his face away. "—and I *know* Kate. I know she's not for you."

"Just what the hell do you mean by that?" Paul bit the words off in a cold staccato.

"Hi, baby," Shaddy said softly. He had seen her in the kitchen but he had waited until she came into the living room to greet her. Evidently he interpreted her movement as a signal that she meant to take part in the scene between him and Paul; and that her decision to take part in it was meant to encourage him.

"Well, I dunno," confessed Shaddy, answering Paul at last. He moved his head as though about to delicately scratch it, but he did not. He merely moved it in a sort of half-circle as though he were trying to adjust his vision: to see both up and down simultaneously. "Let's put it this way. I'm not sure that I'm for her either. I'm open to doubt on that question . . . open, you might say, to her explanation. Yet somehow I feel my *doubt's* what qualifies me . . . . But *here*? No, it doesn't fit. It doesn't fit my idea of Katie." He cast a look around at the neat living room, the carefully arranged prints on the wall, the aluminum pans shining from their hooks in the kitchen. He shook his head, as if he saw something they didn't see.

Stung by Shaddy's air of knowledge, Paul demanded in an involuntary tone, as if he were ashamed of needing an answer to his question: "And what the *shit* do you think you know about Kate's life—or mine either—that makes you an authority on *us*."

Kate was thinking she had never heard so many obscenities from

62

Paul—it was as if it were the only form of violence he could use; and he wished to show that he was not afraid of provoking Shaddy to violence. She decided she must intervene before this verbal abuse became still more primitive.

"Paul, if this is to be one of those so-called modern, civilized 'confrontations,' maybe Shaddy ought to sit down. Sit down and talk, I mean. Not just . . . yell at each other."

"O.K. by me, Katie," Shaddy sang out and eased himself past the obstacle of Paul's colossal shoulders and sat down. He was very thin and wiry. Compared to Paul, he looked like a child. As if to accentuate this difference he seemed to fold himself like an instrument he was about to put in a case. He slipped himself into a corner of the sofa, crossed his feet in front of him. Altogether he seemed to take up no more space than a slim, collapsible pillow. On his feet were blue sneakers which he wore without socks. The flesh at the ankles was pink with sunburn, and with a surprising spasm of attentiveness to this detail, Kate found herself wondering where he had been.

"I don't see why we have to be civilized," Paul said in a cool tone which contradicted his words. "There's nothing in the capitalist system which makes allowances for people who expect to be rewarded for kindness and good manners. So let's get down to it. You didn't come here to drink beer," he added harshly.

"No. I came to get Kate. I'm going to take her with me. We're going to San Francisco. First to St. Louis, Kansas City, Houston and all through Texas. Then back to California." He glanced at Kate. "If she wants to come that is."

"And what are you offering her to come?" demanded Paul.

Shaddy had been slowly moving his neck around with a nervous gesture apparently habitual to him when he was trying to remain calm. "What do you mean, what am I offering?" he demanded, with an oblique glance at Kate. "I'm offering nothing. She can come of her own free will if she wants to."

"You're not, I infer . . . proposing marriage," said Paul sternly.

Kate turned toward Paul in astonishment.

Shaddy was silent a long time. Finally he said: "I think that's between her and me. What makes you think *you* got a right to ask?" he added bitterly.

Paul paused a moment, as if measuring his words. "Kate was a . . . Kate was innocent. When we first met . . . she was innocent."

"For God's sake, Paul!" Kate exclaimed.

Shaddy drawled, narrowing his eyes angrily. "Well. I'm sorry about that. But I mean, what the hell, that was your responsibility, not mine. I knew she was just a kid by the way she acted. I could of taken advantage of her—I see *you* didn't hesitate—though you're a sight older than Kate to my way of thinking and ought to have known better . . . . But I figured I didn't know myself well enough. I mean, I didn't know her hardly at all, and if all I wanted was a piece . . . . I had plenty of places to get *that*, didn't I?" The way he asked this rhetorical question seemed to enrage Paul. He shot Shaddy a look of pure hatred, shifting his weight as though he would have liked to hit Shaddy across the face with the heel of his crutch.

"Look," interrupted Kate. "I think you're both out of your minds. What do you *mean* talking about my sex life as if . . . as if—" She could find no words to express her humiliation.

But the men were silent. They had arrogated the right to talk about her. That was an accomplished fact, and all the protestation in the world would make no difference at that moment.

"Anyway," Shaddy added, after glancing at Kate to see if she were following his reasoning. "I'm here like I promised. I come back. We're staying at the Metro," he added to Kate. "—just like last time, you remember." He couldn't resist a short, silent laugh. "You want to come along, you come find me there. We push off to Toledo, O-hi-o in the morning. I'll be waiting." He rose to his feet. "As for you, Mr. . . ." He looked at Kate to see if she would supply Paul's name for him, but she could not bring herself to speak. "I'm sure sorry to come in on you like this. But I figured you ought to know I had Kate all staked out for myself."

"You sonofabitch. Get out of my house before I kill you," Paul breathed, his voice harsh as steel rasping over stone.

As if in obedience to this command, Shaddy rose to go. He stood by the door a minute, seeking her eyes. But she could not bring herself to look up. "Well, like they say, you can't win 'em all," he added in a consolatory way, whether to himself or to Paul remained uncertain. Then they heard the stomping of his feet on the front porch, the rattle of pebbles as he strode across the graveled path, and finally the purring of an engine.

"O.K." Paul said with cold fury, the moment the car had driven away. "Now *you* can go. You can get the hell out of here."

"But Paul—"

"You sat there the whole time and you didn't say one goddamn word. Not one goddamn word. You didn't say once to that bastard that you wouldn't go with him. That he was out of his mind. That he was a dumb chirping yokel from Arkansas or Texas or Oklahoma or wherever in God's name he got that weird accent of his . . . . *Why didn't you speak up?*"

Bewildered by the question Kate could only reply in all honesty that she couldn't think at the time of what to say, that she felt she had to think about it.

"*Think* about it!" he exploded. "Well for Christ sake go home and think about it. You're not going to think about it in *my* bed!" He began putting her things together for her, her pocketbook, her scarf, a paperback book.

"But Paul," she protested. "Why are you doing this? Why are you forcing me? . . . ."

"Oh. Forcing you, is it? Slut . . . . You're already looking for excuses. You were a nice kid when I met you. Now you're going all-out for a cheap sonofabitch like that. Before he's through with you you'll be nothing but a whore like the rest of them—" He stopped, pale with anger but also with fear at what he had said.

She felt cold, resigned, aching with compassion; still, there was a very real edge of contempt in her voice when she asked: "Why is it that a man can sleep with every woman he wants to and people say he's a Don Juan, a rake, a real man—but a girl gets called dirty names by the very man who's supposed to have . . .'loved' her?"

Obviously there was no answer to this question. So she picked up her things and made a point of going into the bedroom for her easel and paint box.

"So you *are* going with that sonofabitch?" he said contemptuously as she stood by the door, shifting the weight of her burdens from one arm to the other.

"I don't know. I don't know anything about that. But if I do," she added with a wan, whimsical irony meant to cover her real grief, "I'll write to you. Get yourself a post office box . . . ."

She did not make any gesture of farewell. She did not believe Paul was casting her out. She preferred to think of it all as a kind of sham rage he had found necessary in order to purge himself of Shaddy's visitation. In his powerlessness he had used the only weapon he had: a terrific fury. But Kate had seen so much genuine anger from Jacob K. that the heat of Paul's rage, whether real or not, flashed over her, annealed her, and left her dry. She packed her paints and easel and loaded the burden on her back with great care.

5

In her confusion, heavily loaded down by easel and paintbox, and frightened at the prospect of arriving home long after Jacob K.'s curfew, she took the wrong streetcar. (She never allowed Paul to take her home: if her neighbors had seen her with him they would immediately have recognized him as the local high school teacher. Even at night Paul's physical handicap drew the attention of strangers. By some physical law their eyes were drawn to the heavy braces on Paul's legs and moved as if by reflex to Kate's angry green gaze, as if they were asking: *these two? why?*)

In retracing her steps she missed a southbound car and was altogether exhausted by the time she reached home. It was nearly eleven and every light in the house was on: her brother was not asleep, but neither was he hopping up and down to convey his message in his usual kinetic way. He stood by the door of his room, somber and frightened. He looked as if he had been crying, and in spite of herself Kate hoped that the look of chaos about the house derived from some petty sin on Yasha's part. Perhaps her brother had forgotten to do his chores or had failed to show up at Hebrew school.

But the chaos was too absolute for it to have sprung from any fault on Yasha's part. Obviously Jacob K. had been looking for something: clothes were strewn across the hallway—dirty clothes, as if Jacob K. had gone through the laundry bag. The medicine cabinet had been emptied . . . .

As soon as he saw Kate, her brother's eyes filled with tears. "I didn't tell him, Katie. Honest, I didn't tell him," he whispered. "I'd have died before I'd tell him."

Kate began to tremble with fear. She pretended not to hear Yasha's denial, managed not to demand: "Tell him *what?*" but clung, instead, to an illusion of safety long enough to inquire: "But what is he doing? Why all these clothes?"

"*He* came looking for you," Yasha tried to explain, making a visible effort not to cry.

"*Who* came?" cried Kate, though she knew very well, of course. That manic Man of Freedom, who did what he liked, went where he wanted to, danced till four in the morning, then caroused with the jazzing, hallooing, handshaking libertines till dawn: a man who would not be expected to realize that there were still pockets of darkness in the twentieth century where women could be beaten by their men folks for

67

staying out after dark.

"Shaddy Fierhazzi," said Yasha. The sound of this alien name, articulated so carefully and knowledgeably by her brother, wrought a tremor of terror: how long had Yasha known all about this? "He came here . . . to find you," Yasha added lucidly enough, fixing his eyes upon her with a look that said, *tell me, tell me, you can trust me.* "And Papa followed him. He followed him all the way to . . . your teacher's house. Paul Ardley's house." Yasha paused, his eyes begging forgiveness for being the bearer of such tidings.

"Oh God," whispered Kate. "What am I going to do?"

As if in response to her question, Yasha slipped into his room. He dragged his own small canvas clothes bag out from under the bed. "I'd *go.* I wouldn't let him beat *me.* When I get big . . . ." the vague threat dissolved in the air. "But you better go *quick.* He's gone down to the police station. He says he's going to arrest you . . . ."

"Arrest me? Has he gone out of his mind? I mean, can they arrest their own children?"

"Would he put you in jail?" began Yasha, his voice breaking. "How long would you stay in jail, Katie? How long would they make you stay in jail?"

"Oh for God's sake, Yasha! Be *still.* Let me think." Her heart thudded with terror, echoing like great socking masses of clay flung against the wall of her ribcage. She began picking up things to thrust into Yasha's bag; but her hands moved slowly, as if under water. She could not believe this was happening. She could not even feel guilty, she had not done anything of which she was ashamed. Yet here "they" were ready to . . . she did not know what "they" were ready to do.

It was almost with relief that she heard Papa's furious voice rising upward, straight into her room. Evidently he was on the front porch, crying out to all the neighbors who would listen, while his voice rushed up from the rusted rungs of the fire escape beneath her window.

"So what good are they? Officers, they call themselves. They're only good to take a bribe. When you need them, when you want them to *do* something for you, they sit and play cards. They laugh at you for an old man. 'Juvenile Court' I'll give them. I'll *schlug zei kapores* with their Juvenile Court. A man needs a court to decide if his own child is doing wrong? They'll arrest her all right. They'll find her in the street, they'll arrest her. She'll see. They'll see . . . A piece of trash in my own house . . . ."

Kate and Yasha stood staring at each other in unbelief. "He's gone mad, Yasha," she whispered in terror. "Stark raving mad. Talking to himself . . . ."

She realized, though, as soon as Jacob K. stood in the doorway that he had not been talking to himself. His tirade had been directed at Kate, he had intended his voice to carry upwards through the open window—so that she would not for a moment think she might escape punishment.

"A *knafke* I raised in my house, eh?" was his greeting.

She trembled, naively relying on definition for a defense. "Papa, you know what a prostitute is. How can you call your own daughter a prostitute?"

"How can my own daughter run around with tramps, pimps, carnie-men?"

"If you're talking about Paul Ardley, he's a respectable teacher of history."

"A *respectable* teacher of history, is it? That son of a bitch, I'll kill him if I ever see him again. Does he think because he's a cripple I won't kill him? Is that what a *respectable* teacher does? He takes girls into his house at night?" Suddenly he noticed the canvas bag in her hand. "Hah, what are you taking there? You think you *own* something, you can take something away from this house? Everything you have, I gave it to you. And where do you think you're *going*? I'm taking you myself, to the Court, *du herst*? Tomorrow I'll take you. You won't do what *I* say, they'll fix you. They'll teach you something about how a girl behaves. Your mother will die of this . . ."

"I'm leaving," said Kate with as much dignity and courage as she could muster. From the corner of her eye she saw Yasha watching the two adults in terror. She tried to signal him to leave, she was afraid of what Jacob K. in his fury might do to him. But Yasha stood stubbornly by the window, watching Papa's every move.

"Ha! You're leaving. She tells *me* she's leaving. You're leaving all right! I'm taking you where you belong, with the other *knafkes* and thieves . . . First, I'll give you a taste you shouldn't forget what it is to be an *eidige mensch* in a decent house where . . ."

He had begun to unbuckle his belt; the tremor of his hands as he swept it over his head like a lariat frightened her more than the sight of the swinging belt.

"If you touch me with that, I'll jump out the window," she warned him sharply. Her brother's eyes widened at her words; but she could not at that moment reassure him that she had no intention whatsoever of committing suicide; she was perfectly aware that she could make it from the metal ladder on the fire escape to the ground with a single, swinging leap. She had done it many times as a child.

Jacob K. looked at her with contempt. "Go! Jump already! Break your neck. Better I should see you broken into pieces than like this, a piece of trash . . . ." The belt rose and slashed in her direction ripping across her deaf ear. It was a strange sort of pain because she could see the arm move as in a silent film, feel the pain of it on the left side but did not hear the fall of the belt on her stinging ear; it was as if the pain itself had made the sound of falling.

"Out of my way!" she cried to Yasha and swerved toward the window. She could not open it all the way and she scraped her spine as she pushed her way through. She felt the lash of leather on her legs. She wondered why Jacob K. did not yank her back into the room, why he had not pulled her apart like a quartered chicken as she straddled the window. Then she realized when she heard Yasha's howl of pain that her brother must have tried some diversionary tactic, bringing the wrath of Jacob K. down upon his head. Those moments of grace, however, gave her the freedom she needed to climb down the fire escape to the metal ladder. She absorbed with all the nerves of her body the gratifying squeak of the unoiled joints as the ladder sank slowly beneath her weight to within eight feet of the ground. She heard, too, Jacob K. cursing at Yasha and her brother crying, with a single-minded and continuous wail, like a muted siren. For some reason the sound of that controlled despair affected her more than her own condition: it was like a solid core of pain ringing through a dark tunnel, the wail of a spirit discovering that it has left the joys of sky and earth behind him.

Suddenly clothes began streaming out the window, like strange white birds. She did not dare take time to pick them up. She could hear Jacob K. accompanying each falling article with an imprecation: *Nu, nem dass, take this. Du dafts dass? You need it?* and a billowing pair of panties caught on the rung of the ladder. Kate burned with humiliation as she realized that Papa had taken all her underclothes out of the laundry bag, and like an animal had sniffed out her sins. She could see a patch of her own blood on her clothes, and for some reason the sight of it made her retch. She thought that now at least she had finally reached the absolute limit of her hatred of Jacob K. But when he suddenly appeared at the window, slamming it down with a crash, then throwing it up again with an hysterical fury which rattled the glass, she found there might yet be another dimension to hate . . . . From the opened window he called out a few final stinging epithets which fell on her left ear; she could not make out what he said.

But something cold and metallic struck her cheek as she stumbled through the cindery path. It was a silver coin, flying through the air like a bullet, and she realized that Jacob K. was flinging after her the money she had hidden away in her paint box. Her flight took on an added dimension as she ran now in the moonlight, the tears streaming down her face, clothes and money left behind as in a burning city, ran now all the way across the ghetto, remarkably unattended by patrol

70

cars, down a street emptied of all human activity where she sat for a while in a heap and sobbed like an infant abandoned on a garbage heap. Then she rose and calmly climbed aboard the first streetcar that would take her to Shaddy at the Metro Hotel. As she stared into the astonished conductor's face she thought she must look like what she had considered a purely historical image—a savage and wholly destitute runaway slave.

PART TWO

6

The beginning of the trip was like the end of the trip; what Kate remembered was setting her foot onto the single high step of the bus as though it were a strange new planet. The step was lined with new black rubber on which she could see plainly in white letters on the shiny black surface, U.S. RUBBER: *The Chinaberry Nine* had stopped in Detroit long enough to remodel their bus.

Kate could feel Shaddy's hand under her armpit as he partly assisted her, partly lifted her, up the steep step. The sharp change from the bright August afternoon into the subterranean light of the bus momentarily blinded her, it was like hitting the water with a stunning splash. Except for Cricket and "Kleig," the band leader, who remembered that they had seen Kate at the Y'all Come Back Bar B Q, the other men in the band did not recognize her. They knew, however, that Shaddy was bringing his girl—her arrival at the Metro Hotel the night before could scarcely be kept secret because the unmarried men slept four in a hotel room to save bills. When she appeared at the front of the bus, leaning shyly against the driver's seat, a silence descended on the cavorting, chattering, disputing musicians and their wives. What had a moment before been as confused as the post-ceremonial embraces at a wedding or a *briss*, dissolved suddenly into stillness. Each musician stood as if captured in the net of Kate's vision, caught in a slow impressive motion. One silently swallowed the last bite of his sandwich. Another's hands fell away from the suitcase he was pushing into the crowded racks above his head; even their mouths stopped moving in the low intimate conversations they had been having with their women. It was this arrested motion which frightened Kate; but Shaddy pushed her forward. "Hey, you cats, this is my Katie."

Their response was friendly but somehow aloof; there was a subcurrent of tension which Kate could not understand. She strained with special attention to remember all their names, anxious to please them as though she were a newly discovered stowaway aboard their ship: Cricket and Gabriel and Barney and Les and Red and Shorty and "Kleig" and Slick, the piano man. Shaddy gathered her up toward himself in one arm as he introduced her around, as if to proclaim to all present that she was his. In fact he said it over and over: "This is my girl. And keep your cotton-pickin' hands to yourselves, or I'll blow so hard, I'll blast you yonder side of the moon." Most of the musicians laughed warmly at Shaddy's introduction and took her hand and held it awhile, glancing at Shaddy as if they expected to be cuffed like way-ward puppies. It was all friendly and open-handed.

"Don't they like me?" Kate murmured to Shaddy. Her own timidity struck her as strange. She had never before worried about whether people in groups liked her; she had, in fact, grown to expect the opposite. Individually people had seemed to be attracted to her, often asking deep, probing questions as if anxious to understand, as if by understanding her they might learn something about themselves. Then one by one as they became part of a clique, they dropped away from her as if the knowledge they had gained were more fearful than useful. So Kate's sudden need to be accepted by eight men and three or four women (she was not sure how many women would remain when the bus actually pulled out to their first stop in Ohio), made her voice tremulous as she asked.

"Oh, they like you," Shaddy whispered, patting her hand. "They like you fine. Let's sit toward the back a ways, then we can look at each other and not have to look at *them*," he added loudly. At this spontaneous inclusion of an audience, Kate suddenly realized they would hereafter present a united public image, that they would seldom have moments of privacy when they could be, quietly, individually, themselves.

Clutching Shaddy's hand like a child (she refused to admit to her-self how intimidated she was), they headed toward the last seat which stretched in an uncurving, unyielding bench across the bus. "This is the worst seat from any point of view," Shaddy explained. "Least air, least comfort. You'd be the last to get out if there'd be a accident. No air. No give to the springs on a bumpy road. We'll take it. That way we'll never have to knock off anybody's head to get out of our bed . . . . Now, I got to run back to the hotel to pick up a couple more things, so you sit still, y'hear? And don't talk to strangers," he added for public benefit. At once eight heads turned and began hooting and whistling. "Pipe down, fellas," said Shaddy complacently. "You want people to think these here are some crazy musicians on the road?"

Shaddy was gone for nearly half an hour and during the interim Kate had time in which to think that she did not want to think too much about what was happening. She did not want to wonder whether her actions in running away had been wise or foolhardy or whichever of those terms people apply to what turns out to have been an irrevo-cable decision. She was convinced she would never set foot in her father's house again. She had, so to speak, fallen head first out of a social structure which had taken the Jews six thousand years to build; and she was not sure that the net under her was strong enough to break the fall. She sensed the element of risk, but did not at all feel it was courage which drove her on. In fact she was aware only of a certain blind compulsion. She was thinking, perhaps I ought not to continue this mad trip. But at the same time she admitted she was already on it, she could not so readily disembark. She had left all the security of Jewish homelife behind her. She found herself analyzing with an odd ironic detachment how it was that although she had always thought of herself as "different" from other women, she had nevertheless been catapulted into Life precisely like the countless numbers of women before her, merely by having had a sexual experience with a man: so slight a deviation in the pattern could create unending vibrations in a woman's life. Like the fallen woman of the Victorian period, whose husband or father barred the door on her sins, her first wholly independent act had been a "merely" sexual one. The answer to her woman's question: *who shall be my first lover*? affected all other risks, decisions, probabilities, as though a woman's life were computer-programmed, based on a wholly female probability theory.

This insight made her look up at Shaddy with curious detachment as he returned to the seat beside her. He was scowling angrily: "Goddam sonsabitches," he exclaimed as he threw himself into the seat. All they think about is their own skin. Just let 'em try to pick up a horn player between here and Kansas City."

She turned toward him inquiringly, not yet attuned to his oblique way of speaking.

"Katie," he said bluntly. "The guys have been complaining to Kleig about you. And Kleig's been giving me plenty of flak."

"About me?" gasped Kate. "But what have they got against me? They don't even know me." The thought of being condemned to ride thousands of miles with people who for some reason did not want her, so disturbed her that she leaped up as if to rush out of the bus.

"Aw Katie," murmured Shaddy. "Don't be like that. We're gonna get this all straightened out. It's not you they don't like. It's just they're scared out of their minds about you being jailbait. They'll be crossin' the state line in a couple of hours. You know the laws about taking jailbait across a state line can be pretty damn serious if we got sent up by some hillbilly cop to some teetotalin' peckerwood judge. Especially when some of these guys get high . . . Me, I'm no head. But it could all look pretty bad to some Okie from Muskogee."

"What do they want me to do?" demanded Kate bitterly. "Get a year or two older in the next couple of hours?"

"Two? . . ." He looked baffled a moment, as if she had lied to him. "Well, look. The guys are with you all the way. They think you're a great kid. Really. But they don't want any trouble. I could get picked up and they'd be without a horn player—a really *good* one

77

that is, they can always pick up some guy who uses his horn to get the wax out of his ears," he added with a spurt of raillery and defiance. "They want us to be in the clear, in case the cops decide to bust us all in Geetchiegoomie, Wyoming. Baby, they don't have *no* civil rights lawyers in Geetchiegoomie, Wyoming."

Kate fought to keep back the tears, demanding with anger: "Do I look as if I had any influence with policemen? In . . . in Geetchiegoomie or anywhere? What do they expect me to do anyway?"

"Well, baby, they want us to get married." He tried to say it lightly, but he was visibly shaken. She could not tell whether he was somehow pleased at the dramatic twist of circumstances, or whether he was overcoming a very natural reluctance for her sake. He could, she reflected, have asked her very kindly and courteously to get off the bus. As she quickly considered the alternatives—of knocking on the door of her father's house, of entreating her father's forgiveness, of submitting to her father's insults, she felt an unexpected rush of gratitude to Shaddy.

She sat down, feeling slightly giddy. "Oh . . ." she said, not daring to look at him, but looking out the window instead. "Is *that* all?"

About an hour out of Toledo a kind of vicarious joy seized the band. Everyone seemed to become affected by the prospect of seeing one more bachelor voluntarily give up his freedom. The general consensus was that Kate was a lucky girl, Shaddy was doing the Right Thing. At least she had some legal protection in case . . . in case. Anyway, they all seemed to feel better about it. Kate pondered this enigma while the band sang songs: the prospect of the approaching wedding enlivened their lyrics, their antics took on a carnival atmosphere, as though they themselves were about to break forty days of fasting. But Kate could not help wondering why it was unanimously considered that Shaddy was giving up his freedom, whereas she . . . she was being congratulated, as though she had cleverly "caught herself a husband" by a legal technicality. Her pride felt lacerated at the implications. She wanted to protest that she didn't need Shaddy, to hell with them all, she could go on to Geetchiegoomie, Wyoming (if there was such a place!) by herself: but she knew it would have been a lie. She needed Shaddy. She understood at once that if by some sudden animadversion, he should decide to cancel the whole thing, she would be stranded in Ohio, at the mercy of his charity. The thought of such dependency made her furious. While the band was singing an ancient ditty someone had dredged up from his own failures,

> Say, why don't we do this more of—ten?
> How come we do it only—now and then?

78

quick explosions of humiliation were firing Kate's anger. She did not want to marry Shaddy; it was not that she felt she was against marriage on social or political grounds (she was too ignorant for that); but something in her felt degraded by this approaching ceremony which had been taken on so lightly and in which neither her will nor her desire had been consulted: so obviously was it an *economic* necessity for her to be cared for by Shaddy. At its best, then, this "marriage" was to be an abduction; at its worst, it was a venal transaction, and the word transaction brought another, far uglier word to mind. Afterwards Kate was to believe that it was at this moment, when she was being bargained for at less than bargain prices, that she determined never again to be without a means of protecting her identity. The years she had spent in high school had prepared her for nothing. She had no job, there was nothing she could offer in exchange for services, except presumably, the service she was herself willing to render Shaddy. Because she was attracted to him? "Loved" him? Her concept of love was undergoing rapid modification. She had thought that singular blend of compassion and awe she had felt toward Paul Ardley (her *teacher*, after all!) had been love. Yet how quickly she had left Paul when a new sort of freedom had offered itself, the freedom to leave Detroit, home and family forever. And now she was discovering that this new freedom was only to be another kind of subjection: instead of being a work-slave for her father, instead of being an emotional buffer for Paul between the world and his polio-crippled legs, she was to be used in a more subtle and devious way as the wife of Charles Fierhazzi: she was to be flattered into voluntary servitude.

In Toledo there were signs everywhere: *Get Married Here. Witnesses Supplied.*

"We don't need any more witnesses," observed Kleig sourly, flicking the ash of his cigar out the bus window. "How long you think this shebang will take?"

"There's a sign," called out Cricket's wife, Ginny. "Says, '*Licenses and Ceremonies Complete. No Waiting.*'"

"What kind of license?" called out Gabriel, who was polishing his trombone. "A dog license? I should have brought my dog . . . ."

"Cut that out, Gabriel," retorted Red, who was sitting on his drum cases. "This is serious business. We have *already* crossed the state line.'

"O.K. Line her up. Get the kid a hat or something," said Cricket. "Ginny, you got a hat? Make her look like a bride for Chrissake. What the hell kind of a wedding is this anyway?"

"Anybody got a fifth? We'll need a bottle to celebrate with when it's all over."

"What you mean, when it's all over? You talk like it's a murder

79

trial or something," objected Shaddy. "Listen here: this is a wedding. So get ready to play us some music when we come out . . . . Ginny, you come along for a witness," he added, singling out Cricket's wife.

She was a young woman from Switzerland, with a high sweet voice as though the strings of her throat had been softly rubbed with resin. The skin lay so tightly across the fine bones of her face that already lines of worry were creeping like a kind of delicate ivy round her eyes. Kate instinctively liked her because she seemed the only woman on board who was more ill-at-ease with the situation than Kate herself. Cricket had met her in San Antonio while she was visiting relatives and had promptly married her: he boasted to everyone that she had been a virgin, so he had married her before any of those good-looking Chicanos could get at her, he said.

Shaddy was continuing his instructions. "And Kleig, you mights't well come along and see it all done up legal, so you can sleep nights . . ."

The band leader grumbled he'd take their word for it that the deed was done. Besides, they wouldn't let him smoke in there, would they? He would send the piano man, Slick, as his proxy. "Go and be a witness, Slick. You're the only one looks as if he hasn't slept in his clothes. Shaddy," Kleig added abruptly, "why don't you comb your hair? What the hell kind of a bridegroom *are* you?"

Inside, there were a dozen couples sitting around on the office furniture which gleamed under the bright light as though brought to a high polish by the sweat and oil of many bodies. Now and then a prospective bride or groom jumped up nervously to take a sip of water from the white porcelain fountain.

In spite of the No Waiting sign, they had to wait about an hour before a rangy-looking man with an oddly chambered voice, as though it were striking the tiles of an empty swimming pool, entered the room; under his arm he carried a leather-covered book with red edging.

Kate whispered apprehensively: "This isn't a religious ceremony, is it? I mean . . . ."

"Calm yourself," Shaddy assured her. "He's just a j.p. I wouldn't let a cat marry me if he said he went to church. I had enough of that jive."

Shaddy's rejection of a religious ceremony relieved her, but it also reminded her of how little she knew about him. She had no time to think about that aspect of their marriage, however. The justice of the peace was now asking them to stand facing him. Gently he arranged Ginny and Slick to his satisfaction, as though he were preparing them for a photograph. (It later turned out that he had been doing exactly that; during the ceremony a bulb flashed, and afterwards Shaddy was offered a wedding picture "with frame" for five dollars extra. To

Kate's surprise, Shaddy seemed pleased at the idea and bought it.)

While Kate was trying to find a handkerchief in the purse Ginny had lent her, the justice of the peace began reading from his leather book. Simultaneously there was a click behind him and canned music came out of what appeared to be a nickelodeon. She heard Slick whisper irritably, "For Chrissake, *that* Mickey Mouse arrangement!" Shaddy took off his high school graduation ring and before she could find her handkerchief, he was already turning her face up so that he could kiss her. She was startled, as if she had forgotten that marriages were sealed by these physical tokens. The j.p. was concluding with a new depth of hallowed reverberation, as if he were accustomed to gearing himself to a higher intensity at this point: "And by the power invested in me by God and the State of O—High—O, I do pronounce you . . . ."

Kate's search for a handkerchief, Shaddy's kissing her to proclaim her legally his bride, and the j.p.'s proclamation that God and the State would now permit her and Shaddy to cross state lines together—all this occurring, as it were simultaneously, caused a strange comic convulsion in Kate. At first it was a mere gasp, but this was aggravated by a twitching of the mouth, till laughter was wrenched from her throat like an outcry. She bent over as though she were in pain. Tears streamed down her cheeks. *Still without a handkerchief!* she thought, and the thought intensified her laughter, riddled it with hiccups. Then at last it was over, she could cease laughing. Shaddy gently led her away to the water fountain where, he said, she should drink long and deep and hold her breath: it would stop the hiccups, he said thoughtfully.

When they received their license she saw Shaddy's name spelled out for the first time: Charles Laszlo Fierhazzi. Whoever had made out the license had decided that her own name was not Katinou but Katherine, an error to which she was accustomed, it was part of the universal urge to dissolve others into familiar anonymity. Added to this surprise was the loss of her surname, which she had had for sixteen years: she resented it. It was not that she disliked Shaddy's name, but that she had always enjoyed a small private satisfaction from the sound of her own names which joined together like a solid piece sculptured out of a single stone: Anna Katinou Kalokovich. She realized that it was only a trifle, but nevertheless it seemed but one more humiliation, one more whittling down process. Without education, job, or even her own name, she felt herself more than ever a responsibility to Shaddy and a burden to herself. And she was obliged to be more than ever grateful to Shaddy: hadn't he given her his name?

After the ceremony Kleig insisted on taking them all out to dinner, "A wedding feast," he said. The men seemed to want to believe that this marriage had been undertaken in the spirit of romantic illusion. They succeeded in making themselves believe it: they ordered champagne and Rhode Island duckling; they gave hymeneal toasts designed, in the nineteenth century, to make a bride blush; they wagged Shaddy about the long night ahead. Shaddy accepted it all good-naturedly, as if he too believed in their created myth. He bent over to reassure her:

"You got to excuse these guys. They don't know any better. The only women they ever saw were . . . ." She could barely wait for the feast to be over; it had become for her a deliberate lie maintained in order to perpetuate a myth she wanted no part in. She wanted to *know* these men and women, but instead of communicating with her, they veiled her with imaginary confetti and rice and treated her as if she were a calendar dated "June wedding." Ginny even lent her a shawl as if she considered Kate's sleeveless dress too bare for the role Kate was expected to play. They brought out a white cake; she and Shaddy cut it together as if they had been childhood sweethearts all their lives. During the dinner Kate asked herself fifty times why she submitted to all this, and again and again the answer was as plain as a dollar sign: unemployed, untrained and underage, she had hired herself out to Shaddy as an indentured servant. In the problem of servitude there was only one solution: freedom.

So they had barely settled themselves in the hotel room for the night when, sitting on the bed, Kate ventured to ask:

"Do they . . . The Chinaberry Nine . . . ever stop for long periods? . . . I mean, long enough so I could take a course in . . . study something practical, I mean?" She had added the alternative because she was already aware that art was not practical. She had never heard of anyone making money at it.

"Well," Shaddy explained with a sigh which was also meant to be a warning to her not to expect the convenience of season-long contracts, "the longest we've ever stayed in one spot was six weeks. And that was a real drag, baby, you wouldn't believe. There was this guy playing organ in a cafeteria, and we'd come on when he was off and it went on like that all night—the folks shoving their mouths full of food while we played our guts out. 'Course you're never playin' to *them*. We play to ourselves. But now and then some square'll come up and say 'Could you please play Way Down Upon the Suwannnee River? It's our ninetieth wedding anniversary——' " He paused as he realized she wasn't smiling.

"Never more than six weeks! But how do you get anything done? I mean, it's like being a sailor."

He looked suddenly grieved and lonely as he stood up and began undressing in a slow, thoughtful way: "What do you want to get done? That you can't do?"

Her self-assurance faltered. She hardly dared voice her ambitions to herself, much less to the world. But she tried it, hesitantly: "I want to paint . . . ."

"Paint?" He looked around him vaguely. "You mean like pictures?"

She nodded.

He sighed luxuriously. "Well, I don't see anybody stopping you from that. I'm not even back to the hotel room till after one every morning. So who'd be stopping you?"

"But I want to *learn* something. I want to learn about painting first . . . I'm so . . . ignorant," she added intensely, though without any sense of modesty. It was the simple truth. She knew nothing about art except what she had taught herself on the roof of their tenement. She did not even know how to paint a dandelion, she thought bitterly.

He stood facing her; he had taken off the suit in which they had been married and stood hesitatingly, as if uncertain whether to remove his underclothes. He sat down, holding one bare foot in his hands as though to warm it. Kate's attention was drawn to his feet; she took in the odd way the toes lay in a heap, packed very close to each other as if bound into shoes long before they had reached their full growth. The shapeless toes evoked a respectful pity, like the gnarled hands of a man who has spent his entire life in hard labor. Kate repeated softly: "I'm just so ignorant. I want to . . . go to school . . . get a job . . . ." She tried to laugh at herself with an apologetic twitch of her shoulders.

Shaddy sighed. "You know, we're really married now," he announced with irrelevance. "And I want to tell you something. I didn't have any intention of marrying *any*body, not for a long, long time. I always thought: I been through too much to get myself tied down. What I wanted was *freedom*. But I took you on . . . . Well, let's say this: you impressed me that time . . . , you know? You were a clean kid and smart as a whip . . . . Kate, what I'm trying to say to you, is I had no idea of being in love with anybody: I don't know what that is, really, I seen too many guys spilling their guts just to get their wives a piece of the icing on the cake for me ever to want to get tied up thataway. But when I saw you lookin' scared and helpless and beatup on by your old man, I said to myself, 'Well, Shaddy, do the right thing. Straighten it all out so nobody gets in trouble, least of all that kid.' Meaning you. And that's what I mean. I mean . . ." He shrugged helplessly. "Damn if a Bohunk like me can ever get the words out so they-'re strung right!" he exclaimed irritably. "I guess I mean it's not just a matter of getting my rocks off. I think it's like they say, a guy gets this feeling . . . this love . . ." He paused, furious with himself, with his inarticulate manner. "Look, honey, you married a dumb Hunkie, let's face it . . . . What kind of ignorance are *you* talking about? First thing I said to myself was, 'An educated girl. She comes from a nice family. Her old man doesn't work for the Company, you know what I mean? He works for himself . . . What's more, you know, she hasn't been fucking around since she was fourteen like some I've known. She talks like a nice girl. She's not like the Saturday night tramps who wait for you outside the shaft . . . . A real educated girl.' And those books you were carrying. Man! I was *im*—pressed."

Kate sat and listened in astonishment. She realized that what she was hearing was a guileless social confession: because she, Kate, had had no sexual experience, and because her father did not work for others but owned his own "business" (the shabbiness of which Shaddy could not have imagined), Shaddy had considered her a social class above him. All this had been part of her attraction for him. Her "self,"—her faults and failures, her passions, ambitions and delusions—had entered little into his acceptance of her; in fact, he could not have known anything about these. It was merely that she had represented the sort of girl he had never had: one that read books and did not sleep around . . . . Kate did not have time to consider what personal insult was implicit in his choice because Shaddy rose suddenly and began stretching before her luxuriously. "Look, baby," he said with a sudden nervous grin. "You-'re going to be happy with me, right? We're gonna make it together. So don't start thinking about work, jobs, studies and all that. I got plenty of work for you to do . . . ." He gathered her very close. Kate's arms encircled him, consenting. She knew it would have been absurd for her to persist in talking about her future at a moment when her future was obviously bound up with his.

Kate had always enjoyed the shape of his body from the moment they had danced together. Her hand now slipped beneath his shirt to the bare skin: her fingertips, sensitive to form and shape, traced a scar as thick as a knife which ran from one end of his back to the other. She looked at him with no attempt to disguise her compassion: "My God!" she said. "How did you hurt yourself like that?"

His body became rigid. "Half a ton of West Virginia coal," he answered slowly, with a certain mounting tension in his voice, as if it were he and not she who felt called upon to make a first-night confession. "I got out of the mine after that . . . Boy, you should have heard my mother screaming," he added with a short laugh. "My poor old mother, she can't speak a word of English, and when they carried me out—took four of them to carry me—she started screaming in Hungarian that they'd killed me at last, that they were killing all of us (there were eight of us) like they'd killed my father . . . ."

Kate was silent, her eyes riveted to his. She was not sure what love was, but if love was experiencing the pain of others as though it were her own, she understood it well enough.

". . . she was never right in her mind after that. Partly because she thought he killed himself on purpose. I mean, he'd been going down that elevator shaft every day for thirty years: how come him to just *fall* out? . . ."

Kate touched the trough of healed tissue; it reminded her of thick paint, scooped out on the canvas with the edge of the brush.

He pulled off his undershirt. With a deliberate movement he turned his back to her: a jagged line, crude and fierce as from some tribal knife meant to disembowel, ran in a parabola from his neck to his left side.

She was as moved as if a slave had shown her his scarred limbs, his broken chains.

"*They* did that," she said with bitterness.

"Who?" Then as if he had grasped her meaning without understanding it. "Oh, the mine owners. Well, it's a risk you take. A job like any other. You got to do it. Only me, I decided to get out. You know what decided me?" He looked at her obliquely, his tone quizzical. He turned his head slightly so as to look down upon his scar as a man might thoughtfully look at a weapon he has brought home from the war.

She was silent.

"I'll tell you after," he said, throwing his shirt to one side.

7

Shaddy tried to explain to her how it all had been. While he spoke, Kate filled the clichés and routine obscenities with helium; they took on a hemispheric significance, floating in her consciousness like universal pain.

The entire Fierhazzi family worked for the West Virginia Coal Mines. There were eight brothers and a sister; his sister slopped coffee in the company store behind the company counter. Shaddy was already twenty-two years old, and he earned a great deal of money, all the brothers did; but their ordeal below the earth where others walked on them was so horrifying that when the time came for joy, their one freedom was to spend as much as they had earned: only The Sellers would have anything to do with them, they were always so dirty. Even after the scrub-up, their skin was like potatoes, at any moment a bit of dirt could be rubbed off with your thumb.

He remembered one night at the Corona Whorehouse (he didn't know who had named it, but most of the girls were tobacco-colored, so perhaps the name had come from the phallic image of a slow-burning cigar). Shaddy had washed up with particular care one Saturday night and felt himself young and handsome enough to buy his pleasures: whiskies at the company bar, condoms at the company drug store and companionship for the night at the Corona. Because of his loneliness he liked to hire a girl for the entire night, her price was calculated on the basis of what she would have earned during those hours: sometimes the price astonished him.

When he had entered the house, the madam checked him over: it was a well-run house and they checked both miners and girls for V.D. If you didn't like it, she said, drive out of town to one of those places where you could pick up the clap for a dollar. Shaddy didn't mind, and the madam even spurred him on with a provocative grope in her lust for hygiene.

He and his regular girl, Rita, had sat around drinking for a while. He knew very well that with cheap whiskey at a buck a shot he was not paying for the drinks but for the privilege of exercising his imagination, of pursuing his lust with an air of wealth and leisure while The Girls brushed by him in movements designed to evoke erotic memories, which in turn would be transmitted into splendid erections.

He remembered feeling the cutting edge of boredom, something he had never experienced before. And because he was bored he became angry and began being very "ugly" to his girl, Rita. She had been wearing a kind of Hawaiian grass skirt which rustled and rubbed as she sat on his knees; it itched more than it titillated and he began to complain loudly that he didn't like it on her, he didn't like it on her at all: why did she wear it? Was it supposed to be some sort of goddam cocktease outfit? It didn't tickle, it scratched; it was enough to soften a man like the bite of a scorpion. Was she in business to get his cock up or was she trying to scratch her own pussy? And so on. The truth was, it had been a lousy day in the mine, he'd scarcely been able to scrabble together enough coal to make it worth while going down, and he felt the bitter injustice of Rita's taking half his money for lying on her back. Privately he felt he was doing *her* a favor; he was built a lot better than most of those tired old miners. In short, he was mean and ugly because, as he said, he was bored.

In fact, a lot of things had begun to bore him lately; he was bored with the bickering that went on in his house over the price of meat; bored with the chastisings of the Slavic priest to whom he dutifully confessed his sins every Sunday; bored with the smell of goulash in the kitchen and of carbolic acid in the bed springs; bored, above all, with his job which woke him before dawn and kept him in darkness all day. He longed for the money to leave this clapboard town with its company outhouses useful only to feed the steel factories a hundred miles up the river with sputum-flecked gobbets of coal.

He had managed to finish high school. Only because he was the youngest child had his brothers been able to keep the cabbage simmering on the stove for two years after he, Charles Laszlo, had been considered strong enough to go down into the mines. But now, for four years he had gone down every day, many months he had gone down three Sundays out of four to get the doubletime pay which had made him feel, for one day out of the month, like a king. Once he had even bought a new car: but it had been smashed up in a bad accident in the mountains (nobody killed). He could not seem to save enough for what he wanted even if he had known what he wanted. After his quarrel with Rita he knew at least what he did not want.

That Saturday night, after his fifth drink, apparently Rita, too, became bored and "ugly." She began to complain in a loud voice that when he drank too much he was soft as a tomato, she had to work at him too hard. Perhaps Rita thought he was too drunk to hear her, but he had heard her all right, and by the time they had got up to go into their room he was roiling with fury. She had humiliated him, he felt, in front of the others. So he was surly and silent in spite of all her provocations. He began to think up things for her to do, beginning with the removal of that piece of dried shit she was wearing, that Hawaiian crap

88

that scratched like cheap toilet paper. Rita bit her lip and removed the grass skirt and lay beside him. She was not her usual merry self, and he felt cheated. After all, if she would not make him laugh nor (even) bring on an erection, what was he paying her for? He looked down at her wide nether lip and her slightly slanted eyes and he said to her suddenly, "Hey, what are you anyway? An Indian or something? You're not really from Hawaii are you? I'll bet you there's a Chinaman somewheres in the woodpile."

She had narrowed her eyes at him further, accentuating the Oriental look. He could barely see her pupils which were small nets of darkness caught between trembling lids. *"Puerco!"* she muttered under her breath. "When they fuck with a string, they speak with a whip."

"What's that? Just an old Castilian proverb?"

"And you, you Bohunk!" she demanded with rage. "What kind of Castilian *you* talk? Your *madre* can't even talk English."

He slapped her for that. He didn't let people talk about his mother. What did the chippie know about his mother? She'd had nine kids and never done any screwing for money either. How she'd washed their clothes, soaking the blackened pants in an old barrel, then rubbing the spots with homemade soap till her hands were white from the lye. That had been years ago. Now his mother's hands were getting slack. The veins stood out like ropes. The very thought of his mother made him want to crack Rita one on the snout, as if striking her might awaken her to something, get her out of bed, set her to work like an honest woman, like his mother . . . And then suddenly he had struck her again, hard—at least he saw the bruise on her cheek, he didn't recall having moved his hand.

"Dirty gringo!" she cried, spitting on the floor. "You hit me again and I'll call the police." She meant her pimp, of course, but Shaddy was accustomed to these euphemisms.

It was the last drink that must have done it; he found he was shaking, not with rage but with something enraging: could a young man of twenty-two have swilled so much bad whiskey in his time as to be having the d.t.'s? He continued shaking, shaking, as though something terrible were about to happen. "Je*zus,* what do you bitches put into that whiskey? Salt-petre? So you won't have to do any fucking for your money? What I want is . . . ." And he described it to her, his mouth enjoying what his body told him he would never be able to share in, not on that night, not for a million dollars, but he thought: if she can even make me remember what I'm supposed to be here for, it'd be something . . . .

But he had not counted on the stinking, lurking vanity of whores, like the sulphur in a match, it was like a dying smell which clung to

89

them till the final Over Dose or V.D. or Abortion. Rita began to poke at him, jeering at him, showing him how *dirty* he was. "Pig. *Puerco!* Dirty pig!" she kept repeating, jabbing at him with her hard index finger, showing him the layers of dust which had accumulated like mouse turds in the corners of his eyelids, in the webs of his palms, in the mass of ugly toes heaped up on the bed like bruised bananas.Rolling her thumb and forefinger she prodded loose from him small fetid ulcerous balls of dirt, from his scalp, his armpits, his testicles. Even his face, she said, was pitted with dirt, small bubbles of coal dust like hardened wax around the nostrils: nothing he could do would ever get them out, they were like black warts. And she brought a fancy mirror framed with artificial red and white carnations in which the flowers surrounding his face, flushed red from drink and fury, made him look like a festooned steer. The knowledge that he was naked came to him as a kind of shock: it was with a sad and sentimental regret that he understood that Rita's present fury was to be all that had survived their months of hired lewdness.

He was not sure how he was thrown out of the whorehouse. He thought he must have socked Rita again, right in the jaw, because he saw her jaw go askew like a walnut broken open but with the two halves clinging; he saw the nutmeat of teeth suspended in a cry of surprise as she fell screaming.

He hadn't meant to hit her at all. He had better things to do in life besides beating up whores, he said to himself. And all the next day down in the mine he was gloomy and could scarcely wait to get through with their final load because he wanted to go over and apologize to her. After all, she had to make a living, they all had to make a living, the screwed and the screwing . . . And that was when the cave-in had taken place.

It had been toward the end of the working day. His watch had stopped but he could tell, nevertheless, that it was near quitting time. He did not know how he had learned to tell time in the blackness: some change of light, some diminution of the beam of his head-lantern focused on the coal which would turn to waves of black light, churning. Perhaps it was only his fatigue, but at the end of that day there had seemed more coal in his area than at the beginning. He had loaded his train toward the very ceiling of the vault in which he worked and had begun to pin the gigantic walls back, hammering the wooden beams to support tomorrow's diggings. He had laid his tools aside; the light in his head-lantern glowed with a sudden brightness as though a swig of air or gas had charged through his helmet; he heard a low rumble as of water going over a dam in the distance and realized it was the very earth of this world, a colonic gripe which had seized the bowels of the mountainside; then, from his partners working nearby—screams, oddly muted, as though he had cotton in his ears, or dust. When he came to, he was lying under a mountain of coal, his arms and legs splayed out under him like an insect crushed by an angry and impatient hand. And it was absolutely black, a blackness of oil or dust, of masses of bodies, trees, stones, rain forests beaten down into a black wound of coal. In spite of his terror he could feel how the urine left his body, could smell the fear soak his armpits. He was sure they would never find him. He would be left to die here alone among the rats and runnels of wet which he could feel seeping around his feet. He knew he ought not to struggle; any violent struggle could make the earth shudder. But he tried, nonetheless, to ease his body. He could do nothing, the pain was so intense that he must have fainted several times. Once, upon reviving, he tasted his own blood. He believed himself to be dying then, that the blood was coming from his mouth or lungs—but it was from the wound across his back which had slowly trickled down. Then he heard the shouting through the solid walls of death. He heard the tapping, the hammering, and he thought, my God, let them rescue me: *only let me die out of this hole, let me die in the light. With people, not rats ...* And he sank his head down into the blood. He tried not to waste his strength sobbing, to save it instead for the tapping, tapping, against the solid darkness with the chunk of coal he was already clutching like a weapon in his powerful fingers. He lay there for hours, almost gracefully, like a man washed up on the beach—water and tears and urine moving like the salt water of the sea around his mouth.

And the taste of his own embittered saliva suddenly sharply recalled to him the memory of another taste, the first time he had tried to blow his brother Georgy's saxophone. Unbelievable as it now seemed (Georgy's muscle and manhood had since melted down to a solid cylinder of mindless fat), his brother had once been the owner of a saxophone which he used to play around with on those Saturday nights when he claimed to be sick and tired of the Corona women: he had had them all, he said, and they were all alike. Georgy, of course, had never taken any lessons and had no idea how to play the instrument, but would sit around teasing it into giving out short, sharp notes like an old dog barking. One night he had demanded irritably of his brother: "Why in hell don't you learn to play that thing if you're going to make so goddam much noise with it?"

"I got to get some reeds," said Georgy. "Some real good reeds. Maybe then it'll sound O.K. They told me down at the hock shop you got to get them at a music store."

There was no music store in their town. So he and his brother had hitchhiked into Wheeling, arriving at around dusk. The music store owner, upon seeing two dirty-faced boys (one of them barefoot), with an instrument, had assumed they had stolen it somewhere, and had kept them waiting a long time while he checked out the number. Georgy said afterwards the sonofabitch had even called the police. The joke of it all was, of course, that they hadn't needed the sax with them at all to buy the reeds, but they were that ignorant . . .

The reeds had seemed to Shaddy strange, fragile things to be able to affect the entire quality of sound. At the sight of them in their box he was seized by covetousness. There was a kind of orderliness about them he had never found in his own life which appealed to him: he wanted them all, just as they lay in their box. Shaddy had begged his brother to let him try out the saxophone with the new reeds. Because Georgy had trench mouth (which they both believed to be a venereal disease brought on by contact with the Corona girls), Shaddy had taken a fresh reed from the box. "Suck on it," instructed his brother. "Work up your saliva . . . ."

Shaddy, feeling rather strange, had sat down on a chinaberry stump; dragging his toes in the surrounding dust, he had sucked the reed. He had been astonished at the taste of his own saliva; it had been a hot day and the perspiration around his upper lip, which was just beginning to sprout a few hairs, had mingled with the saliva and the reed, and he had been pleasantly surprised at the combined flavor of wood, salt and the flow of his mouth. It was as if, on the spot, by the sheer exercise of his physical force, he had done something significant. Like a spinning spider he had emitted a secretion from which something could be created—something with a power all out of proportion to its merely visible strength. Then something else happened. As he blew on his brother's instrument, he discovered that his brother knew nothing at all about music. He, Shaddy, made the saxophone come to life. He ran away into the woods with the saxophone, refusing to give it back to Georgy. For which, naturally, he had got a beating when he had got back that night, and Georgy had never again let him play the saxophone. But the memorable thing had been that he, Shaddy, had brought the thing to life, not his brother; he had even fingered it till he could play an Hungarian polka.

And now as he lay tasting his own blood, he knew that what he wanted was to create something again from the saliva of his mouth, the fluid of his brain, the power of his gut. He did not ever want to let himself down into the mine shaft again. The first thing he would do, he promised himself, if he got out of that place would be to buy himself a horn. And so, like some simple priest offering up a vow to save his life, he promised the God in whom at that time he still believed (although he had already separated Him out from Religion), that if the rescuers reached him he would never again go down into that funnel of death, he would save his hands and lungs for music, he had found what he wanted.

Since a horn had been what he wanted, Shaddy had decided the best place to get one and somebody to teach him how to play it would be a big city. So he had left West Virginia, intending to explain to his mother later why he had gone in the first place. But somehow it had all seemed easier merely to vanish, writing a postcard now and then. He went out and bought a horn for fifty dollars, and then he discovered something about himself. He found he was a man of patience: he could practice for hours every day while other guys were tilting pinball machines or popping pills.

He explained to Kate that you couldn't get fooled by the horn: "You're only as good as you can make it. No amount of bullshit will make you a horn player if you're not."

Kate said eagerly: "That's true of painting too. You paint something, it's there for everybody to see and hear. If it's a failure you can't just put a sauce over it and call it something else. It's not like baking a cake."

"Oh baking a cake's not such a bad idea," said Shaddy. "When we get to Houston maybe we'll take us an apartment. You can bake us a cake . . ."

"I'm being very serious."

"Well, *I'm* serious. People need cakes. Man does not live by bread alone . . ."

"But you just said yourself . . . How can you reduce what I'm saying to a . . . *cake*?" She gasped angrily. "We were talking about . . . your horn."

"O.K. we were talking about my horn. That doesn't mean I can't like to eat cake does it? I'll bet Heifetz, he puts away a *storm* of cake." He grinned.

"What about my painting?"

"What about it?" He stood with his chin up, trying to button the collar. He slewed his eyes around questioningly. "Damned if I can see how baking a cake now and then is going to keep you from . . . whatever it is you think you want to do . . . You can't paint every minute of the day, can you? Be reasonable."

"Do you think it's reasonable to play your horn day and night?"

"Ah, but baby that's different! I make a living playing horn!"

"You mean I don't have a right to paint day and night—if I wanted to, if I were able to—if I don't make a living by it?"

"Hey, come off it. What's the point of getting mad? We're . . .

93

friends aren't we? We're even married . . . ." He chuckled as he moved his hands with a faint smile over the body which had been so responsive to him the night before. "I don't see what's wrong with celebrating with a little cake now and then? . . ." He slid his hand under her skirt. "Just to warm up the kitchen . . . . I like my women warm——"

She moved away from him. "You know we're not talking about any goddam cake!"

He seemed baffled at her anger. "What's the matter with you, Katie? What have I said? You mustn't pay too much attention to a Bo-hunk when he shoots his mouth off. Remember I haven't read all those books."

"Stop that. I *mean* it. Stop that. What has *that* got to do with it? I tell you I want to be an artist and you tell me there's an art to baking a cake *too*." She was trembling. "Do you thing there's a shortage of cake-bakers?" she demanded with contempt.

He was finally angry. "And do you think there's a shortage of artists? Do you think the world out there is just waiting for Anna Katinou Fierhazzi to paint 'em something so they can hurry up and write her a big fat check for it? Well you sure are living in a fool's paradise. You got to have something they can *pay* for."

"Is that what you thought of when you left home? Spending your last dollar for a horn?"

"Baby, I'm a *man*. I could take chances. But one thing you can't forget—and I don't *want* you to forget it, either," he added solemnly, "is that you're a woman. A woman just couldn't hardly walk off the way I did. You'd been beaten up on the road first thing, I guess you know that. Goll—*ee*, when I think of the chances I took, hitching rides, taking odd jobs. Like I took me a job baling hay for a farmer that near to broke my back one summer. Could *you* do that?"

"No."

"Could you have walked into the union hall 'way I did—a place full of a hundred men and said: 'Look here, you got yourself a horn player. *Have horn, will travel*,' I said."

"Would they let me into the union?" she demanded.

He looked at her, frankly bewildered. "Well, yes. I reckon so. We got women musicians. Kind of *Symphonettes-type*. But have you ever heard of a really good jazz trumpet player who was a *woman*?"

"Oh God! You're just asking that same stupid question, 'Has there ever been a female Michelangelo?' "

"So I'm stupid, am I? What's so stupid about that? It's true, isn't it? There never *has* been a woman Michelangelo, has there?"

She was silent. He had finally buttoned his collar. She could see by the way he was checking his trumpet case that he was plan-

94

ning to go directly from rehearsal to the dance they were booked to play.

He added: "That's a pretty cheap way of winning an argument. Anybody disagrees with you, you call 'em stupid."

"I'm not trying to win an argument. *I'm talking about my whole life.*"

He snapped the lid of his trumpet case, hefted the handle like a skilled artisan weighing his tools. She could see how his body changed as it came into contact with it. The touch of the leather case seemed to remind him of his true role in life, as an actor becomes himself when he walks on stage. At the assumption of his role, their argument was no longer relevant to him. He looked down at her cheerfully: he had serious work to do. He appeared to decide that they had been engaging in a merely intellectual discussion in which, of course, she was bound to shine because she was "educated." But it was he who was the horn-blower, after all, not she: and that was what mattered.

"You sure do exaggerate," he said with a happy grin. He was proud of his wife; she had ideas and education and that made life more interesting for him.

"Listen," he said at the door as he left. "Why don't you get all the Houston papers and see can we get an apartment . . . I sure would like that cake!" he grinned, and went whistling down to the elevator.

8

It took them six months to get to Houston. They went by way of
a week in Memphis, two weeks in Minneapolis, three in Kansas City.
Then they plowed through an endless furrow of one-night stands across
the Deep South (Kleig had not mentioned this in his original itinerary),
playing to tulle-gowned girls and penguin-suited boys in the honey-
suckled Southland. It seemed every daughter in Dixie was getting ready
to go away to "school," in honor of which the town felt called upon to
have a celebration.

For the first two months Kate sat in the darkened ballrooms
watching them. It struck her that these people did not really care for
dancing; the dance was merely a commemoration of something far
more important. There were times when she wanted to rush out on the
floor to impose her choreography upon the gently swishing bodies who
danced as if they were drinking iced tea: sipping it from long spoons
while being careful not to get wet.

These couples bore no resemblance to those she had watched on
the night she had met Shaddy, when the dancing had been not only a
disguise for their sexuality but had expressed a deeper longing, a desire
for something which they might never have, did not even know existed.

These dancers were not covering up anything. They were genu-
inely listless, as if the life-force in the women had been attenuated.
Kate did not know at that time what a long cultural struggle it had been
for the Southern Lady to cultivate her passionless etiolated look, the
look of a pure spirit tolerating solid flesh as it was allowed to pass
through her ectoplasmic self without soiling or touching. She did not
understand that it was not even hypocrisy, it was the rigidity of a code
so long imposed on them that even their mimetic actions were believed
to be real. In that sense it was a true art form in which shadows were
as real and important as the painted subject.

But the dancers were so extraordinarily alike that afterwards she
could never remember whether they had been in Monroe, Louisiana or
Pensacola, Florida or Gulfport, Mississippi or Fayette, Alabama. It all
became for her a diaphanous mise-en-scène in which the same girls in
white satin shoes were whirled about by identically tuxedoed young
men, their faces still flushed from the Lifebuoy in their evening shower.
It seemed to be a world forever young and to be enjoyed: it made Kate
feel simultaneously that she was missing her youth and that her youth
was precisely the thing she should be missing in this case. Eventually

the dances became as unreal as seances in which the ghosts were trying desperately to fill the empty space with spectral evidence that in their youth, at least, they had existed.

One night in a hotel room in Covington, Kentucky Kate did a Blakean sketch of the dancers—joined together in a flowerlike chain around an etherealized center in Hell, around which they were obliged to bow and pirouette, their bodies turning spools of grace, their necks pure-white stalks of love. But their faces were the mummified heads of women for whom absolute and permanent death without consciousness would have been their closest view of Paradise. That night the men in the band admired it immensely; it seemed to carry for them the easy significance of Good and Evil. They gathered around the drawing where she had pinned it onto the wall, and pointed out to each other the hideousness of old women . . . . So that was what they thought she was saying, Kate reflected somberly. When they had gone she took down the drawing and hid it at the bottom of their suitcase: it got lost somewhere between Pass Christian and Texarkana.

When they finally reached Houston Kate had had enough of one-night stands across the Southland and was ready to remain in one place —any place, where she could enroll in art school. She had not done any oil painting in their six months of travel; their late arrivals and immediate departures had barely allowed for drying time for oil canvases; their limited space, both on the bus and in hotel rooms made it impossible to carry easel, paintboxes, canvases from place to place. In an effort to overcome the problem of drying time she had tried a mixture of poster paint and plaster of Paris, creating a thick *impasto* effect. But the results had been disastrous. The paintings had indeed dried quickly enough to be packed away and shipped to the nearest big city, but the southeastern swamplands had infiltrated her canvases: the moisture had literally dissolved her work. Roaches and moths had ruined two sable brushes. In addition, the unexpected loneliness of their way of traveling (they had no time to make friends on their journey) had made her conscious of art as a form of intellectual exchange. She wanted to talk to other artists at work; she wanted to learn what she was certain she needed to know. She saw that the very things which had attracted her most in Shaddy's way of life—its restless mobility, its happy flux— were now a threat to her as an artist: that she was still too ignorant to survive this rolling like a mindless pinball from one corner of the country to another. What she needed was time to master her craft: to stand still long enough to learn how to paint. One morning, impulsively succumbing to this need, she had mailed away for the proper registration forms and applied for acceptance to an art school scheduled to begin classes at about their arrival time in Houston.

The last ten dances before their arrival in southeastern Texas passed in a blur. They drove like the riders of the apocalypse all day, arrived in town an hour or two before the Chinaberry Nine were scheduled to play—and left immediately after the dance, forsaking the hotel room which they had not had time to sleep in. They barely had time to stop at the local post office to pick up the mail which was their only contact with the stable, "normal" world which did not eat its dinner on the run.

Since letters were their only contact with people other than the Chinaberry Nine, Kate and Shaddy always looked forward to getting mail as eagerly as if they were in another country. Immediately upon their arrival in a new city they would drop their bags, shower and walk down to the Main Post Office. Shaddy's letters were almost invariably from his mother. Written in Hungarian, he would sometimes translate them aloud to her, interrupting himself with an abrupt silence as he cautiously censored the old woman's grievances: his mother had been first shocked, then hurt, and finally enraged by Shaddy's marriage.

Kate's mail was usually from Channa or Yasha—and to her surprise —from Paul. Since he knew her habits he had taken a chance on writing to her at the Main Post Office in Atlanta and had managed to follow her around with a postcard or letter ever since. Paul still seemed to her, in spite of his jealousy of others, a heroic person worthy of love. It seemed to her, even, that she had ungenerously expected a generosity of spirit from him which she herself did not have. Wouldn't she envy everyone who had eyes if she were blind? Not everybody could be Homer: most were like Tiresias—bitterly exulting in the downfall of those who had thought they were seers. The truth of the Sophoclean tragedy was, that if Oedipus had been blind from his youth, he would never have done much of anything, never have got around to sleeping with his mother; and certainly Jocasta would never have married him.

Their first day in Houston Kate hurried into the post office while Shaddy stood outside talking to Kleig who, as the official letter-runner for the band, had already picked up most of their letters and packages. At the General Delivery window the postmaster handed Kate their mail: she saw at a glance that the blue form which she had filled out several weeks ago for art school was being returned. ACCEPTED had been stamped across her personal data in black ink. She at once stuffed the card into her handbag. The other mail was, predictably, a letter for Shaddy, and for herself, several postcards—one from Yasha, she saw at once—and a letter from her mother, apparently written for her mother by one of the nurses at the Sanatorium.

She stood at the window reading while people moved politely around her.

Yasha had written:

Uncle Mark died of dibetes. Im going to have a baby brother. There are a lot of cowboys in Texas. Did you see any? Mama's dr. at the San. says they have the best onkologists in Texas. That's canser.

Your brother,
Yasha

Kate's reaction to this news was complex. First: *The dirty old man. She's hardly been home long enough.* Evidently the Sanatorium must have allowed Mama to go home to attend her brother's funeral, and in that interval . . . . Her second thought was: Yasha will have someone to love—someone nicer and pleasanter than myself: a baby. She experienced a surprising sense of having been supplanted.

She tried to concentrate on her mother's role in this astonishing news. She found it hard to think of Channa as a willing collaborator. The last time she had seen her mother, she had seemed too weak, too remote for Kate to imagine her as Jacob K.'s sexual partner. And it was absolutely impossible to think of her taking on the duties of Home, Motherhood, etc. even if the doctors were again to pronounce her "cured."

Kate had impulsively gone to visit her mother while the band was settled in Kansas City for an entire week. Plucking up her courage she had decided to fly to Detroit to tell Mama about her marriage before Jacob K. could poison Mama's mind against her. She had taken the plane in the naive hope that perhaps some of the "glamor" of air flight would rub off on her marriage; that perhaps Channa, who had never been out of Detroit, would think her daughter had married a prosperous artist who could afford to let Kate do nearly anything she wanted to do . . . . In the loneliness of the Sanatorium, Kate had hoped, even such shabby illusions might console her mother. And in fact, for the first few minutes of her visit her mother had forgotten to burst into tears. Then it came.

"Why did you do it, Anna? Weren't there enough Jewish boys, you had to run off with the first boy who asked you?"

She bridled at this, feeling in spite of all common sense, that she had been insulted. Childishly she tried to think of all the boys who might have asked her to run off with them, so she could tell Mama about them: there were none. Any Jewish boys she might have known would have been altogether too young for marriage—were being programmed, rather, to emerge from their studies a decade later as heads

100

of the Empire: doctors, lawyers, merchants, chiefs. She felt at the same time ashamed of this impulse to lie, and resentful of Channa for having forced her into such childishness: parents kept one fixed into childhood, no matter how old one got to be. How did they manage to do it? Kate wondered, even while, as if in conformity to an ancient law, she continued talking, talking, trying to explain the inexplicable.

When it was her mother's turn to talk, Kate realized that Channa saw it all in terms of her daughter's having made a "bad" marriage: *her* daughter could have, should have done better. With a little coaching and primping and a little stylized entertaining to show that, after all, the Kalokoviches were not so poor as all *that*, they could have afforded a fine wedding and maybe a nice little house of their own for the new couple. With all this, and her *"talente,"* (her mother averted her eyes, not really believing, as Kate clearly saw, in the negotiability of Kate's "talent"), with all this, Kate might have married, at least, a-Poor-but-nice-Jewish-boy-with-a-Future. Papa would have staked him to a little store of his own (again Channa averted her eyes, not believing in Jacob K.'s willingness to stake this hypothetical son-in-law). Why, then, did her mother offer so many lies, as if they were dainties on a dish which a guest might accept or refuse? To convince herself, or to convince Kate? Altogether, Channa went on, it would have been better if Kate had learned such things as how to purify the home for Passover, for example; but she was worse than a *shikse*, she was ignorant of all Jewish ways, she had stubbornly refused to learn even the simplest of kosher cooking; and now look at her, see what had happened as a result: what would happen to the children?

Kate stared at her mother, her heart wrung with pity. The cultural gap between them was so great that they could never make any discovery about each other when they talked. Once the tone of their conversation was set, her mother would begin to mourn the loss of all that might have made her life meaningful. And since there was absolutely nothing Kate could offer to replace those losses, since her own generation's freedom would not be considered freedom at all but Degeneracy and Sin, it would be no consolation to her mother if Kate now insisted that Channa's imprisonment was not to be inflicted upon her children and her children's children forever.

"Children?" Kate echoed, as if this were a strange new idea. "We don't want any children. We hardly know each other . . . ." This sounded so grotesque that she almost laughed in spite of the melancholy surroundings.

"You don't *know* him?" Her mother turned away as though from a bad joke. "Why did you marry him, then, if you don't want children? *What kind of marriage is that?*"

A good question, Channa Kalokovich. In your day a marriage came with dowry and tears. The absurd explanation, that she and Charles Laszlo were married because there was a law which forbade people from transporting minors across the state line, seemed too cruel. Her mother would think that she was laughing at her. The only acceptable explanation could be that trap her mother had been warned about in the strange New World: *love*.

She looked at her mother, wanting to weigh her words carefully, feeling that her very silence was a rejection of all that Channa had forced herself to accept. The first time her mother had seen Jacob K. was when she had arrived in Detroit, a tall, slender girl of eighteen, not knowing a word of the new language, with a long chain handbag dangling from her wrist, the fringe tickling her bare arm as she had slid it firmly into the crook of her elbow: it contained all she could claim as her share of the riches of this world: her dowry. She had extended her hand to Jacob K., her suitor. So, he was pock-marked . . . . So he was a head shorter than she . . . . So he had this predisposition in his lung—nothing serious, only painter's colic, they called it, and he was giving up house painting to buy his own store: he was really a businessman, the *shadcan* had assured her before she left Russia. From behind the mist which now gathered in Channa's eyes Kate now experienced as if it were her own life, Channa's longing for life, more life, *more, more* which had brought her alone to the United States—trading herself off for passage fare, as it were, only it was all legal and aboveboard, conducted through the proper channels. No promiscuity or bartering, but a handwritten contract by which she became the betrothed of this strange little man who had really wanted to marry the daughter of a rich leather maker from Gloversville. But the daughter had rejected Jacob K. at the first sight of his face, seined with gaping holes and broken capillaries like the map of a river gone off into twenty directions.

Because of Channa's loveless marriage, *love* would have been the magic word. If Kate had said simply—lowering her eyes and folding her hands, "I love him," her mother would have been comforted; she might even have taken some vicarious pleasure in it. But she could not force herself to say that. What she had discovered she wanted to affirm, as if it were a manifesto which had been thought of for the first time in this world was: I married him to be free. And *that* was the only truth. By running off with someone as alien to her family as Shaddy, she had been as lost to them as if she had defected to Red China. By this "criminal" act she had set herself free from the rules which guided and restricted the women in Channa's world.

At the end of the visit, as her mother walked down with her to the lobby of the sanatorium, it had seemed to Kate that Channa was distraught, preoccupied, as if she were listening to distant thunder.

"You're looking . . . better, Mama," Kate had forced herself to say as she became aware that her mother, though looking more exhausted than ever, had seemed to gain some weight.

Her mother had shrugged, adding with a baffled look: "They think I can go home soon, a month or two more. I'm gaining weight fast. Twenty pounds."

Kate regretted having spoken. In spite of the new fleshiness her mother looked bad. The extra pounds seemed to have gathered round her jowls like a kind of imminent corruption. Only a few years ago her mother's hair had been worn in glossy braids curled about both ears, like gigantic earrings made of her own hair. Now her hair was short and coarse—almost calculatedly unkempt, expressing her disdain. In the strong light of the lobby Kate now saw the lines, like incisions, which had deepened about the mouth. The lines were engraved as though in wet sidewalk cement with childish untutored hands; the dark smudges under the eye seemed to betray an artist's unsteady hand. It was as if the artist, in correcting his sketch, had overdone it: *who had botched this work*?

Channa did not seem to regard the prospect of going home with any pleasure. "But I'm not in a hurry," her mother said. "There's a word . . . . The doctor says: 'institutionalized.' That means you get used to it. Out there, everything looks so hard to do. You ask yourself, 'Is it worth it?' "

Involuntarily, Kate's eyes filled with tears. "But Yasha needs you," she pleaded. "You mustn't get—'institutionalized.' For God's sake, Mama, don't leave him alone with that crazy husband of yours!"

Her mother grew pale with vicarious insult. Her throat moved imperceptibly. She looked as if she were about to strike Kate; then her gaze fastened itself on Kate's wedding ring, as if this ring somehow sanctioned Kate's right to criticize: "Ah, so you see it all now? . . . ." she murmured with a new resignation that did not even have any bitterness in it, and turned her emaciated body away, dismissing her.

Perhaps she had stirred up Mama's desire to be near Yasha, if only to protect him from Jacob's conflicting doses of Idolatry and Repression. But if so, her mother's letter in Houston revealed no such desire but only a weariness of this world which, after the birth of the new baby, Kate was to remember over and over . . .

. . . So what is the use of it? And if it will be a boy, does America need more soldiers? And if it will be a girl—where will I be when it's time, like you, to find for her a husband? I can't

103

help you yet—can I help her, who's not even born yet? Anna, why did you do this crazy thing? At least write that he's good to you, he doesn't drink? A son-in-law I've got that I've never laid eyes on.

So you'll come see me in the San? This time it'll be *naches*, not death waiting in the halls. Better to bring a new baby home than to rot like an onion in that place (you know Mrs. Neselbaum died two weeks after you were here? A hemrage.) At the same time I ask myself, did I need this too? I'm so tired from morning till night I can't stand on my feet and I feel the baby already waking me up as if to cry in my womb.

I'm sending this to the place Yasha told me. Don't write me postcards. I think everybody looks at it before Chin-Chin—we got a Chinese postman—brings it me.

The unsigned letter had no date, a deliberate omission perhaps: Channa unwillingly thrust out of the magic mountain back into the "real" world where real time and total responsibility must descend on her again.

There was still another card, an oversized postcard intended for tourists, with a picture of Niagara Falls on the back (where had he found such a thing?) which was from Paul. Kate stood by the light of a window, trying to decipher the cryptic message written in a nearly illegible scrawl. In that scrawl she could see no vestige of the fiercely logical teacher who had stood at the blackboard and calmly explained the causes of: The Ten Days That Shook the World, The War in Europe, The Revolution in China, The Stock Market Crisis, The Black Days of October, The War in Europe (II) and The Beginnings of Fascism. The truth was that her own impact on Paul had come as a surprise to her. At the beginning of their affair she had been a child with everything to learn; it had not occurred to her that she could have a catalytic power over others. She had naively accepted the belief—with that sort of ignorant humility which resembles egomania—that people could change *her*, could cause *her* suffering. But because Paul was so much older than she, she had somehow thought him invulnerable to change: the revolution was to take place entirely within herself. But since her marriage she had grown to understand—partly from Paul's letters—that flimsy as she was, she had been the linchpin fastening Paul's life together. She often brooded over her responsibility for the change in Paul: to what extent is one responsible if one is the final straw on the camel's back? Surely a Talmudic question.

She did not understand, really, why he continued to write to her. What was his motive? Did he perhaps hope she would tire of her endless voyage, or was it simply enough for him that she read his letters and did not return them? Later she was to realize that she could not understand Paul's motivation because Paul had reached the point in his life where he was living without motivation: therefore, his actions were inexplicable, even to himself.

She read:

> After you left I threw the gin rummy deck on the floor.
> I can't play gin rummy alone. They're still there. I look at
> them and say, Paul, you worthless crawling thing, get down
> on your *hands* and pick up those cards. You could stand on
> your hands. Stand on one hand. Do tricks, Paul. Pick up
> one card at a time with your teeth. But don't bite. Why not?
> Paul wonders. Answer: Because it ruins the deckle-edge.
>
> Still, The Queen of Hearts has two heads—she'd hardly
> miss one.

Tues.

> If I'd never met you I'd been better off. I had my hate. I
> could stuff everybody's condoms into the sand. Nobody could
> get to me. Love's a bait for fools and fishes. Worms, worms,
> worms. It's hot on the beaches this year. I don't even try to
> get wet anymore. Let them swim.
>
> How long will you be there? I'm planning to drive down
> anyway to see ....[illegible]. The gas averages out
> about 8.6 per gallon. It's about 1200 miles from Boston to
> St. Louis. Could you meet me in St. Louis?

Scribbled on an ordinary card, as if it were a postscript was:

> People are always asking you like what book if you could
> only and I think I know why I'd take it. Because Camus is
> the only one who makes suicide reasonable. As if you needed
> reasons.
>
> P.

When she left the post office, Shaddy and Kleig were already waiting for her on the sunlit streets. Kleig was shading his eyes from the intense light with a paper which looked very much like a new contract. Kate had already learned to recognize a new contract; the band leader would wave them around like a college kid with his first college pennant.

"Got plenty of reading material there, eh?" Kleig asked her with unabashed curiosity, as though her mail might be of general interest to the Chinaberry Nine.

In reply Kate carefully folded her letter and cards into her pocket-book so that neither the handwriting nor postmark was visible.

"Pretty secretive, isn't she?" Kleig observed with a suggestive wink. He tapped Shaddy lightly on the shoulder with the contract. "Don't forget. Rehearsal for the new gig on Monday. First night, September 20. That doesn't give us too much time. But on the other hand, it doesn't give us too long a vacation. Vacations leave you broke."

Shaddy laughed in agreement. He was evidently pleased with the new terms Kleig had arranged for them. "This climate was getting on my nerves anyway. A steambath of a town. Can't even walk to a restaurant without working up a sweat."

Kate watched Kleig's slightly stooped figure disappear down the avenue. " 'New gig'?" she echoed. "How far?"

Before replying Shaddy looked up the sunswept streets as if the shimmering heat waves were smoke signals: he stood quietly interpreting their significance.

"Salt Lake City. Six weeks. That's like a whole season. And it'll be cool there. Wow, what a relief from this heat."

"I'm not going," Kate announced abruptly.

He stared. "Where *you* going? To Timbuctoo?" He seemed to be trying to treat it as a joke.

"I'm going to Art School. There's a good one here."

"What you mean, you're going to art school? You talk as if you're still in Detroit, going to high school with your old man taking care of your expenses. This here's a whole new ball game."

Somehow the cliché which under other circumstances she might have found amusing, irritated her as much as anything he said. "I don't care what it is. I've already made out my application: that's what I *intend* to do. That's what I'm going to do."

Passersby were pausing to stare. One middle-aged woman murmured to an unseen audience as she passed: "Trash . . . . Fightin' in the street like niggers."

Shaddy lowered his voice, glared at Kate. "Let's see those damned letters." His face was livid, his eyes narrowed to two jets of fury.

She was somehow astonished at the direction of his rage: what had her correspondence with Paul to do with it? "They're postcards. From Paul," she said, as if that explained everything and should satisfy him.

"I don't care who the fuck they're from, I want to *see* them!"

"Let's get off this public street," she murmured coldly.

He gripped her arm while they crossed over to a nearby public

106

park. It was one of those treeless squares of sparsely cultivated grass that soak up so much heat from the burning Texas sun that they usually remained deserted till twilight. Shaddy now threw himself onto a bench and sat for a while in silence, his hands clenched between his knees. Kate stood staring at a couple of sparrows who looked as if they had fallen asleep in the mid-afternoon heat.

"You gonna give me those cards?" he demanded at last. "I don't care *who* they're from. I can't see any wife of mine carrying on a correspondence with *any*body without I know who she's writing to."

The phrase *wife of mine* settled in her mind like a fog. Since she had nothing concerning Paul to conceal she handed him the cards, but kept her acceptance card from the art school carefully put away. "I'm not just a 'wife of yours,'" she objected. "I'm a person. As a person—"

"Well, as a goddammed *person*, you're coming with me. I pay for your food, your clothes! You'll do what *I* say." He bent his head to the postcards as if having made this pronouncement, there could be nothing further for her to say.

When he had struggled through the reading of Paul's difficult scrawl, he handed the cards back, shaking his head. "That guy's gone off his rocker," he said emphatically, but with a certain satisfaction, as if this made everything clear to him. He looked sharply at Kate. "Now you just sit right down here," he pointed at the place beside him on the bench in the tone of a man determined to talk reasonably to unreasonable people.

She resented the command, but felt she had more important things to argue about, she had to guard against being diverted by the trivial.

"Let me remind you of a few facts. Like one of them to begin with is that you're married to *me*, not that poor bastard up there. He couldn't do a thing for you. He had his chance . . . . For six months we been getting along good, haven't we?" He paused, awaiting her answer.

Kate just barely nodded.

"I give up fooling around, didn't I? I mean it. Women come up to the bandstand, I just say 'fuck off, baby: my girl's got it all' . . . ." He tried to smile, but there was a tremor in his voice. "I didn't ask anything of you when I brought you with me—except to *be* with me. Now you tell me, cool as a cucumber, that you are not going to go to Salt Lake City with me. Do you really think I'm all that stupid? Do you really think I believe all this about going to school and all? What I want to know is, *who's* in that school? A wife who picks up her own private exclusive mail at the p.o. is sure to have something very good going for herself . . . wherever she is. Well, whatever plans you had, baby, you just better cool it. You're coming with me."

107

She shook her head. "I can't get anything done while we're on the road. Can't you see that? I can't produce any body of work on the run. I can't *learn* anything."

"Jesus Christ," he said wrathfully. "You sure do use the most high and mighty language when you want to shit on somebody's head, don't you? *Produce a body of work*, my ass. You want *me* to pick up the tab, while you suck up to every fancy art teacher in town. Well, baby, find yourself another sucker. I'm not into Being Had . . . Jesus Christ, how do I know how many guys will be in those hot pants of yours between now and Christmas? A cunt not everybody's had his finger in—I figure that's the *least* I can ask——"

She drew her hand back and slapped him across the face. Shaddy was the wrong person to do that to, she knew: a physical instrument, his reactions were instantly physical. Within seconds he had spun around and hit her three times, so that her cheeks were blazing, her nose bleeding.

He continued punching his right fist into his left hand, as though waiting for her to say one more word and he would finish her off.

She cursed him under her breath. "You think *that'll* change things? I wouldn't go with you to Salt Lake if you killed me." Nothing aroused her obstinacy like violence. A moment ago she had been pleading, excusing, asking for what had in fact seemed a privilege. Now, in a fury, she demanded her release from a contract, on the basis of the violation of herself as a person.

"You'll come," he said. "Just don't imagine I'm about to finance your little party. Hell, you can't even make yourself enough money to buy you a bag of paints!" he added contemptuously.

In humiliation she realized this was true. She sat at the edge of the bench, sobbing with impotence. It would have been more dignified to walk away, but there was no place to go. She had not a dime that Shaddy did not give her.

"You know damn well I could divorce you. Desertion. A woman *supposed* to go along with her husband. That's the law. That's *my* law. If you don't like it, if you don't like *me* enough even to be with me, well you might'st well get yourself a lawyer." He stood up. The sun was hot as flames on their faces.

"You coming back to the hotel?"

She shook her head fiercely.

He sighed and walked away.

When that night, hungry and exhausted after stubbornly wandering the streets of Houston for hours, she returned to the hotel room, she found that Shaddy had checked out. On the mirror, using her white watercolor paint, he had left her a note:

Baby, this is it. I'm not fooling you. Here's our address in Salt Lake. MEET ME THERE OR I FILE.

Love?
Sh.

P.S. A longie in Mormon City. Six weeks!

Stubbornly Kate washed away the address, prepared her clothes for job-hunting in the morning, and fell asleep without a tear.

9

In spite of her exhaustion she woke long before daylight, determined to prove Shaddy wrong. She found herself carried along by an excitement which veiled her fatigue like the shimmering afternoon heat which had veiled the whiteness of the park the previous day. Before she left the hotel room she experimented with a crayon and chalk drawing in white and ultramarine: the treeless park surfaced out of the green-blue haze like the white whale from out of the sea. A shadowy evocation of Shaddy's body, his back turned to the viewer, sat hunched and ominous; the heavy whiteness enveloped the seated couple, swelling to a huge bubblelike surface as though she and Shaddy and the park were enclosed in an airless white balloon which would explode at any moment, dissolving its inhabitants. Kate placed the drawing opposite the wall mirror; the bathroom door was open and the drawing's reflection in the bathroom mirror seemed to reduplicate itself around the room: she felt as if she had created a true image of her fears, and she fled from the hotel room.

In a nearby coffee shop she sat, pale and alert, reading the classified ads. Her stomach slowly tightened as if some gigantic screw driver were nailing down her insides. She felt some unspeakable danger threatening her, she would never have believed herself capable of being so frightened. She did not realize she was experiencing the most dangerous threat of all—the economic threat. If she could not expect help from Shaddy, she must have a job. What kind of job? With plummeting self-esteem she scanned the ads: Typist wanted, Model wanted, Drug store needs part-time help. Insurance clerk, File clerk, Mother's helper, Salesgirl for cosmetic line, Lingerie, Waitress. Experienced only need apply.

Rage and helplessness gathered in her at the realization that "they had taught her nothing useful." Twelve years of schooling and she could not even earn enough to eat. *Experienced only need apply*: down here they did not hire white girls to do the kind of work she had done for Jacob K.—the cleaning and slaughtering of fowl, the filling of shelves with heavy canned goods, the haggling with farmers for produce; she felt herself thrown back into the nineteenth century just as surely as if she had been taught nothing but how to pick cucumbers for the czars of Russia. Down here they hired black men or Mexicans to do peasants' work: old men who were called boys when the work was light, strong boys who were called men when the work was heavy. By a grim irony of a racist society she was classified out of all jobs using unskilled help.

Even as her stomach was grinding into a new and tighter panic her gaze fell on an ad in the MALE HELP WANTED column: Cairns' Taxidermy. Clean-up work. *Some art experience preferred*. Apply in person.

Without a moment's hesitation Kate gathered her things together and was on her way to the Cairns' Taxidermy. While, nervously, she listened to the taxi driver's meter tick her lunch and supper down to the size of a grilled cheese sandwich, she began inventing a whole history of "art experience." She tried to think of what she had ever heard or read about taxidermy. Nothing. Nothing at all.

But her life with Jacob K. had taught her the uses of bravado, if nothing else. She hiked her shoulder bag high on her back, like a hitch-hiker she'd seen once trying to look as if he were on an adventure instead of just trying to get out of the burning sun. She wondered if her face bore the same look of disdain, of exhaustion, of tight-mouthed bitterness against the cars which had abandoned him to the dusty highway.

She now produced a smile for what she expected to be the inevitable black servant at the front entrance to Cairns' Taxidermy, a rambling corner house cutting across the highway on which their busload of musicians had entered the city. She recognized with faint surprise the very roadside restaurant, Nini's, at which the bus had pulled up when the entire band of Chinaberry Nine—famished and exhausted from the long ride from Texarkana—had lined up at the counter for breakfast, kneading their cold hands. She remembered the restaurant because Slick and Barney had started up a chant to accompany their entrance into town: "Eenie *Nini* Miney Moe/Catch a Nigger by the Toe"—a rhyme which any white child from the ghetto would have known better than to sing: she had been amazed at their childish bigotry.

But at the home of Cairns' Taxidermy no "black boy" appeared. No one at all answered her ring. Perplexed, and fearful she may have come to the wrong place, Kate wandered around the side entrance up the long driveway. Behind the house and dominating the land-site in much the same way a farmer's barn rather than his house will seem to dominate the landscape, stood a long metal shed. The windows were open and Kate could hear a faint humming sound, as of an eléctric blade or saw, or perhaps an air conditioner. As she entered she was struck by the distinct odor of leather, glue, turpentine, paint and even (she thought) blood. Later she was to understand that she had not mistaken the smell of blood: many small animals, owls, quail, pheasants, doves, were brought direct from the hunt to Cairns' Taxidermy and were at once stripped down to their skeletons—to be rebuilt to a kind of immortality by Caleb Cairns.

With a timidity unusual in her, Kate tapped on the metal walls of the shed, announcing her presence. From the end of the shed came a hailed invitation from a man who she hoped would be Caleb Cairns himself. The man, whoever he was, was leaning over a table while yelling at her to *come over, come on over, he couldn't look up now, it'd spoil his* . . . . She couldn't quite understand what it was that was in danger of being spoiled. She moved through the long tables as if in a dream. It was as if she had fallen out of the Texas sunlight into some subterranean circle where she was surrounded by the transmigrating souls of the dead who had taken on the forms of otters, skunks, chipmunks, squirrels, pheasants, weasels, quail, peacocks, eagles, sailfish, marlin, tarpon, barracuda. Above all these, as if tranquilly guarding their empire, were the mounted heads of antlered animals. The taxidermist had arranged them so that their eyes turned toward the entrance: any newcomer at once confronted these Lares on the wall.

At the work table in the far corner stood a tall man whose hands, covered with thick chamois gloves, gripped a pair of clippers with which he was twisting wires into a body form. The form appeared to be the skeleton of a bird; it stood daintily on one leg; though still fleshless it seemed about to wing into space. Cairns was bent over the form, shaping the wire into still another claw which stood poised in the air. A pair of blue-tinted goggles rested high on Cairns' forehead.

At Kate's approach, he glanced toward her with the mild proprietary courtesy of someone who dislikes leaving his work, but knows a certain minimal courtesy is necessary to the "buyers" of the world, especially trappers and hunters.

"Looking for something special?" he asked laconically, as if he hoped she weren't. He gave her the brunt of his entire vision, lifting his head slightly to look at her. Kate was surprised at the shock of it. It was as if with a single artisan's glance he had looked at her vertebrae and had immediately fleshed out for himself the size and shape of her breasts, her bones, her heart.

Kate flushed slightly and raised her chin with an air of courage (trying to look like that moose or elk or whatever it is up there, she reflected).

"Yes. Very special: a job." She held out the newspaper as if to explain.

He seemed to smile, but his mouth did not move except to ask, " 'Kind of job you looking for?"

Kate had become aware that a water cooler was splashing away behind him which partly accounted for the mysterious mood of the place, as though it were an underground grotto with water seeping from the walls. Words seemed to be caught up in the atmosphere and vanish in the air: or was it the effect of the silent antlered heads?

Cairns took the newspaper from her hand, looking down at it as if he did not already know what was in it. He was silent a long while. Then he slid the goggles over his eyes and leaned forward to the form he was shaping. He said finally, speaking very slowly and (she imagined) with disappointment: "That's for a man. We don't have women around here. Can't stomach the dead animals. I mean, there's a lot of blood, sweat and tears goes into taxidermy. No job for a lady."

"I'm not a lady," she said firmly, risking all. "I'm a working woman." In the South, she knew, to affirm one was not a lady was like announcing (instead) that one was a prostitute.

This time he straightened up with a sort of grunt, his hand gingerly touching his back at the precise point where moments before he had been bent over the emerging form of the bird. She noticed now that close at hand stood a crockery barrel filled with papier-mâché which was apparently used to fill out the animal forms.

"Never heard of a lady denying her own sex. What are you then?"

"I'm an artist," she said, determined to enjoy the challenge whether she got the job or not.

Cairns shoved his goggles as far back on his brow as they could go, then turned off the water cooler. Instantly the Texas heat enveloped the shed as though they had stepped out of a sheltered embankment into a dark tunnel of heat without air. But the voice of the water cooler had been like the presence of a third person; the silence which pervaded the shed made them drop their voices into unexpected intimacy. Kate stepped back, as if the silence, the heat, the presence of this stranger constituted a kind of assault. For a moment she was afraid.

"I'm an artist," she repeated, her voice strangely fervent as it rebounded on the heat. "You asked for someone with artistic experience."

"Sit down," he ordered, pointing to an empty crate. "I need someone to work. And I need someone smart. You look smart enough—" he grinned slightly. "I'm not sure you mightn't be *too* smart. But it's heavy work too. I mean: see those heads? Some of 'em got horns three feet long. They didn't get mounted to those armatures and hoisted in the air by any ninety-pound girl in dancing shoes."

Kate kept her legs neatly together beside the wooden crate. She was not wearing dancing shoes, but his metaphor was clear enough.

"And . . . you're married," he said slowly, reaching into his blue coveralls for his pipe, slowly tamping it down while he watched her.

114

"What's your husband going to say to your working with . . . a ranch hand all day? In a place like this?" He scrutinized her as he waved his arm toward the long tables with the half-created forms of animals drying on their platforms.

Kate wanted to say something about the antlered heads, how she was mysteriously moved by them as by a phantom race, but she was afraid that under the circumstances Cains would be suspicious if not insulted by compliments. So she answered only part of his question, "As for my husband," she said slowly, twisting the gold ring on her hand with a faint sense of surprise that she was not only legally married but that she did in fact feel obliged to wear this ring of ownership during Shaddy's absence. "He's gone. I mean, he's out of town—"

He ignored her embarrassment. With an obvious determination to be precise in every detail he probed: "You mean he's gone and left you? Deserted you? Or do you mean he's out working while you're—" He snapped his teeth to the stem of his pipe and with a sudden awkward gesture pushed the table so that the bird skeleton trembled precariously, about to fall. Kate at once put her hand out to rescue the trembling form.

"Look," she said desperately. "I can really paint. And I can draw. And I can learn anything. If you'll teach me." Her voice shook slightly as she followed the bite of his lip to the stem of his pipe. The mystery of sex: she had seen the tincture of his eye, felt the pull of her bosom. Even if he hired her now, she would never know whether he believed she had any ability at all. She tried to explain how she wanted to attend Art School, that she wanted to learn all she could, that Shaddy's migratory profession did not permit them to stay in one place long enough for her to learn anything about art or anything else, that it was becoming impossible to carry her easels and canvases from one hotel to another, and that, besides, she wanted to experiment with sculpture, metals, murals, sandstone, pottery, ceramics, metals, plastics . . . . Even as she explained all these "truths" there was under his pale gaze that flicker which claimed her, which she had later to admit was the real reason Caleb Cairns said slowly, lowering his goggles again as he walked her back into the light of the Houston highway, out of the surcharged heat of the shop: "Bring all your painting stuff tomorrow. Not too early. I don't start before ten—though like as not, I'll be working till dark. I want to see can you paint like you can talk."

He stood at the curb watching her as she crossed over to Nini's Restaurant. It was not till she had returned to the hotel that she realized he had not even asked her name, her age, her experience, her telephone number or her address. He had left it entirely up to her whether she wanted to come back and spend her days with a ranch hand.

Her job during the first week was to tear newspapers: piles of shredded, confetti-like paper disappeared into wooden barrels which Caleb kept beside the armatures: around these armatures he would model his own papier-mâché forms for the animals. Kate shredded the newspapers by hand. By the second week at the Cairns Shop she felt every newspaper in the country must have passed through her hands. Pictures of the world-in-crisis sluiced around her fingers like oysters: pictures of grim-faced leaders of juntas in Latin America, pictures of hungry people in India, in Pakistan, in Biafra, Asia, in Appalachia, passed through her fingers along with the smiles of reelected incumbents and the manacled hands of assassins. Her gloves became black with newsprint; she felt herself physically absorbed into history: she caught time on the rip. Princes and princesses dissolved into masses of gluey paper to be transformed into bird-mounts, fish forms, turtle backs, antelope heads.

One day when she was too tired to stir the mass any longer, she climbed into the wooden barrel with her bare feet and trod the shredded news like grapes. When Caleb arrived at work that morning, she had the radio tuned up to the loudest possible country western and was pacing to and fro, emulsifying the news of the day. Caleb stood watching her in astonishment for a while, as though she were one of the Bacchae performing her ancient rite in his temple; then he gently took her by the hand to help her out of the barrel.

"Here. Come on out of there. Lean on me, else you'll tip over, barrel and all."

He led her to the stall shower, a crudely constructed metal box with a concrete floor. "Wash all that off, and when you get dressed, come on out, and I'll put you to some real work." He threw his bathrobe over the side of the shower stall with the self-conscious manner of a man determined not to exploit a situation.

"No call for you to work like that," he said when she had come out. "You use up all that steam, you won't have anything left for school." Caleb always referred to the art classes Kate was taking four nights a week as "school," as if she were attending a little red school house where they were teaching her to read and write. "Anybody willing to put in ten miles of walking in a barrel ought not to *have* to. I reckon it's time to put you on Ears."

Her own ears seemed to twitch nervously at the thought. Caleb's work was at times so strange to her that her imagination flinched at what might be expected of her next. She felt she had little stomach for the flaying and tanning which went into the preparation of animal skins; fortunately Caleb had all his larger animals done at a local tannery. He handled the birds and fish himself, regardless of size; he said

116

they were too delicate for other people, too perishable.

To her relief she discovered she was simply being promoted to a higher level of paper cutting: she was no longer to prepare newspapers to be jellied to a homogenous mass, Caleb informed her, but was to cut out "ear forms" instead. Caleb showed her how to cut out the ears from paper soft as chamois, resilient as flesh: the diamond-shaped ears of the buck, the paddlelike ears of rabbits, the dainty inner cups of night animals.

For several days, this new task absorbed her; the variety held her interest. Luckily, just when she had decided she could not cut out another Ear (she remarked plaintively to Caleb that she was beginning to feel like one of Santa Claus' elves), Caleb called her into the painting room to let her work on Eyes. On a long table with grooved fissures like an old-fashioned school desk lay a row of transparent glass eyes. He claimed he was about to trust her with the most important aspect of his work. "Anybody can paint up the body to look like a fish. But only an artist can paint the soul. These are *souls* I'm giving you," he said, showing her a handful of eyes. He carefully assembled them into the grooved row of her workbench, then placed a sample chart on an easel-like rack before her. "These are the eyes of a deer, these of a bobcat. These? Who you think these'll belong to?" He indicated an enormous pair of saffron yellow orbs on the chart; Kate glanced from the chart to the spheres of glass which she was expected to endow with color, vision, soul. The eyes on the chart looked back at her like a Cheshire cat which had left, not a smile, but this ineffaceable gaze.

Kate shook her head, as much with awe as with ignorance. "I couldn't imagine. They're enormous."

"Fit to see the Invisible," he said with a faint smile. "Only thing more beautiful than the eye of an owl is the eye of a human. Which can also see the Invisible. Though, like it says, there are some 'which have eyes and see not; which have ears and hear not' . . . ."

He was leaning over her as he spoke, pairing off the bits of glass according to size. Kate began to feel that his own eyes were the most compelling force she had ever met. She decided, however, to sound professional, to distract herself from this physical lure: "Will I be able? . . . . Do you think—once I've painted them, you'll let me tamp them into the mount?"

He rose, straightening his back. She noticed that he was continually bending over to talk to her. "Not yet, not yet. Don't be in such a hurry. God didn't make eyes in a day. He took one hell of a long time about it . . . . But I want you to look at 'em good. Study 'em. There's a lot you can learn from studying eyes. You can almost tell

117

what kind of animal it was, how he lived, what he thought . . . ." He was looking directly down at her now and Kate wondered whether he saw in her own eyes . . . what she was thinking of. He stepped away with a faintly irresolute movement. "Yep," he added as if summing it all up. "Nothing more beautiful than the eye of an owl. Some say a deer, and I guess I'd go along with that as far as you can see, but there's something about the way you sink right *into* the owl-eye . . . . Do you believe in the transmigration of souls?" he asked abruptly.

Kate discovered in herself no urge whatsoever to smile: transmigration of souls? O.K. by her.

He sat down on a bench, close enough to see her, but far enough away so that his voice echoed slightly in the narrow room. She became suddenly aware that Caleb was not at all concerned with how much work she did: he wanted someone to talk to. It struck her that Caleb was a very lonely man; that although dozens of hunters came in to see him during each season, none stayed to talk to him. There was even a kind of restrained hostility between Caleb and the men he depended on for his livelihood. A couple of days ago, for instance, the Wainright boys had come in, each bearing a brace of mourning doves they had shot while on their vacation. They had set the birds down on the table proudly: their first kill.

Caleb had stood in silence, his pipe cradled as if for warmth in his right hand. Although it was still early in the day he had suddenly seemed to Kate very tired. He had stood poking the velvety grey birds like a surgeon looking for the wound. The blood had coagulated to round red buds at their beaks.

"Y'all did some good shootin'," Caleb commented laconically without looking at the boys. They nodded enthusiastically, their skin radiant with health, their eyes an identical shade of blue. "Who taught you to shoot so good?" Caleb inquired, as if deferentially.

"We got our first rifle when we weren't but ten," offered one of the brothers. "Had to. Shot my first snake on the ranch with a twenty-two. After that Daddy said he'd see to it, we had plenty of practice. Took us out to a turkey-shoot. We did real good, and he bought us a pair of rifles come Christmas."

"Ummm," Caleb had said thoughtfully. "How soon you want these birds? I'm mighty busy right now." He shot a guilty glance in Kate's direction. "Might not be able to get to them for a few days: and I don't like to just stack up a whole passel of birds in my cooler. They don't *keep* too good."

The brothers had seemed disappointed; Kate herself had wondered at Caleb's tactlessness. Then, as if to prove that the hunting of doves was not worth the expense of taxidermy, he had asked her to do the job. Stunned by this responsibility, Kate had spent the rest of the afternoon drawing sketches of doves. She had produced for Caleb about a dozen sketches, all of them different—not in size and coloring, but in expression: she was disturbed by this variety. What she needed to do, both she and Caleb felt, was to stabilize the expression, to catch the essence of mourning doves.

Caleb had explained: "That's because you're starting to work from the dead ones. You can't do resurrecting till you've had a good look at the living." Asking her to wait, he had at once walked over to his house which adjoined the shop, and returned with a pair of doves in a wooden cage. "Take these on home," he said. "Do your homework first. And above all, take a good look at those eyes, the living eyes. The big problem is how to make an eye that's been dead-blind look like it's come back from the dead and don't intend to give up seeing ever again . . . ."

"An animal's got a soul," he continued as if confessing to secret knowledge. "In this business the body is secondary."

She looked up in surprise.

He nodded as if she had said something, and continued with conviction. "They bring 'em in to me dead. And I bring 'em back to life. That's a kind of religion, isn't it?" He smiled, leaning forward, his elbows on his knees; his jeans were worn to a delicate skinlike thinness; as he moved forward the flesh seemed to stir beneath the faded cloth, as if by his movement the cloth had taken on an intenser light. "It may seem strange to you for *me* to be saying this, but I just wish they'd stop killing 'em. I can't stop 'em from killing 'em, the only thing I can do is make 'em look good again afterwards. Oh, I'm bootleggin' *life*, that's what I'm doing, just bootleggin' it. I'm a subversive organization. A big lie."

"Back in Florida," he went on, "my old man was a gospel minister. He'd stand up there before these dried-up old folks and say, 'I am the Resurrection and the Life.' And he believed it. He thought a belief in Jesus could bring eternal life. Well, that's what I'm doin' too . . . ."

Kate prepared herself to listen; she was beginning to understand that there was a moment-of-truth when a person was willing to tell you all about his life; if you let it pass, if you turned away with a shrug, a joke or a look of boredom, you lost the moment forever. The astonishing thing was that, as though it were a religious act, a confession which absolved him from repetition, the person seemed never to wish to refer to that part of his life again: just as Paul had never again mentioned his paralysis and as Shaddy seemed to have willed himself to forget he had ever been in the mines.

Kate fixed her eyes on Caleb, trusting him, wishing to be trusted.

119

Caleb was no longer a young man when Kate Kalokovich had walked into his Taxidermy Shop. He recognized that fact with mild astonishment as a man would who, in spite of his ignorance, had managed safely to cross a desert. If he had known there was a desert he would have come better prepared: water bottles, snakebite kit, hiking boots, protection against sun and sand; in short, supplies for survival. But as it was, he found himself merely astonished that he had come such a long distance: unprepared, uneducated and unloved.

Brought up on a small cabbage and cucumber farm in north Florida, he had come to his profession through successive acts of violence which had turned him to taxidermy as a kind of antidote. From the sandy Florida earth his father had earned a dull living excited to pleasurable ferment by the threat of damnation which lurked perpetually over their heads. "Yaweh" Cairns, as some of the younger members of his congregation had secretly named him (his real name was Uriah but he was not fond of the biblical reference), had elevated repression to the high oratory of sin-and-salvation. In the small town of Reed he had drawn to himself a modest congregation of about seventy people who came Sunday evenings to hear Cairns preach the life of the soul to cool-eyed women in magenta-colored dresses who did not believe much in the flesh anymore anyway. After Caleb was born the Carinses had no more children, having decided that the surest proof of their purity of mind was the minimal family. Preacher Cairns vigilantly safeguarded the life of his congregation; their physical and spiritual well-being were the main subject of the pulpit and constituted in effect the social life of the rural town—a life arid and landlocked, as though being so far from the ocean had kept it from loosening up.

For their son, Caleb, the hard-working Cairnses aspired after the symbols of earthly and heavenly favor: land and education. Land so Caleb could prosper, and education so he could hang onto it. They quietly preferred the ministry for Caleb, but were willing to settle for the law as an extension of God's justice. Quickly they allowed their little ten-acre farm to bleed into the land nearest them, so that it soon coagulated into several properties alongside Uriah's.

Uriah had begun to feel God was truly rewarding his efforts till one Sunday night after his preaching one of his congregation was frightened out of her skin by a black man who followed her home. The distance from his church to the home of his church member, Pinky Sutton, was about two miles, and in that distance every possible configuration of violence had crossed her mind. By the time she had arrived home where she lived with a widowed sister, she was hysterical and could scarcely recall whether the man had mumbled an obscene threat, terrifying her with hooting owl-like calls, or had in fact exposed his huge black sex to her, which (she later swore) was red at the tip, like mashed huckleberries. He must have followed her all along the highway, slipping in and out of the rigid pole-like pine woods which stood up like prison bars on either side of the highway, a labyrinthine woods winding about itself as far as the eye could see: he could at any moment have seized her and carried her off into the woods. It had all taken place directly after services when it was nearly dark, though not so totally dark but that she could recognize the man if they found him.

It was an old story, of course. The men of Reed County all knew it by heart, they knew the offense and the remedy. There was no point in verifying the testimony of a woman who had gathered at the feet of old Uriah for nearly a decade, soaking up faith and chastity like money to guard against a gaunt old age. At least a dozen members of Uriah's congregation had retained their membership in the Klan, a membership always valid though rarely used; and unhesitatingly Cairns made the necessary telephone calls from his farm and started out at once in his truck—calling to his son, Caleb, where he was out in the fields spraying for cabbage worms, to come see justice done in Florida. Caleb had just graduated from high school, and what better introduction could a boy have to manhood than to see how women were protected under the old laws? If in the old days white adulterers were stoned to death, what death should be decreed for a black man who spilled his seed on the ground, terrifying women so innocent they did not understand when he, Uriah, arraigned them from the pulpit, reminding them, "and if Mary was not *known* by Joseph, it was because God *knew* better than to sully the body of the mother of Jesus with such *knowledge*." One woman had come up afterwards to ask mildly if God did not "know" everything. Of such was his congregation.

Caleb had not especially wanted to go, Pinky Sutton had always bored him, and personally he could not see how even a sex-starved buck could have cared enough for Pinky to have followed her for two miles; but perhaps the man had been drunk, which in itself would warrant a solemn rebuke from his father. He was annoyed at the affair because he knew it would keep his father rhetorical and flamboyant for weeks and he would not be able to approach him in any sensible way concerning what lay nearest to his heart at the time—which was that he wanted to go to medical school. Cairns, of course, wanted his son to sit on the right hand of God. For Cairns, the medical profession had a certain taint along with its aura, like the alchemists of old, and he was sure it led men away from the Lord. Uriah rarely had a good word to say for the medical men who had "cured" members of his congregation, often affirming that it had been prayer and faith and not medicine which had cured his folks after they'd been to one of the big hospitals down to

Dade County. Besides, all the accumulation of cabbage plots had really been for Caleb's sake, Cairns argued, and now if he were to run off to the city and be a doctor, what comfort would he be to Uriah and Myra in their old age? Cairns barely believed in Sickness anyway. He had never been sick a day in his life, he said, and that was because his soul was well, and it continuously, day by day, kept his body healed. The day Pinky Sutton was obscenely spoken to, or assaulted (not that it mattered much to Uriah which, the black man that would do the one would do the other), old man Cairns took the hoe from Caleb's hand and said, "Come on boy, you got a man's job to do today." So they had all piled into Ted Poole's truck, about twenty of them, and they were so crowded they had had to stand up in the truck, their rifles lowered to the floor, looking oddly like those revolutionaries of Latin America who are always off to fight in some improbable war.

It was nearly four o'clock when they started the hunt, pursuing every black buck of Pinky Sutton's description—"tall and skinny with a gold ring on his left hand"—she did not at that time describe his red, "blood-stained" sex; that came out later. The men were getting more and more angry as they rode through the "quarters." They felt the black women were protecting their men, the alibis were altogether too probable, as if a warning had leaked into every shambling cottage in niggertown. As the riders were standing about, all of them, outside one woman's house, she was swearing up and down that not only was her boy not there but that he had been in Georgia all week working for a lumber company, logging pine. "Here's the number, you can call 'em. Come right on in and use the phone, you'll find my boy been workin' like a man for that company, though he ain't but fourteen. They ain't like the white folks down here in Reed County . . . ." As she stood talking, a field hand who had been picking potatoes drove up in a muddy truck. He was alone, he stood in the dusk—a rare, mute species, neither friendly nor hostile, like some lorris-eyed vegetarian from a time neither forward nor backward in history. He was so close they could see or feel his breathing and the faint flush of his cheeks. His color was a perfect sepia on skin as smooth as though it had flown together toward the bones out of water. He had, Caleb remembered, a high delicate nose whose nostrils moved, delicate and inquiring like the antennae of one of those butterflies which live on liquid and never eat . . . .

Quickly the men seized him. With something like paternal pride old man Cairns ordered Caleb to bind the boy's hands (this nigger wasn't the one, but that didn't matter, he was to be an example to the rest of his people on the your-brother's-keeper-principle, Uriah explained) and threw him into the truck. All the way to the shooting range the boy lay at their feet, his terrified eyes near the toe of Caleb's boots.

The boy did not struggle. It was as if terror had immobilized him, his body lay limp and lifeless before they tied him to the fence. Since he was gagged, he could not plead for his life, nor cry out, so he died in silence. The men had gathered close for the first execution bullet; they now stood loose and waiting, dressed in plain farmer's clothes; they did not wear white sheets in that town because the punishment of blacks for these offenses was serious business and did not need theatrics. What was important, like the killers of Caesar, was their communal obligation to protect the people of the country from tyranny. They did not, however, wash their hands in the blood of the boy, but instead each man with his rifle was given a certain number of shots. Afterwards, no man nor woman in the world, not the boy's own mother would have recognized the boy: they buried him with a rake, like leaves.

Caleb, who had thought he had the stomach for whatever gristle and bone a man would have to contend with in the medical world—inflicting pain, of course, but doing it to reestablish the just equilibrium of the body—Caleb, after his permissible round of shots which he did not follow to the bull's eye (they had drawn a circle around the boy's private parts), had turned into the woods, saying coarsely he had to take a piss (he knew he was being initiated into manhood and the language of it was part of the ritual), had gone into the pine woods and vomited. The next day he announced to Uriah that he was going off to med school, as if being a doctor was simply something you signed up for.

And he even sent away for the college forms to fill out, for they thought the business of Pinky Sutton was all over. No one had seen them pick up the black boy, he would simply have disappeared. The distraught family would hunt for him for weeks, fearing the worst—and then would finally begin to wait to hear from him from wherever they would have persuaded themselves he had run away to, to stake out a new life for himself somewhere, "done run away to the North" perhaps. It was better than believing he lay somewhere coiled within coils of water moccasins, or just staring up at the Spanish moss which scrimmed the sky. Caleb felt that those eyes (which had not even dared to expect pity but which had gazed at them from over the white gag across his mouth like some shapeless ghost to whom nothing was left but eyes) would never close but could still, doubtless, penetrate darkness, might even now be gazing upward through the leaves under which they had buried him, warding off the bombardment of cosmic rays . . . . But his voice, at least, was silent, and he could not testify against them.

But they had not counted on an ambitious governor, nor the rash of new residents in Reed County, who without their noticing it, had infiltrated the town under the guise of illness, retirement, or opening a new business. 'These few new residents, more afraid of Klansmen than they were of niggers, had demanded an investigation. They had heard horror stories from somewhere, from the back streets, from their maids, from women weeping in the grocery stores. Could it be true? The incumbent governor wanted all those Dade County votes at the next election and he meant to do a thing about it. Before the night riders had realized what had happened, the leaders were brought before a grand jury. Hunting dogs had been used for the first time, not to trace the living, but the dead. In an effort to dissociate themselves from their leaders several of the men turned state's witnesses. Yet all of the men, strangely enough, as if in instinctive tribal protection of their medicine man, refused to implicate "Yaweh." As if to balance the scales of their sacrifice, however, they turned their spite against Caleb. For some reason they all remembered that Caleb had tied the boy's hands before he was thrown into the truck. When all the "evidence" was in, convictions were given out as though the State were raking in a crap game: ten years, five years, three years—and for Caleb, two, because he was the youngest.

Although old man Cairns was stunned, he did not rush to deflect the verdict to himself. Instead he intimated to Caleb that he was a lamb chosen by the good Lord for this sacrifice. Doubtless the good Lord knew that Caleb was strong and would survive. For him, Uriah, to rush in and denounce himself would destroy his church: his entire congregation would be under suspicion.

Caleb had sat in his cell, his hands splayed and lifeless between his knees, his head bowed, avoiding Uriah's eyes. He was neither spitting nor swearing nor shouting, and definitely not sobbing. But he had said his last prayer. Before they drove Caleb away to be put on the chain gang, Uriah came to see him every day, but Caleb pretended he was ill and did not get up to come to the door-grill, on the other side of which his father was mumbling. Uriah said tearfully he would pray for him every day, that he was a young man, that God would give him strength to bear up under it. And he might even get out in less time if he behaved right.

But Caleb was to discover on the very first day at Reed Prison that behaving right was a meaningless word in prison. You were guilty, you were criminal, you were a wild beast, and the only way they had to protect themselves against you was to remove your fangs.

For nearly a year Caleb had been growing a mustache, great fine brown-brush handlebars which he wore with pride and dignity as though he were an extinct animal, the Irish elk, or some rare Arctic reindeer; he measured their breadth as though they were antlers. While working on old man Cairns' farm he had liked to stop now and then in the sun-drenched field and thoughtfully appraise the span of his mustaches with his outstretched hand. He did not think of himself as a handsome man. True, he was tall, which was some help, but his features were spread-eagled around in an unkempt way and it seemed his head was altogether too large for most girls to contend with. The mustache gave him a certain manly validation; it had finished off his face with dignity.

On the very first hour of his arrival at Reed Prison the Captain, as he was called, had lined up Caleb and two other new arrivals for inspection. The captain had at once interpreted the mustache as a personal offense, perhaps feeling that a man who took such liberties with his appearance was capable of anything. Or perhaps it was that those handlebars reminded Captain Gorman of his time in Mexico; he despised Mexicans even more than he hated niggers, because, he argued, we had brought the niggers here ourselves; but who had let all those wetbacks in? He had therefore (apparently) decided that he hated Caleb, not because he was a murderer, a man might kill in a passion, he understood that, and secretly he did not feel Caleb's crime worth mentioning . . . but Captain Gorman had had a grim life, nobody had ever given *him* anything: and it was the civilized freedom from care or public judgment, the protection of state, family and church allowing Caleb the freedom to grow whatever he wanted on his own face, instead of scraping it down to suitable anonymity which infuriated him. He could not understand Caleb's audacity in not having shaved the damned thing off before arriving at the prison.

Caleb, deeply depressed and still in a state of shock at old man Cairns' hypocrisy, was quite unaware of the impact his mustache had on the captain.

"What the fuck is that *shit* on your mouth?" demanded the Captain.

Caleb moved his hand questioningly across the offending brush, as though its shape would explain the Captain's fury: but there was no explanation in the touch of it.

"You'll get rid of that piece of shit at once," ordered the Captain.

"For cryin' out loud," protested Caleb with a faint grin, moving his legs in a shambling, irritated way, feeling the whole thing was too petty to be believed, as if the Captain were just another school principal calling him on the carpet for reading paperbacks during assembly.

But before Caleb could make the grunting joke he intended, the Captain's fist shot out, striking Caleb straight between the eyes as he had meant to. Caleb could feel the blood spurt from his nose, and with a howl of rage he instinctively clenched his fists. Before he could recover enough to remember that men condemned to the chain gang didn't clench their fists when surrounded by ten guards with rifles at the ready, Captain Gorman had shot his fist out again, knocking Caleb flat to the ground.

As Caleb fell he could feel his teeth cut through his tongue; the blood in his mouth tasted like spoiled wine. For some reason the idiocy of having bitten his own tongue (it required nine stitches before he could talk, sewn up by a prison doctor who thrust a needle through his tongue as though he were putting a worm on a fishhook) which humiliated him most, turning his sense of injustice to fury. Springing to his knees, Caleb positioned himself for a leap at Gorman's throat; he had never before felt himself so ready to strike regardless of consequences. But Caleb was at once ganged up on by the ten guards who rained blows on him as though he were a pestilence of lice and they were going to destroy every living thing on him, eggs and all.

While he was unconscious they stripped him naked, twisting his shoes from his feet with such force that when he recovered consciousness he thought both legs had been broken; that he might never walk again, his immobilized feet were pointed in opposite directions. But naked, in that icy cell, with neither blanket nor pallet nor bucket to keep the urine from first steaming up, then chilling—coagulant—on the concrete floor, he soon learned that the only way he could survive was to walk.

The temperature at night at that time of year in north Florida frequently went down to 25 degrees. He had to walk to live, so he walked. From the time he awoke till he fell asleep again in exhaustion, he walked up and down a cell eight by four feet, imagining himself at times an insect crossing and recrossing the eighteen-foot ceilings, so as to give himself imaginary space.

Yet those sixty days of solitude in "the hole" when he himself was rationing out his four slices of bread and one quart of water per day so as to have some way of enduring nights more lonely than madness were, he considered afterwards, the easiest time of his sentence.

The chain gang has become a myth. Even recently Caleb had read a story about a couple of brothers from Tennessee who tried to dupe the sheriff so as to avoid going on the chain gang. Surely nobody in his time believed (in spite of seeing them on highways) that there were still places where men with shackles on their legs were obliged to break rock in a sun so hot that resting on one's pickaxe could mean serious skin burn. Caleb himself would not have believed it, though he had seen the gangs in his youth. One day, while eating his lunch from a lard can, Caleb had dozed for what had seemed a moment or two on his axe; the metal surface had burned the entire side of his face like a flashburn from an oil fire. The skin had soon curled up like shavings and in the continuously blistering heat his face had taken weeks to heal. He had decided he had skin cancer and, preparing to die, had thought he might kill off that Captain first—it would be Caleb's last good deed before disintegration, saving the men who would come after him from the curse of Gorman.

It turned out he did not have skin cancer, but even if he had, he would not have been spared Gorman's vengeance. Gorman bore him an invincible grudge: that was the only explanation Caleb could arrive at for the punitive fist which managed to strike him down every week for some real or imagined infraction of the rules which Caleb was never prescient enough to foresee. Finally he grew to accept the iron fist as he accepted the iron chains and the smell of hot stone and the ridiculous grey-striped uniform, like some parody of early movies in which Buster Keaton or Laurel and Hardy might have starred. Later, when they marched onto the state highways, they wore plain government surplus clothes, as if they were performing a patriotic duty for their country and not building roads to improve Florida's public image from Orlando to Key West. Evidently the State was far more concerned with the reaction of tourists than with humiliating the prisoners: it looked bad, the tourists' seeing those striped, shackled prisoners while on their way down to enjoy the sand and sea.

When, finally, Caleb was set free, the wars which had once gripped the world everywhere except on their peninsula of stone and sand seemed to be over forever. But there was still enough left of the old hostilities to allow for a peacetime army, so he got himself sent to Germany. He thought himself lucky at the time, the girls were so friendly. Caleb had been lonely a long time and his head was not filled with tales of atrocities, the atrocities he had seen were closer to home: on the whole, he did not believe much in Good Guys versus Bad Guys—remembering how prisoners who were supposed to be buddies or even lovers would buy their safety at the expense of the other guy.

So when Caleb met Monique (her real name was Berta but she had decided to adopt a French name and a French grandmother as well as Gallic mannerisms: since she was a girl of many talents, she was a success at all three), he became a victim, not of the weakness of his political theory but of his vision. Monique was simply the most beautiful girl he had ever laid eyes on. She wore her hair to her waist as if she had never heard of Geman efficiency, and her eyes were a china blue which fixed themselves upon his face with concentrated and effective guilelessness: he felt bound to save her. Her accent was British, not French, and she chattered away, speaking English far better than the folks back home, and Caleb was struck dumb with admiration. She was like some brilliant bird, calling, calling; and Caleb rose to the lure of it, he felt sorry for her and at the same time amazed that such a stunning creature should need him. He was ready to forgive and forget: only individuals, they had been, the victims of events.

In addition he found that Monique was kindly and patient with his awkward attempts at sexual freedom (he believed, of course, in every kind of Freedom, and sex, he insisted to himself, must be one kind of freedom—whatever Cairns would have said about it) and he felt that it was good that a poor girl who had obviously been through so much could still be benign in bed and not turn her head away from him. On the contrary, her eyes would fasten to him in that inimitable way of her, would seem to change color at his climax, as though his pleasure wrought electrical changes which turned the color from a guileless blue to deep indigo. It was a startling metamorphosis but because it was his pleasure which wrought the change and not hers (of that they were both certain) he never commented on it, though it made him think sometimes of a squid. Otherwise Monique was, as he noticed the first time he saw her, the most beautiful girl he had ever laid eyes on, with a body like those of the Sabine women.

It seemed that in no time at all they were married, though Caleb never remembered the exact moment he had proposed. It just became something they wished to do. It was the convenience of it that attracted them: how else could he take Monique back to the States with him? So they were married and went to Florida for their honeymoon. He had thought Cairns and the old woman would be pleased to see him again, he had not realized Cairns didn't want him back because it reminded the whole town (which was getting to be a city), of the Pinky Sutton scandal, and his mother hated Monique at the first sight of her. He found that hard to understand, Monique was making every effort to be charming, her accent trilled like a canary through the big farmer's kitchen Cairns had built himself. Yet something in Monique's manner made Caleb ashamed of his parents' poverty, it seemed suddenly not right that folks born in a country which built empires both at home and abroad should be so poor: his mother's harsh glances and plain dresses seemed out of tune with the world of affluence. At the same time he was ashamed of Monique too, for wearing those shorts that showed her thigh and the slit of her buttocks, and for forgetting to knock her cigarette ash before it fell, so that he saw his mother looking nervously from the tablecloth she had embroidered herself to Monique's slender fingers curved toward the cigarette she held in her mouth as though she loved the loll of it on her lip. The atmosphere soon became so tense that suddenly one evening while Monique had sat cooling off on the front porch in an outfit that would have "bugged out the eyes of a nigger in a whorehouse," as Caleb had overheard the old man complain wrathfully to Myra, Cairns had suddenly offered to stake Caleb somewhere—Texas or Arizona or maybe Oregon. Caleb was surprised at how far his mother (if not Cairns) was willing to see them go, he had naively thought she would be anxious to see the family perpetuated by Monique and himself—just as soon as he could get Monique pregnant (they were having a little problem along that line for some reason). But Myra and Cairns seemed mainly concerned with getting the bride and groom started before they should be exposed to the brunt of the summer heat since, Cairns explained, the old car they could let them have was not air-conditioned. Since Caleb had never lived in an air-conditioned house nor driven in an air-conditioned car, and even the word *air-conditicned* seemed to belong to a world which was not yet part of his time, he had lost so much time in prison; and since, moreover, he was conditioned to breaking rock in the sun when the days ran by the dozen into a hundred degrees, old man Cairns' solicitude had seemed a bit irrelevant. But at the suggestion, Monique's *yes* had changed to that deep indigo, and without a word she had gone to pack their bags. She did not even say *thank you* for the car, and although the Cairns stood on the porch and nodded goodbye (his parents never waved, they thought it looked frivolous), Monique sat in the car without turning her head. As they curved into the highway, she did extend a couple of fingers, but they had an ironic curve to them, as though she were about to take the cigarette out of her mouth and was not really waving at all.

The trip was no hotter than Caleb was accustomed to; indeed, with his pocket swollen with a cashier's check as big as a ransom, and driving the first car he had ever owned, he was enjoying his freedom; he felt like singing. But Monique suffered from the heat, the sweat poured off her like oil; she found his touch unbearable in all that heat and told him so. She said she had not thought America would be like Africa, she had thought it was a civilized country. There was not even anything to see as they drove—nothing but woods as thick as a jungle on one side and alligator swamps on the other.

"Oh, you want to see something? I'll show you America!" sang out Caleb good-naturedly, still not taking her rancor seriously. "I'll show you mountains, valleys, canyons—the most beautiful in the world." Actually he had been thinking that he might get a job around Flagstaff as a kind of tourist guide through the Canyon. But to cheer Monique he began talking about Texas instead: he knew Texas would be more meaningful to her (she had seen hundreds of western films). Besides it was a kind of country in its own right, romanticized abroad, everyone had heard of its oil kings and cowboys, and perhaps the exoticism of it would appeal to her. So at once surrendering his fantasy of himself as a genial knowledgeable guide who assisted people and mules around the curve of the Canyon, he began, rather wildly, speculating on a ranch in Texas.

But Monique sat silent and absorbed, one slender leg folded under her thigh while she plucked listlessly at the blanket Cairns had spread on the front seat to protect their skin from the coarsely woven seat covers, now shredding into blades. Idly she picked up the cosmetic case she had bought for herself while attending a beauty contest in Orlando (she had wanted to enter as a contestant but old man Cairns had said he would rather die than see his son's wife strutting on the stage with her breasts and thighs displayed to a crowd like a blue ribbon cow). So it had been the one thing Caleb was forced to refuse her since they were married; he had not realized how deeply she would resent it, she had mentioned it a dozen times since they had left Florida. Now from out of the cosmetic case she pulled polishes, creams, tubes, pencils, brushes, jars, rattling them around in her box like bones. Caleb talked on and on about buying a few acres and starting with chickens and eggs and then adding some livestock, till eventually, maybe, they would be able to expand into cattle, with the best black Angus in Texas: they'd be as good as landed gentry he added, laughing at himself for the phrase. He did not say anything about medical school, though at the back of his mind lay the wish like a raging appetite which he sensed must be kept quiescent. In silence Monique began using the creams and colors from the cosmetic case. Slowly she massaged her face, as Caleb had seen Cairns massage the belly of a cow, to help her deliver; then step by step, without looking up, she transformed herself into a movie star, there was no other way Caleb could describe it. Her skin became white as sugar, her lips were a blossom of orange, her eyes the black circles of the tragedienne . . . . Caleb did not know whether to laugh or be frightened as she raised her face to his with a look of triumph. "I don't want to go to Texas," she said slowly, as if that explained her transformation.

"But honey, I just told you, that's a place we can get rich at. A man can work himself into a good ranch—if he's strong and can work sunup to sundown. Which I can." He couldn't help boasting about his physical strength: at that moment he felt it was all he had.

"I want to go to California," she said with slow precision, as if she were memorizing the words for a part she would soon play.

He tried to look as if he were seriously considering the idea; after all, considering their free and uncommitted condition, it did not seem too irrational. Folks were lighting out for California, he thought, like they were scared the Okies would get all the land tied up before they

130

did. But without wishing to make much of the fact to Monique, he believed he had a better chance in Texas: because the people, like himself, were Southern, because he suspected land would be a whole lot cheaper there, and because of the unalterable fact that their car was so old that he did not think he could ever cross the California desert with it. They'd be lucky if they got to East Texas, let alone all the way to the Pacific Ocean. So he shook his head, trying, though diffidently, to smile her notion away. But Monique kept her face riveted to his with such intensity, it was difficult to keep on driving, it was as if she were saying to him, *Look, look at this beautiful face and dare deny me what I want.* She then stated what she wanted:

"I want to be in movies. I want to go to California. This ... person I met at the Beauty Contest . . . he told me I should go take a screen test. I even have this card . . . ." She was already holding it out stiff and white for him to see. He said irritably he didn't have time to read that kind of junk, he had to drive the car.

"What do you mean, junk? I tell you I want to go to Hollywood. I know I can be a star. Look at me. Don't you think I can be a star? I'm beautiful, aren't I?"

Caleb did not dare look at her; in the first place, the roads were terrible in that area, they were driving a spavined, two-lane road at once rutted and rocky. *Don't they have chain gangs here?* wondered Caleb as if from a great distance, even while he was aware that Monique was thrusting her face forward, leaning over her cosmetic case, the glint of whose mirror scattered in bits like a broken diamond across his rear-view mirror. "Shut that thing down," he snapped irrelevantly, turning all his hostility toward the mirror. Inarguably, Monique was more beautiful than *he*–a mere cucumber and cabbage farmer with a prison record–had any right to expect her to be: yet didn't that beauty, in a sense, belong to him now? But he had not realized that those china blue eyes saw her own beauty so well: and if so, what had she seen in him, with his face like a walrus head? . . . . The shock of something inadmissible was turning his hands to ice on the wheel, he was glad it was broad daylight, everything was turning to darkness within him. When Monique whispered with a familiar fierce intensity which in the darkness of bed he would have thought was unsatisfied lust but which now a sweeping glance from the corner of his driver's vision forced him to admit was rage, he felt the threat to his potency as though she had cursed him with some medieval curse. For seconds they struggled for power, eye to eye, he not turning away, Monique finally lowering her gaze as if in defeat–just in time for them to see the stag which stood as though it were guarding the road.

It had all the characteristics of a dream, except that when they woke up they were still in it. The animal approached them like some Grand Conciliator, a broad-tined magnificent beast who in the old days in the bright sunlight might have become a legend of the unicorn. His antlers were broader than a man's embrace, they seemed frescoed on the immovable air; instead of fleeing, the stag turned his head toward Caleb with eyes at first mildly questioning, then growing wider and brighter, as if illuminated by fear itself into a new kind of intelligence: a perfect prince of a stag who forgave him his own death. Caleb had somehow been unable to accept that death; he swerved to avoid killing the animal. It had all been too much for Caleb, the intransigent indigo of Monique's eyes pitted, as it were, against the brown eyes which were pleading to be freed from this death which it nevertheless accepted.

It was not one of those accidents where the car is heaped up on itself like a platter of steel spaghetti and where Caleb always imagined severed limbs and concussions and broken necks. In fact, Caleb always swore afterwards that he had slowed down many moments before the moment of impact and that he had been driving well under the normal speed. They should have hit the pine woods with a hard thud and, maybe, a bad whiplash. Even the windshield was uncracked. But the quicksilver mirror of the cosmetic case had splintered like exploding shrapnel into Monique's face, taking the print of every piece of glass like a soft white pillow smashed by brutal and indifferent fists. She had required so much plastic surgery even before she left the Louisiana hospital that it had taken Caleb four years to pay the surgeon.

Long before he had finished paying the bills, Monique had gone, not to Hollywood, but back to Germany—a bitter and disillusioned woman barely twenty years old with one drooping eyelid. With the new mask of skin welded and stitched to what was left of the old face, they discovered that Monique had lost not only her youth, but something he had not known existed, a mimetic flexibility of nerve and muscle which had given her the ability to take on any personality she chose: now, suddenly she was Berta, and only Berta, and even the old name, Monique, skidded on her tongue as though with the dread screech of tires on the highway. The color of her eyes became permanently indigo. She never forgave Caleb. She claimed it was entirely his fault, that he had sacrificed her to a senseless beast. What was unforgivable, she said, was that Caleb had pulled the buck from the highway as though to save it.

It was true: Caleb had seen the slowly dying stag in the road—its great tawny suns of eyes eclipsed. Suddenly, while the interns who had arrived with the ambulance were treating Monique for shock, assuring her that her eyes were clear, there was no glass in them that they could determine, suddenly and inexplicably Caleb had moved into the highway and pulled the dying deer to one side.

It would have been easy for someone to mistake his intention, he did not himself understand it. He had acted on instinct, not wishing to see the stag smashed into dead meat by the oncoming cars. So he had pulled it out of the way as he might have any dying thing.

A local taxidermist had come to take away the still-breathing body. When Caleb saw the deer again, it was as if it were still breathing. The taxidermist's shop was not far from the big hospital where Caleb was visiting Monique almost daily during her first treatments.

One day the taxidermist had recognized Caleb and had called him in, as he said, to show him a sight for sore eyes. At the sight of the stag, taller and more graceful than he had been in the dream that had been a true accident, Caleb had stood struck dumb with awe and wonder. The man, Osgoode, had been a wizard, nothing less: he had resurrected the deer. The stag stood in the center of the shop, surrounded by the living habitat the taxidermist had created for him, his head turned toward them, gazing at them with a mild wonder which never ceased.

The entire medical profession, Caleb thought, had been unable to restore Monique; it was as if Monique herself had vanished with the face she had borrowed. But this man, Osgoode, had transcended the limitations of bone and flesh; he had made the corruptible incorruptible. Caleb longed to be able to do that, it was what had attracted him to medicine; and at once he apprenticed himself to Osgoode. By the time Monique was preparing to return to Germany Caleb had already learned what he could from the Louisiana taxidermist.

He drifted to Houston—a city, the taxidermist had assured Caleb, with a future: since Caleb figured at the time that he himself had had no past to speak of, it had seemed a good idea to go to a city with a future. With his last hundred dollars he had rented a quonset shell and had quietly begun his mission, recreating animals as though they had souls in those bodies which he was called to save. Gradually he had built up a reputation for being Houston's most sensitive taxidermist, a man who transformed dead animals into living.

10

"So that's what I do," Caleb repeated. "I'm carrying on the ministry. I'm bringing eternal life to . . . *them*." He pointed to the doves in a somber but whimsical way. "Work hard on 'em now," he said, as with a groan of weariness he rose from the grooved table on which he had been resting.

That evening she placed the doves on her worktable, examining them long and affectionately. She wanted to impress Caleb with her drawings: she wanted him to feel that she had listened most attentively to what he had intended to reveal to her that afternoon. After supper she went to work at once, sketching. Over the weekend she did dozens of drawings, took out books on the anatomical structure of birds, read histories of doves and pigeons dating back to the nineteenth century. She had begun with delight, wanting to please Caleb with her thoroughness; but she ended by being overwhelmed by her ignorance: there were people who devoted their entire lives to the study of doves. The thought shriveled her pride. She would never know enough. Easy for Isaac Babel to cry, "You must know everything!" In writing, it was easier for a person to disguise his ignorance, she thought: he could just not write about it. But in painting what she stupidly left out would show up as clearly as what she put in. Caleb wanted her to paint the soul. What was the soul of a dove?

She experimented with colors. White, she discovered was the mystical color. Like Melville's whale, it wrought changes everywhere. At last she succeeded in achieving the perfect tint of "mourning dove-gray." But the eyes were incredibly difficult. Caleb was right: every living thing looked at you. The mystery of Van Gogh's flowers was that they stared at you from their table. *What is the source of my beauty*? they demanded. The eyes of the doves gazed out at Kate from their cage. It seemed to her they, too, asked their sorrowful epiphanic question: *why are you here? why are you here?*

Nearly a week passed before she had done a few drawings which satisfied her. She wished to show them to Caleb at once, so she walked over from her apartment, bird cage in one hand, the drawings in the other. Even though, officially, at that time of evening the shop would be closed, she knocked first at the workshop rather than at his home: he often worked till late in the evening.

There was no reply. Except for the guide lights posted along the walls, the shop was in darkness. Kate picked up the cageful of birds and crossed the patio over to Caleb's house—a rambling frame which dated back to Reconstruction days. It was badly in need of repairs. Her practiced eye took in the nails which protruded carelessly from the wooden steps of the porch, and the peeling paint on the door: Caleb clearly did not think of his house in terms of beauty and architecture. Even from where she stood, in spite of the half-dozen rusty but growling air-conditioners projecting from various parts of the house, she could detect the powerful odor, the smell of live animals—droppings, ammonia . . . . Kate thought with amusement that it would take an intrepid salesman to go farther than the porch of Caleb Cairns' house.

Caleb flushed with pleasure at the sight of her. At the same time he seemed understandably reluctant to invite her in. "Kind of messy in here. No place for a lady."

She raised an eyebrow. "Thought we'd been all *through* that one the first day I came here. I want to show you my drawings."

"Well, you still a lady to me, whatever you say. Just because some folks can't tell the difference between a coyote and a red wolf doesn't *make* a coyote out of a red wolf, to my way of thinking. I see you got the doves with you. Did you enjoy 'em. You can keep 'em, you know. They're good company . . . . I can still get plenty of doves. It's the others . . . that are hard to get."

She winced at the thought. "Oh—but no thanks. I just don't care for birds in cages. No personal offense intended. It's just that once I saw this hawk at a zoo. It was in a big cage, supposed to be a *natural* cage, a kind of grotto. But it kept banging its head against the stone ceiling: it was in a prison all the same. I'll never forget it—this magnificent crested head, and that powerful useless beak. And such a baffled look on his face. I felt . . . sick."

He looked at her a long time as if examining her motives. He put his hand into the cage: the birds fluttered nervously. "They don't know I don't mean 'em any harm," he said sadly. "Or else, they figure I've already done 'em the worse thing I can do, putting 'em *in* there, so they don't trust me . . . ." As they stood on the porch a startling apparition came to the screen door; for a moment in the twilight as it stood behind the crosshatched screen door, it resembled a child.

"Why Caleb, whatever are you doing with that monkey?"

"That's Jezebel . . . . Jessie, get *back* in there. Sit down!" he scolded the animal, shaking his fist.

Kate laughed as the animal imitated Caleb's motion with a stubborn emphasis, as if it had been taught to respond to interference with some well-timed obscene insult.

136

"She's my watchdog. She keeps people out. The minute they come in the door she starts screaming like a banshee. Scares 'em half to death. If she gets real mad, she'll start throwing things at 'em. She and the others don't get along *too* well . . . ."

" 'The others'?"

Caleb looked embarrassed.

"I've got a kind of time capsule . . . . I'm a sort of collector you might say."

"Caleb, you do look positively guilty—as if you were hiding a *body* in that house!" She stood stunned at her own words while the muscles of Caleb's face broke into a kind of havoc: hurt, surprise, chagrin, disappointment. She put her hand on his in apology. "I'm sorry, Caleb, Forgive me."

"Fact is," Caleb said heavily, "I *do* have a body in there. I got a body on my conscience that'll never leave me rest in this life again . . . " He rose quickly from the railing on which he had been resting, as if he feared her compassion more than her ridicule. "You like to see my collection?"

His mood, however, now seemed to her forced and unnatural. She wanted to offer him something in expiation of her unthinking remark. Instinctively she held up the drawings: were they good enough? She thought she had never before wanted so much to transcend her own limitations. They stood on the porch, facing each other in the twilight. In the grasses the crickets toiled, tuning their cries to the oncoming heat. A few bats had begun to weave their path across the sky. Caleb stared at the drawings such a long time Kate wanted to run. Then he touched his hand to his eyes with that slow motion one used to shut the eyes of the staring dead. Without looking at her he said heavily: "Come on in. I want you to see . . . ."

Instead of entering by the screen door where Jessie stood beckoning to them (whether in guile or friendship was unclear) they walked around to a side entrance where Caleb had built an annex onto the house.

The annex was a single large rectangular room, well-insulated with asbestos. A powerful air-conditioner roared out like an organ fugue as they passed through the hallway. At the threshold Kate stood transfixed by the spectacle of antlered heads. She had, of course, seen some of Caleb's collection in the Cairns Shop, but it was nothing compared to this.

In this specially designed corridor, like a gallery of saints, Caleb had mounted all his antlered species. Every kind of deer which he had been able to save from the hunters' skinning knife he had brought back and miraculously restored to life. All the animals were carefully labeled for posterity. As Kate looked up she was dazzled by the apparition of fifty pairs of eyes staring down at her from their magnificent heads: antelope and ibex and white tails and eland and kudu and bison; mountain goat and caribou, elk and gazelle and all sorts of sheep she had never seen before—horn sheep and desert sheep and stone sheep, and Dall and Fannin . . . . There were many animals she had never seen anywhere.

Caleb hastily explained that there were naturally quite a few he had had to reconstruct from photographs and zoology books—that they were already as extinct as the passenger pigeon.

"But Caleb! Why are you doing this? It must cost you a fortune."

"All I have," he retorted dryly. "You don't see me stashing it away for the future. No future to be had anyway."

She was afraid she understood him all too well. "You mean for people?"

"Well, last of all for people. But all these'll be gone long before people. People are still multiplying faster than *they* are. And people are pullin' down the trees faster than they can ever find a place to go to instead of the woods. So I've got me my own little museum here. My own little Noah's Ark, you might call it. I figure they're going to need it someday: there won't be a hoof-footed ungulate left in the entire continent pretty soon, the way they keep up. Look at that whitetail there. Used to be plentiful as wild turkey. Kill one for dinner you could. And now what? Barely a hunter's brace of whitetail left. What beats me, is that they let the hunters keep on *shootin'*. Call it responsible hunting. Well, far's *I'm* concerned any hunting that doesn't bring 'em back alive is *ir*responsible."

"But Caleb, *you* go hunting? Aren't some of those yours?"

"Now and then I bag one. Only to allay suspicion. I'm a kind of double agent . . . ." He smiled ruefully. "No . . . . I let *them* do the shootin'. They're a whole lot better at it than I can ever get to be. What I do, is resurrecting . . . ." He glanced at her with a shade of pride. "You think I'm losing my mind over it?"

She was not sure what he meant by "it"—whether he meant the loss of the world's future which he identified with the loss of all the beautiful animals: or the death of the black boy in Florida.

"If you are," she said cautiously, "it's a pleasant sort of insanity. But how on earth do you get all these species?"

"Correspondence. And money. I keep in touch with the hunting market. I keep a runnin' ad in the magazines, like I had a live herd I was adding to. Also the zoo market. Also the world wildlife clubs. It's going to be profitable one of these days to save the animal race, then I'll be right in there with all my ideas."

138

She sighed. "You have ideas?"

"I got a lot of ideas. Only wish I were twenty years younger. I'd hotfoot it around to all the legislatures in the States, I'd get sanctuaries and aviaries set aside in every last one of them before it was too late. I'd not let 'em take a *twig* out of the Big Thicket. I'd put the water where the fishes are and the mountains back where they belong."

"And the oil?" she asked ruefully. "Where would you put that?" She knew that from time to time when Caleb had been completely out of cash he had hired himself out to the oil-hunters, to Gulf and Shell and Standard and Humble. "A hired killer," Caleb referred to himself on those occasions.

"I'm not rightly sure where I'd *put* it. Only I'd make it a man-slaughter charge every time there was a spill and *my* birds died down on the Gulf."

"*Your* birds?"

"Well, I think of 'em as mine . . . Whose are they anyway? God's, they are. They sure as hell don't belong to the oil companies. Those slicks are killin' off the waterfowl faster than the railroad did the buffalo. One goddammed oil spill and you can count off ten thousand birds . . . . Look what happened when that American steamer, the what's-her-name, oh, I'll think of it in a minute—anyway, she spilled into the Weser River. The place was like the tenth circle of hell. It stank of dead and dying fish for weeks. Same thing happened right here in Corpus. Me and a bunch of kids, we rented a big truck and went down to see if we could save any—"

"You mean—bring them back to your shop?"

"No, no. I mean *before* that. Alive. And you got to really work. Only the most primitive methods do 'em any good. You got to hand-clean 'em, like giving a bunch of mud-caked kids a bath. First thing, you know, most of 'em drown. The oil makes their feathers water-soluble, so naturally they just sink right into the Gulf. But even the poor bastards that get to land just *starve* . . . ." Caleb's voice broke with anger. "A waterfowl's got to have fish—not putrefied fish, but clean, live fish right out of the water. If they can't fly, they can't eat. Well, anyway, we did save us a few. I just camped out there on Padre Island. Closed the shop. Hired a man to feed Jessie and the others. . . " He jerked his head toward the other side of the house. Kate's eyes followed the direction, but she could only faintly hear the barking of dogs.

"You mean you just left everything here and went off to clean the beaches? Were they angry about it? I mean, like the people waiting for you to get their heads mounted? Like the Wainwright boys: they

139

didn't take it too well when you shrugged off their work on the doves as not too important."

"It's *important* all right. That's why I gave it to you. I figured you could do it. Those pictures . . . . You keep on painting like that and I'll give up mounting birds: you can be the new Audubon. What kind of painting they teach you at that school?"

She smiled ruefully. "So far they haven't let me touch a real canvas. Canvas is very expensive, I'm told. If I want to learn on it, I have to supply it myself. They're very convincing on that score. Anyway, so far it's been strictly drawing. But I'm drawing better—I think."

"You draw real people?" he asked. "I mean from models?"

"Well, we get a few models, but the school naturally doesn't pay them enough. Mostly they're kids from the university who need money. And they sit there, very tired and very bored. Hungry too, I suspect. So we haven't done much from the model. My problem seems to be that I started painting in oils before I was told that oils were hardest to do. Before I was ever told *any*thing, really. I'd never even heard of *gesso panel*, for instance." She cocked her head wryly to see if he were surprised at such ignorance, but he seemed to take it in calmly enough. "I'm not sure now whether I've got to *un*learn all those 'bad habits' I got into that I learned by myself, or whether there's room for both of us."

"Both of *us*?"

"*Both* of us. The teacher and me."

"Oh." He looked relieved. "I thought you meant both of *us*. I thought maybe I was taking up too much of your time—on your job, I mean."

She considered this a moment, trying to be honest. She could not afford to give up her job. Shaddy was sending her no money. He had not yet filed suit for a divorce, but he was making her aware of his power. The rent of her small apartment within walking distance of Taxidermy Shop took nearly half what she earned, and the rest went for food and art supplies.

"I can't afford to give up my job," she said as delicately as she could.

He flushed. After a pause he said, looking away: "*He* . . . doesn't send you anything?"

"No. Why should he?"

"You're his wife."

"Why should he, just because of that?"

"You're his wife," he repeated.

"We went through some kind of legal ceremony: if that's what being a wife is."

"But he loves you." He apparently had tried to state it as a fact, but his voice rose faintly to a question.

"I can't speak for him."

"And you? . . . ."

"Yes, I guess I do. I love him and I love Paul Ardley and I loved a boy in high school once, whose name was Antinous Walski. I used to call him Przewalski's Horse because he seemed the last of his kind—"

"Who was Paul Ardley?" he demanded, interrupting her forced gaiety.

She explained.

"This man who—couldn't even *walk*? This man who was twenty years older than you, you mean to say you were in *love* with him?"

She was silent a moment. They were standing beside a deer which had been mounted by Caleb ten years before. Beside the date on the platform someone had carved his initials. Kate took it all in, even while her mind was reexamining with intense clarity what it was that had poisoned her relationship with Paul, had made it impossible for her to remain at his side—as his lover, his pupil, his nurse . . . . As Caleb took his hand away she saw that he had left a small moist spot on the flank of the deer.

"He was not old *enough*," she said. "He was not old enough to . . . forgive . . . everything."

"And what about *him* . . . your husband?" he asked in an angry, personal tone. "What had *he* done wrong to you, besides not being perfect? I mean, you sure are a hard girl to satisfy."

She touched the spot on the flank of the deer where Caleb's hand had rested a moment before. "No. I'm not hard to please. That's not true. Maybe, even, I'm too *easily* pleased."

The faint bright bristles of his brow came together, scowling: "Aha! Miss Charity!" he exclaimed with anger.

"No. No. You don't understand. Didn't you just ask me if I loved Shaddy? I'm trying to answer your question."

"That his *real* name?"

"I'm trying to *tell* you something. What *difference* does it make what his name is?"

"Well, for God's sake, you're married to the man—I thought the least you can do is tell me his right name. It's your name, too, isn't it?"

"Caleb, Shaddy's name is . . . *irrelevant*. I'm trying to *explain* something to you."

He sat down, leaning against the wall; he pulled his knees up before him, and his long hands, already ridged and gnarled hung loosely at his knees. "Love doesn't need explaining," he said. "Either you do or you don't. It's still the one idea left where the biblical *yea-nay* holds good."

"Well *I* think it's childish! You mean I can't love people without being *in* love with them?"

"So that's the kind of distinction that lets you run off and leave that poor sonofabitch, what's-his-name, *Paul*, and then get married to another guy right off the bat. And now—" He faltered, shook his head. "Reckon I'm getting old. I don't see it too clearly."

"Well, what kind of answer do you *expect*?"

"*Yes* or *no*. Do you love your husband?"

She repeated, with a kind of strenuous honesty, the very effort of which was somehow self-defeating: "Yes. I *do*, dammit. The thing is, there are plenty of things I *don't* love about him—I don't even *like* them. But he'll always seem to me just as charming, just as sadly exploited—and just as *stupid*," she burst out inconsequently, tears rising to her eyes. "Why do people have to *label* everything? A man can have a dozen women, can't he? And nobody starts labeling his emotions?"

Caleb raised a skeptical eyebrow. "*Can* he now?" he countered.

Kate ignored his skepticism. "And if a man can do that, why not a woman? Seems to me I could keep right on caring about Shaddy or Paul or . . . anybody I ever loved . . . in *exactly the same way* for the rest of my life."

A defeated look settled around his eyes. Wearily he shut them as she had seen him do when the Wainwright boys had brought the doves to his shop.

"That's not love," he said.

"How do you know? Are you some kind of authority?" She tried to sound as if she were very sure of herself, but she could feel her voice quavering. Caleb, she knew, was basically a man whose beliefs derived from the Old South, from traditions of southern chivalry and good-and-bad women. She felt certain she had debased herself in his eyes. To defend herself against imminent insult and humiliation she demanded: "And besides, what right do you have to speak for *me*?"

"I love you, that's what right. I need to know what you think love *is*." He pulled himself up beside her on the bench. "I need to know, do you think this is all there is *to* it?" he asked, placing his hand on her breast.

She shook her head. As he bent to kiss her, instead of closing her eyes she widened them. Above her, the canopy of antlered heads seemed to turn to stare.

Caleb cradled her head under his arm. "Because if you think that's all there is to it," he said, "I sure got a lot of hurtin' to go through."

Kate shut her eyes against the vision of animals, adjusting to the steady tremble of the wooden bench at her back.

A few days later, at Caleb's suggestion, she went to be fitted for a diaphragm. She felt happy, loved, guiltless. She would have preferred to continue as they had begun, but Caleb was not a man who could endure condoms while making love. He was an idealist, and the art of love seemed to him to require spontaneity: there was nothing spontaneous about unrolling a condom. Furthermore, Caleb's association with condoms was as a means of avoiding venereal disease while having sexual relations with prostitutes: condoms cooled him like a cake of ice, he said. Kate had thought it best not to enter into a dispute on the social injustice of his revulsion (she was still too young to understand the terrific revulsion men feel for the prostitutes they exploit), so she obediently, even joyously made a trip to the nearest physician to be fitted. She believed such a fitting to be a simple process which any doctor could do respectably well—like getting one's teeth cleaned at the dentist's; so she had naively stopped in at a nearby doctor's office on her way to the Taxidermy Shop.

The doctor was alone—Wednesdays were actually his day off, he said, as he ushered her into the examination room himself. He was a short, squat, husky fellow with a mustache, built rather like a midget wrestler, with a barrelled torso. When she had explained her mission, he at once looked down at her hand to see if she were wearing a wedding ring. Unconsciously Kate clenched her hand into a defiant fist. She was still wearing the high school ring Shaddy had slipped onto her finger at the marriage ceremony in Toledo. A growing sentimentality about Shaddy's action that day, his good-natured acceptance of the situation and surrendering of his "freedom" had endowed the ring with the unique quality of one's personal history; she had grown attached to the ring and continued wearing it.

"Don't look much by way of a weddin' ring," the doctor observed dryly. "Wouldn't fool an old-timer like me. I seen 'em all: cracker jack box rings tryin' to look like the only family jewels buried in the War Between the States."

"I'm not *trying* to fool anybody," said Kate with acerbity.

He lifted an eyebrow; he smiled what he must have imagined to be the smile of the *pater familias* who has seen everything. "You and Who Else sez so?"

Stung by the insult, Kate glanced toward the wall of the examining room where the doctor, Gerald Butt Stillwater, had hung his credentials on the wall. "That paper says you're a doctor," she said caustically. "At least that you're a doctor in Texas . . . . How do I know it's not a forgery?"

He flushed angrily. "I did my internship at Mass General. Best in the country," he added as if there could be absolutely no doubt of *that*, at least.

Kate observed him sullenly. "You mean you don't have to wear a ring to prove that you can fit a diaphragm?"

She could see that he was furious; she fully expected to be shown out of the office. A settled look had rounded out his jaw, as if the sands of rage had shifted down to the bottom. During the examination he barely spoke except for what seemed to Kate an intentional insult or to warn her abruptly: "Quit movin'." He did not once address her by her name but referred to her as *you*, by which he seemed to mean all women rather than herself alone.

Kate lay on the examination table, her legs in the stirrups; she was too angry even to protest against his rough handling. She could feel herself sweating profusely from this bitter comedy of sexuality in which every touch was somehow an implied insult: there was a kind of genius in it, Kate thought, as if he knew precisely where her points of humiliation lay. Although she had (she thought) carefully douched before leaving her apartment, a faint odor of vaginal secretions welled up between them; it became suddenly a symbol of mutual assault, as though she had deliberately contrived to exude this effluvium in order to annoy him, and he in turn had deliberately found a way to evoke the odor in order to prove her foulness. My imagination is running wild, she thought; but at that moment he said: "Still got a lot of jissom left in there, you ought to clean yourself out afterward." Tears of humiliation filled her eyes, as though he had taken Caleb's love and rubbed it in the dirt. She had just decided not to take another minute of this when the savage shock of cold steel entering her vagina made her cry out with pain—precisely, she thought a second later, as though it were a rape, not a medical examination. Then the instrument was being screwed into her like a man tightening the lid on a mason jar; the doctor's eyes riveted to her face. Tighter and tighter.

"Least you ain't been at it long. Nor had too many. You ain't hardly bigger'n a hazel nut." Somehow the smallness of her vaginal opening seemed to have excited him. Kate watched in fascination as he dipped his index finger in, running it around the rim of the vagina as if measuring its perimeter. His face turned crimson, his eyes dilated as he watched her face intently. Why the sonofabitch thinks he's exciting me, thought Kate with disgust, but pretended to be blind to the glistening invitation of those eyes. He'd take me right on this table if I gave

144

one consenting glance, she thought, and nausea filled her stomach. She gagged, and apologized; her gagging interrupted his work. At last he began to insert the diaphragm, testing it for size. He squeezed jelly on the small cup as though he were preparing his breakfast, then with a conspiratory look at Kate plunged in with a small plastic applicator shaped like a catheter with a hook. It was all so sickening Kate could barely wait till he had finished. At last there was a grunt of satisfaction, so personal that it sounded—to Kate's overwrought imagination—downright obscene. "Now you try it," he commanded, and put the plastic instrument in her right hand. He stood as close by her as he could without changing the rhythm of her movement, but she could feel him leaning against her, moving his body vicariously as she doubled over to remove and reinsert the diaphragm. Each time she pulled out the disc, her vagina felt the insult of it, but he seemed pleased with her progress. "Aaah!" he breathed at one point as he instructed her to squat down while inserting the diaphragm. "Spread your legs apart." Kate could not help feeling that their physical postures were somehow gratifying to him; her own was acutely humiliating—abject, as though she were being forced to perform her excretory functions before him. When she had done this exercise three times to his satisfaction, he became himself again. He took the diaphragm from her with a reshifting of the disapproval in his face; he dusted the small cup with powder, wrapped it in tissue, and asked for his money. It was astonishingly expensive. Kate did not have enough money with her and asked if she could use a counter check. He looked at her suspiciously. "You sure it won't bounce on me? I got no *patience* with hot check *patients*," he said with such arch facetiousness that she saw that it was an old and oft-used pun which he had fallen into out of irresistible vanity; he had not meant to break the stony surface of his disapproval by even this stupid joke. But having fallen into the *wording* of it, he was forced to accept her promise that the check would not bounce (she'd get the money from Caleb and deposit it that very morning, she vowed to herself). So she signed a counter check—he had an assortment in pastel shades from four different banks in the city—and he handed over the diaphragm as if she were redeeming something from a pawnshop—worthless to him, of course, though of tremendous value to her: he was only getting a bit of interest on it. She wanted to sock him, she was so angry, but walked out of the office, grinding her heels to the office floor with indignation, carrying the diaphragm folded away in its Christmas tissue as though it were a jewel of immeasurable price.

When she arrived at the shop (diaphragm in hand) and told Caleb about it, she was astonished at his lack of surprise. "Probably not an O.B. at all," observed Caleb knowledgeably. "Even if he *was* to Mass

General. Did he actually *claim* to be an O.B.?" Kate couldn't say he had. Caleb added probably just about any doctor would have treated her the same way. Kate refused to believe it, but added that she had had no other experience in purchasing diaphragms, (Caleb smiled with pleasure to hear her say this), she really could not compare. "Next time," he said, "try a taxidermist." They ended up by laughing about it.

But it turned out to be no laughing matter. Kate swore to Caleb that the doctor had done it on purpose; he had incorrectly measured the diaphragm, it had slipped out of its position in spite of (or because of) all the wisdom and know-how of medical science. She was pregnant: of course.

Kate discovered that the abortion laws were inflexible: no less than a clear threat to the mother's life would satisfy the medical authorities that Kate should not bear this child. Her own wishes had nothing to do with it; she should have thought of that before she began fucking, the doctors implied, turning away with a severe look. The fact that she was a married woman ironically militated against her; she had a cover behind which she could conceal her crime; unlike thousands of others she need not have her child at a home for unwed mothers. Her child would have a name: what else did she, in her condition, feel she had a right to—a reward? a stipend? Other doctors, they implied (unlike themselves) were getting altogether too lax about such things.

The fact that she did not want to exploit Shaddy's name, that she would have to bring up the child alone (unless she married Caleb); that at this time in her life she wanted to study art—all these were considered callow, selfish and even irrelevant grievances. You can always study later, they said. Or in a more surly, even envious tone which she had grown to recognize, as if she were preempting a freedom they themselves coveted, one man and wife team of physicians observed dryly: "Why are you so different from everybody else? We all want to do things we can't. We have to assume responsibility for our actions."

She tried to argue logically that she had assumed "responsibility" when she had undertaken to prevent this birth. The physician himself had incorrectly fitted the diaphragm: why wasn't *he* responsible? To this she received only angry, suspicious looks: what was Kate trying to suggest about the medical profession? Doctors were not perfect. Did she think this was a Margaret Sanger Clinic or something? This was a busy hospital. They had no time for women who wanted to sleep with every tomdickandharry and then expected doctors to get them out of their predicament. *They* hadn't had the fun of it, they didn't see why they should risk disgrace and imprisonment just because she . . . .

She would not be able to get a professional abortion, that was clear; so Kate began inquiring of the girls at the art school. At the school she discovered there was a cordon of silence protecting every girl; the subject was taboo. Some pretended to be scandalized; some offered sympathy; one or two "knew a woman who . . . ." Only one knew a practicing abortionist who charged a thousand dollars and Kate would have to arrange to meet him across the border in Mexico. The thought was intimidating: suppose there were complications? Why should the Mexican government care what happened to a sick American girl whose own country would have permitted her to ship herself across the border like cattle. In desperation Kate wrote down the (pseudonymous) names of a couple of women who were actually classified as *curanderas* by the Mexican-American population. Kate rationalized that they were women: after all they would have personal knowledge of their own bodies. One girl offered the amazing statistic of a woman (name unknown) who had performed eleven such "simple" abortions on herself, so it could not be difficult.

As the difficulties of obtaining a legal abortion mounted, Kate's anger and stubbornness intensified. She was barely eighteen years old; she had neither money nor education nor strength to undertake the rearing of a child by herself. She had tried to protect herself (*and* the unborn) by taking pains to be measured for a diaphragm. Clearly they were trying to punish her, to rub her nose into guilt and shame: where would *they* be if their mothers had decided it was inconvenient to have babies?

"She's all right," whispered the art student Magenta, handing Kate the name and address of a *curandera*.

Magenta's real name was Margaret, but the other students, flattered her by calling her—like "Mauve"—by her favorite color. Actually the poor girl was only a moderately talented watercolorist, but her obsession with Texas sunsets was something everyone could understand; the Impressionists had done such things to perfection, their teacher told them, and it was natural to imitate until one achieved a style of one's own. Kate's own conviction was that the girl ought to be whipped for painting sunsets like the Impressionists: it might be good for her technique but very bad for her soul. The girl ought, Kate felt, to be set adrift to sink or swim in some passionate medium of her own. But Kate never criticized her art teachers: her sense of economic determinism spared her that particular sin of pride. She never for a moment believed that they were teachers of painting because they could not paint, but only that they were obliged to teach, for the sake of bread and (perhaps) a little wine . . . .

"Is it far?" asked Kate, "I'd rather stay right in town."

147

The girl looked at her incredulously. "You can't be too choosy. You've got to get it done as soon as you can. You'd be surprised . . . ."

But Kate did not want to hear horror stories. It was going to be hard enough on her nerves; so she interrupted: "Can I get there and back the same day?"

"Well: San Antonio's not far if you're just driving to see your folks . . . . But if you're on the bus and you don't feel so good . . . ." The girl shrugged.

"Do you bleed much?" Kate felt she couldn't very well sit on the bus for several hours, saturating the seat; that would be asking for trouble. She tried to remain lucid, but panic was rising in her. Even the simplest problems could become overwhelmingly complicated when one was alone. "I mean, do I have to stay in bed? Will I need to take stuff along? Food? There won't be anybody visiting me." The thought of Caleb's moral indignation at what she felt it was necessary to do, made her quail with guilt. It was hard enough to sustain one's will about such an action without hearing moral arguments: *what are you fixin' to do with MY child?*

"Well, no. Not till it starts coming, at least. It's not like a D&C, you know. It causes contractions, more like a miscarriage, you know."

"Oh." She felt fortunate at that moment that such words did not evoke associative responses from her. She preferred her ignorance: ignorance kept the anxiety from watering down her courage. She decided to ask no more questions, but simply wrote down the name and address of the woman in San Antonio.

"*Perdita?*" she observed with heavy irony. "That's one hell of a bad symbol."

She packed her bag for a weekend in San Antonio. Instead of a confrontation with Caleb she decided to send him a note which would, in fact, arrive Monday morning, by which time she hoped to have been through the worst. She thought she could face his recriminations afterwards, but not his moral arguments before: he made her feel like a murderer.

But by the time the bus rolled into San Antonio on Saturday morning she felt more like the victim. Her body ached from what felt like an oncoming case of flu. The lunging and growling of the bus had given her a headache. She had risen at six in order to catch the express; then the bus had turned out not to be an express after all, had seemed to stop at a Stuckey's every twenty miles. She had bought a San Antonio newspaper and map at the bus station and she now mulled over the classifieds, carefully scanning the columns for a cheap room in the event she should have to stay over. A hotel would be out of the

148

question; it would cost her as much for one night as a room would cost for the week: she carefully outlined her itinerary on the map, calculating the distance between a well-known Mexican-American neighborhood where the rents would be cheapest and the distance to the house of Señora Perdita. As she descended from the bus the first sight that struck her was a billboard for a tourist company: SEE OLD SAN ANTONIO. Blazoned across the name of the company, like flying pennants, were pictures of Spanish missions, of the Alamo, of antique bridges and mossy riverbanks lined with Spanish-style restaurants.

It took about two hours after her arrival to find a room, wash up in the bathroom (which was on the second floor), and make her way to Señora Perdita's address. It was, as she might have predicted, a slat-strewn shack with outdoor plumbing. Chickens roosted on the twisted metal fence which separated the Perdita territory from the unpaved streets gullied by gas pipes which the city was in the process of laying down. Two long-haired brown and white dogs, very dirty and of uncertain breed, barked hoarsely at Kate as she climbed the splintered wooden porch. Corn feed had been strewn on the porch, apparently for the chickens. A sign on the bell in Spanish said the bell was out of order, and an arrow pointed to the rear. Kate wearily shifted the bag of clean towels she had been instructed by Magenta to bring along ("Take along extras, in case," Magenta had added warningly. *In case of what*? Kate had wanted to know, but had not dared ask).

Her heart sank as she plodded through the backyard. The outhouse was open; flies buzzed like bees over the atmosphere, scenting out the decomposition of the race: *human beings, human beings*, they seemed to be repeating, their buzz rising to a crescendo as Kate passed and they moved away in a triangular swarm.

She did not need to knock. The old woman, who was apparently Señora Perdita, had heard the dogs barking and seen the chickens scuttle away, clucking at Kate's approach. She now stood at the screen door, nodding at Kate in that friendly mute way of people who expect not to understand the language they will hear. At her side was a dirty barefooted boy of about eight who stood nervously clutching at his crotch as if he had already been punished into believing that these parts were the cause of mankind's Sin and Suffering.

The old woman continued to nod to everything Kate said. She spoke from time to time to the child at her side and Kate realized with horror that the boy was her grandchild, (he said *sí, madre* to everything she instructed him to do), and that he was also her assistant. The thought that the boy could be in the house at all during this delicate procedure made Kate miserable: there was no end to the psychological damage one inflicted on people, she thought in despair. How many

149

women had this child witnessed his aging, impoverished grandmother performing abortions on? "He's not going to *be* here? . . . " she demanded at last, plucking up the will to this decisive question at last. If he were to be present, Kate would leave at once.

"No, no. He helpin' me," said Señora Perdita. "He gonna play. You gonna play later, Fernando. First, you put the teakettle on."

Kate closed her eyes briefly; she felt faint. She saw the boy unhook a huge white enamel teakettle from the wall and place it on the black stove (Kate's habitual eye managed to take in the stove: it was obviously used for heat in the winter; there were three black burners on each side while the oven was overhead—its door a soft Delft-like blue enamel finish, strangely out of place in that house). If the old woman had been a witch about to roast Kate alive, the sight of her standing over the teakettle could not have been more terrifying. At the same time Kate could not overcome a feeling of sadness, of compassion, for the slovenly grandmother who managed to keep herself and the boy too from going hungry by practicing these ancient arts.

The old woman said with pride: "He my grandson. He go to school." She patted the boy on the head as he carefully dropped into the teakettle what looked to Kate like a small rubber hose, a pair of thick rubber gloves and some sort of arrow-shaped object which Kate could not see clearly. It was in fact difficult to see anything at all: every shade in the house was drawn against the blinding sunlight outdoors: Kate wondered how the señora would see to do her work if there were no electrification in the house. But as if sensing her thought, Señora Perdita now cautiously hauled a long outdoor extension cord in from the porch. This she placed on a hook in the ceiling of the kitchen and screwed into the open socket a blinding bulb of about two hundred watts. *An experienced surgeon*, thought Kate bitterly, and waited to see if the woman would wash her hands.

The señora did not in fact remember to wash her hands until she asked Kate for the towels. Then, with a confidential grimace, she gestured to Kate to wait *uno minuto* and hobbled over to a sink in the corner of the kitchen where she self-consciously washed her hands with what smelled to Kate like naphtha soap. From where Kate stood, nervously waiting and watching, she could clearly see long brown and white hairs on the soap. Then with a surprisingly gracious smile the woman summoned Kate to a cracked leather chair which boasted an adjustable head rest, like a dentist's chair. Evidently Señora Perdita was proud of this reclining chair. She patted the head rest for Kate to be comfortable on: but first she dramatically (and admiringly) took out the towels Kate had brought and covered every inch of the shredding leather couch to her satisfaction. She then ordered her grandson out to play.

Kate was so relieved at the boy's departure that she forgot for a moment to be frightened.

Señora Perdita then plucked out her sterilized instruments from the teakettle, lifting them with ice tongs. Kate watched from her semi-reclining position on the couch as the woman put on the black rubber gloves. Then, evidently remembering something, and still wearing her gloves, the señora walked over to a closet commode evidently used for storage, and took out a white sheet with which she wrapped herself from bosom to toe. So much for sterile conditions, thought Kate grimly, and thought that in a moment she, Kate, would start praying to be released from this grotesque but dangerous nightmare. She could still get up and leave—but what then? She tried consciously to whip up her courage with admonitions, but had to admit she was scared. Her terror increased when, suddenly, during the insertion of the catheter, the two brown and white dogs began scraping and whining at the door. Tenderly cursing them, the señora abruptly left Kate's side: while holding her hands self-consciously in the air, she slewed her body sidewise at the screen door to push it open for the dogs . . . . The dogs promptly ran over to Kate and began sniffing at her with curiosity and excitement. Señora Perdita shoved them into the bedroom and latched the door. "Lotta trouble," she observed affectionately of the animals, and returned to Kate.

What followed took only a few minutes; the insertion of the catheter seemed ludicrously simple when Kate considered the terror which had preceded it all. Kate stood up gingerly, and handed the woman two twenty dollar bills. It was with mild surprise that she realized that in spite of her poverty, the woman had trusted Kate to hand over the money after her work was done and had not insisted on receiving cash beforehand—a kind of *cortesía* which had not died with the indignities of poverty and old age.

"That's all?" asked Kate incredulously. "Finished?"

"Ahhh . . . . " Señora Perdita shrugged ambiguously. "Later, later. You'll see. All gotta come out." She indicated by clenching and unclenching her fists the labor contractions Kate might expect to feel. Kate sighed with discouragement, already exhausted from the psychological fear and trembling, and dreading the ordeal to come. Enough, she wanted to cry. I've been through enough already.

The señora took the bills Kate had given her and pushed them into an empty milk bottle on the kitchen sink; the bills moved languidly, unfolding and spreading themselves in the bottle like green leaves floating upwards from their watery depths. The two women stood a moment watching the money float in the glass bottle, fascinated by its movement as though it were a living thing, a snake or water plant. But

151

the dogs had begun whining again impatiently behind the bedroom door. With a groan of feigned impatience (it was obvious that the woman adored her dogs) the señora allowed the dogs out of the room. Then she rolled Kate's towels into a paper shopping bag and returned them to Kate. At the sight of the shopping bags, the dogs began sniffing around the bag, nuzzling Kate's crotch as though the smell of her body had put them in heat. Kate quelled a rising nausea long enough to say feebly: *Adiós,* smiling what felt to her like a smile of complicity between two women who had been forced to use each other to disadvantage: what we ought to do is beg each other's pardon, thought Kate, and stepped out into the air.

She did not feel giddy, but she was too emotionally upset to eat. The strain of the past two weeks had exhausted her, especially the grueling and humiliating interviews with doctors in an attempt to get a legal abortion. Now, at least, she was free. She bought some milk and a few cans of food and returned to her room. She fell onto the unmade bed as if she had somehow survived a disaster.

When she awoke the room was dark. Several mosquitoes were tasting her blood, but she was too tired to beat them away. One of the things she had neglected to buy was insecticide, she would either have to get up to fight the mosquitoes or allow them to feast on her blood. With an effort she struggled to her feet; she at once began trembling with cold and realized she had been lying under a heavy blanket for hours: yet the sunlight streaming through the paper windowshades as though through heated glass testified to the relentless summer heat. Flies buzzed inside the shade, trying to get out; their bodies, elongated against the parchment-colored paper, made flying shadows big as bats.

She tried to open a can of sardines, reminding herself that food was necessary to recover strength, but the smell of fish oil as powerful as iodine sucked into her lungs and nostrils as though she were drowning in oil. There was no wash basin in the room; if she wanted to vomit she'd either have to use an empty can in the clothes closet or walk down the hall, then upstairs to the bathroom. She chose to stay motionless, fighting nausea. It was as if there were no air left in the universe, the face of the earth had been taken over by tropical fauna, these buzzing flies and snarling mosquitoes. Kate put her head down on the table and resisted an overwhelming impulse to cry.

Her head on her arm was hot, and the realization struck her (what seemed her first rational thought since she had arrived in this *barrio*): fever. The concept was as clear as her first vision of sunflowers years ago followed by that illness which had struck the sound from one ear and left her with those star-shaped scars which were only beginning to fade. Fever, she knew by heart and experience, was not something sardines could do anything about. With relief she pushed the food aside. Stick to water. Feed a cold and starve a fever, as the ancient almanacs said. She finally forced herself to stagger out to the hallway and climb the twelve steps to the bathroom (the fact that she counted them seemed to her a miracle of pure clearheadedness). Here she filled two empty milk cartons with water.

All night long she carefully remembered to wake herself and to *sip water, sip water, it prevents dehydration*. But by morning her mouth was parched, her skin like coarse blotting paper spotted over with small bites from the bloodthirsty mosquitoes. The flies which had quieted down resounded like helicopters in her brain. She must do what was necessary, she must manage to climb those twelve stairs (*again!*) to where she had seen a phone not far from the bathroom and telephone for a taxi. Otherwise she was certain to be found in this room a week later when the rent was due, stretched out on the bed, her body blossoming with flies, her tongue hanging out with thirst . . . . With an effort she pushed all her things into the sack Señora Perdita had given her and made her way toward the pool of light which lay upon the stairwell.

In the street she waited anxiously for the taxi. She stood leaning against a fire hydrant for support until she saw a black driver moving his cab cautiously up the unpaved street, avoiding the ditches ploughed by the gas company. He looked at her suspiciously as he approached, afraid, perhaps, that she had been knifed, or would bleed to death in his car.

For some reason, perhaps the fever itself, perhaps because she was in a Mexican-American neighborhood and the driver was black—she was inspired to tell the truth. Luckily her instinct did not betray her. The driver understood at once and, clucking his teeth sympathetically, scolded her like a child all the way to the County Hospital. "Look like you ought to of knowed better," he said, and helped her out of the cab. She smiled at him tenderly—she was all her life to remember the scar on his forehead as though someone had meant to cleave him in two and the axe had slipped; by then her fever was so high, her brain so giddy that she never noted his company nor his name nor anything about him but his voice. He vanished, having unwillingly stuffed the five dollar bill she insisted on giving him into his pocket.

By the time they had laid her on the table to prepare her for a dilatation and curettage, her temperature was 104. She could hear the doctors in the clinic cursing her and all those ignorant *curanderas* who kill off more people a year, they said, than diphtheria; they were like a plague upon "the people." Until these ignorant people learned to go to real doctors, she heard someone say, they would continue to die off like flies. Someone then quoted the San Antonio annual death rate, but by this time Kate was staring, half-blinded at the blazing light which hung over the surgery table. She could feel them quickly and expertly shaving her pubic hair: an anesthetist hovered efficiently over her with fumes from a cone-shaped cup: *why couldn't I have had all this before? NOW they want to save me, when only a day or so ago they were willing to see me murdered?*

She had not time to separate the "they" from the "me" however; for with the first whiff of ether (*if that's what it is*, thought Kate doubtfully—adding to herself with what she imagined was enormous lucidity: *je doute, donc je suis*), she seemed to hover over and fall into the bright light which was pouring into her eyes; and she shut her eyes until she waked to a clean bed with a spotlessly white nurse pushing penicillin into her hip with a sharpness which felt to Kate like the distilled savagery of the world and who was saying: "There, that wasn't so bad was it?"

12

She awoke in a seven-bed ward, a white canvas shower curtain separating her from the others. It seemed very quiet. Later she was to realize that her bed was at the central apex: the beds on either side were empty except for two Mexican girls, the nature of whose illness she never learned.

Caleb was admonishing her and kissing her hand. "Oh you baby. Oh you foolish child. 'Katie, Katie, Katie. What am I going to do about you, you don't have any more sense than to run off and—" His eyes filled with tears. "Like to of killed yourself, I guess you know that?"

This idea stirred her drugged body to anger. "I wasn't *trying* to kill myself. They *force* you."

He shook his head in silent reproof.

"How'd you find me?"

"That girl with the purple name. You know who I mean? Magenta."

"But how did *she* know? About you? I never mentioned your name."

Caleb shrugged. "You got to understand The Southern Lady. She may *act* like she doesn't know what's going on, but she knows *everything*."

She tried to smile. The nurse brought her some pills which she said were vitamins and left them on the nightstand. Kate at once reached over to take them with water but found to her surprise that it was painful to move: a tearing pain as if she were being slowly flayed, burned at her navel. With a groan she sank back to the pillow and cursed. "What've they done to me, the bastards?"

This was apparently more than Caleb could bear. "You did it to yourself. There was no sense to it. You knew how I feel. It was my baby and I had as much right to it as you . . . ." His feeling had begun erupting in spite of his evident determination to remain calm.

"Is that what you came here to tell me?" she asked wearily, gentling her body into a more comfortable position. "I tried to avoid all that. It's over now, and I'm the one lying here, not you . . . ."

"You had no right to do it. I'd of been glad to have taken the child and brought him up. He would have had everything in the world to make him happy."

"Goddammit Caleb," she said with slowly rising rage, as if he had tapped at the center of her, where the pain lay, "you keep talking as if

155

that baby were real. You even call it *him* as if it were bound to be a boy. I'm telling you it had no reality to me. It stood between me and freedom, whatever that is. No unwanted child should have to come into the world anymore: *there are enough people!*"

"*He* wasn't unwanted," Caleb said bitterly. "I wanted him."

"You wanted it. But I'd have had to carry it, give it birth. I'd have to nourish it, keep it alive. And I'm hardly alive myself yet. I've only begun to live, to free myself. Was I supposed to spend the rest of my life worrying about another human being so *you* can have a child? Go adopt one, then. Go have one yourself if you want one so bad ...." she concluded irrationally, the tears rising to her eyes.

Caleb studied his fingernails as though reading the white scars on them.

"I tried that once," he confessed, looking away. "I tried to adopt a little black kid got orphaned by a fire. They wouldn't let me have him, the social workers wouldn't. Said my motives were too 'obscure.' I thought they were clear enough."

Ah, so that's it again, thought Kate, and rested her cheek upon the boiled surface of the pillow case—chemically clean and uncomplicated: a luxury of simplicity. "Caleb, if you've come to visit me just to share in my 'guilt'—"

He lifted his head sharply: "What do you mean by that?"

"You know exactly what I mean. You're just *not* going to manage to 'expiate' your Everlasting Guilt by keeping other people from doing what you think is sinful."

His lips were clenched so that she could see the faint white line where the blood had been. He picked up the water glass from her table, holding it fast in both hands. "So that's what you think I am. Just a murderer going around preaching against murder."

She tried to reply but the pills lay in her throat like fumes; their gelatinous skins had dissolved to a powdery air, choking her. She began to cough harshly, but Caleb did not seem to notice. He appeared to have physically and emotionally removed himself from her as though he had suddenly leaped off a cliff and all she could hear now was his low scream. "Would you *mind*?" she gasped, taking the water glass from him, angry and hurt that he had driven so far only to end up tormenting her (as she felt) like everyone else. Wearily she swallowed enough water to loosen the grains in her throat. "How hard it is to swallow even the stuff that's supposed to keep you alive," she murmured, and waited for the spasm of pain at her navel to subside.

"Well, I guess I'd better let you rest," said Caleb awkwardly. "I guess the reason they sent me right on up to the ward was 'cause I said it was my baby."

156

"Oh Christ, Caleb. Did you *have* to? What did you achieve by that? A public act of contrition? Do you think if you suffer enough about this baby, it'll save you from hell-fire?"

The gentle eyes turned upon her the incredulous look of a child who has been unjustly punished. Kate instantly regretted her words, but an irritability, caused perhaps by the pain in her womb, had made of her tongue a retaliatory weapon: perhaps she even held him responsible for her ordeal. After all, neither Paul nor Shaddy had . . . . She closed her eyes, overcome by the stupidity of it all. It had been neither Caleb's error nor hers: an incompetent doctor had simply failed to fit her properly—a simple error in calculation that could cost you your life.

Caleb rose to go. "I'll be back day after tomorrow," he said.

"It's a long trip for you." She refrained from adding *just for me*.

"It's not that. I'm going on a hunting trip down near the border. Should be a good season, as they say. They're expecting to bag 'em a deer apiece."

She signed. "Caleb, I can't see—"

He shrugged impatiently. "*You* can't see. But it's my life. It's the way *I* got to do things. These men have been my friends for years. They're not killers. They don't see it my way yet, but they may . . . . I keep talking it up. You don't go to Mahatma Gandhi to preach love and non-violence. You go among the publicans and sinners."

" 'Publicans and sinners . . . .' " she murmured thoughtfully. "I'm sorry I can't be of any help to you. I mean, after the hunt you'll need all the help you can get."

"Nothing for you to worry about," he said curtly. "All I want is for you to get well. Then it looks to me like we got a lot of thinking to do about this. We've got to do one thing or another—we can't keep on killing kids."

"Caleb, if you use the word *kill* once more, I'll—"

"What'll you do? Kick me out of here?" He looked around scornfully. "Place like this, they can't keep *any*body out. They don't give a damn *who* they let in here. I saw a bunch of teen-agers runnin' around the halls a while ago, smoking pot and horsing around in front of an open door said *intensive care*. Nobody looked very intensive about caring to *me*. Not a soul around to keep those kids from bringing in a whole entire Mariachi band if they wanted. That nurse that was here, she didn't stick around to see if you took your pills." He looked down at her sadly. "Want anything 'fore I go?"

"All I want is to *not* hear any more about this. I've already done the 'one thing or another' as you call it. We can't change that."

"And next time? How many times do you think you can take this sort of thing?"

157

She felt her hands clench in anger: "It won't happen again."

"Well, if it does, it won't be *mine*."

If she had felt up to it, she believed she would have begun to quarrel, demanding to know "exactly what he meant by that," but the pills (probably not vitamins at all) were making her groggy. She closed her eyes.

"See you Wednesday," he said.

"Better by then," she murmured, and wondered who or what would be better by then.

She was sitting up in her bed reading Proust when he arrived on Wednesday. She had never seen Caleb in hunting clothes; when he appeared at the hospital (he said their party was passing through on the way to the border) he seemed transformed. She thought with unexpected clarity that he might deny with every breath the true function of The Hunt, but physically his whole being was in tune with it. The high leather boots, the colorful hunting jacket, the vizored cap, and above all the oblique sling of the rifle (not loaded yet, he assured her at once: but why should he think she would even care to see it?) created a striking effect.

In the hallway stood several of Caleb's hunting friends, similarly attired, who for reasons of their own had decided to wait in the corridor instead of in the parking lot: they stood peering into the women's ward as if they would have liked to be invited in: but Kate had no such intention.

The presence of these men standing in the corridor produced a titter of hysteria from the two young Mexican women. They became suddenly bashful and giggling, as though a man in hunting clothes were more sexually suggestive than the male orderlies in white smocks who came to take their temperatures. The attraction, Kate dimly realized, lay in the royal caparison—the special apparel of gentlemen with hunting dogs gazed upon from their thatched huts by an admiring peasantry. Their bright uniforms sent out flares of power, like firecrackers in a darkened sky: a man with a rifle going out to kill something, whether usefully or not was a symbol of blood and capitulation. The women smiled at the men as if they were conquerors—new masters who had just liberated their villages and were now to be propitiated. From time to time one of the men gravely bowed to the young women, sending them into smiles of ravishment.

"You look very—sportsmanlike," said Kate guardedly, not wishing to anger him.

"Beware of a woman with a tongue like a viper," Caleb cautioned himself as he arranged his chair at her bedside.

"Well, I've about decided," he announced, glancing with suspicion at the volume of Proust she had been holding in her hand, as though this were a factor in the situation he would have to learn to deal with.

"What have you decided, my Prince?" asked Kate, smiling. He looked so handsome in his clothes that she found it difficult to take him seriously. Her imagination was already arranging a cartoon she would like to do: of Caleb standing at the door of his Taxidermy Shop (built like Noah's Ark), wearing a cowboy suit, his boots polished to a high blood-red. Quail, pheasants, 'possum and deer would be passing through the doorway of the shop, on their way to the Ark. At Caleb's side would be a trusty-larait (not a rifle), which Caleb would be unfurling. The balloon above his head would read: "When I'm through with you, you'll be immortal."

"I've decided," he said without answering her smile, "that as soon as I get back, you and I are going up to Juarez to get you a divorce. Then we're going to get married quick-like."

She felt herself childishly pleased that Caleb should want to keep her, legitimizing their affair.

"*You* decided." She had decided to take it lightly.

"Well," he said challengingly, "you got any sensible objections?"

She laughed. "This surely must be the most romantic proposal a girl ever had."

"We've *had* our romance," he said pointedly. "It's time we settled down to—"

"—to having a family," she finished for him impatiently. "But Caleb, I've already told you, I'm not ready to settle down to *any*thing."

". . . or anybody?" he insisted. "You just going to go promiscuously from one man to another? No strings attached? No future?"

"You've said yourself there's no future. That's what the 'Noah's Ark' is all about, isn't it?"

"No future for the environment is something different than you and me. We've got everything going for us. We like the same things, we do the same kind of work . . . in a way," he added humbly.

"Caleb, I'm not ready for that. As for going from man to man, what you call 'promiscuity,' I certainly don't *feel* promiscuous. I feel fine. Only I feel, a little older, a little wiser. In fact, maybe it's a good idea, what I've done. It's been . . . an experience. I've learned more about life in this past year than in my entire life before this. In that other life, the one I'll never live now, I'd be waiting for my husband to come home from work, wondering what name to give my son so he wouldn't be marked forever in this crazy System—" She paused; at the word *son*, his look of supplication turned to anguish not unmixed with hatred: it was as if she insisted on being stupid and stubborn about all this.

159

"Look, I've said we ought to get married and you give me this line about some other life. I know you don't want to go back to Detroit just to be a good housewife and all . . . . But I'm offering something different—a good life, really. A ranch, maybe; a place to entertain your friends and have plenty of time to draw or paint or whatever you think you want to do."

It was, finally, the carelessness of his phrase, DRAW or PAINT *or whatever you think you want to do* which triggered her impatience. "Painting is not my *hobby*!" she burst out. "I don't want to be an amateur painter! It's what I want to *do*. My thing: you know?" She stopped abruptly, embarrassed. She had a high distaste for oracular statements. When people talked about "the Personality of the Artist," it always made her wince. Yet all the other activities she and Caleb might engage in—the farming or ranching or raising of children or even the luxurious hobbies they might cultivate—were meaningful only in so far as they might make of her a better artist: if riding cattle trains would make her a better painter of cattle trains, she was prepared for an unending ride on cattle trains from one end of the United States to the other and back again forever.

"It's not that I'm against marriage as an institution," she said after a long silence. "It's just that I'm against anything that makes it awkward, difficult, and even dangerous for people to change, that rewards people who remain static. Because if they don't, they're in danger of outgrowing each other."

"People who love one another to start with end up by loving one another," he said stubbornly.

"Well marriage seems to demand a kind of love which I've never seen. I don't really believe that kind of love exists and if it doesn't exist why should people kid themselves into believing it does?"

"Just because *you* don't believe it exists, doesn't mean it doesn't exist. What you're saying is you don't love me." He picked up his cap, thrust his rifle loosely into the crook of his elbow. "Well, a lady has a right to change her mind. When I come back we'll talk about this," he added in a light-hearted tone meant to deny that anything was settled.

"That's not true," she said sharply. "I do love you. But the fact is, you've stopped living . . . . You want peace, tranquillity, silent days and long sunsets: well, what I want is . . ." she laughed at her own dramatics: " *'life piled on life,' 'the wine-dark sea,'*—that sort of thing."

He stood silently thinking, then sighed with almost visible sacrifice: "We'll sell the shop and go to New York. Or San Francisco. How'd that appeal to you?"

She sighed. He was willing to give up his tranquillity for her sake;

160

but it was not for something he really wanted. It was useless to insist that someone be more adventurous, imaginative and daring than his nature intended him to be: and who was she to set up such standards?

She was relieved when Caleb bent to kiss her goodbye. "Take care of my girl," he said good-naturedly. As he leaned over her the buttons of his hunting jacket stabbed into her side; the gun seemed to float momentarily above their heads. From over Caleb's shoulder she could see the soft dark eyes of the Mexican women watching her with vicarious pleasure; then the boots in the corridor began to pace to and fro restlessly, and Caleb had gone.

About a half hour later a nurse came in with an airmail letter. Those four handsome men, the nurse said, the ones in the hunting jackets, had come all the way back when they were ten miles out on the highway just because her husband—he *was* her husband, wasn't he?—had forgotten to leave this letter. "And he sent you this too," she added, handing Kate a carved eland which Caleb had evidently picked up at a curio shop. "Such a nice man," the nurse murmured. "Not many men are so considerate of their wives nowadays."

With irrepressible irritation Kate exclaimed: "He's not my husband. We're not married, and we don't *plan* to be married!"

Visibly shaken, the nurse stared at Kate. She piled the bedclothes from the foot of the beds on either side of Kate as though they were infected, and pushed them quickly out of the room on a cart.

The letter was from Paul. How Caleb had managed to get hold of it was difficult to imagine. Perhaps he had been to her apartment to see if there were any message for himself and instead had found this letter lying in the mailbox. With Caleb's usual self-effacement he had brought the letter to the hospital, then apparently forgotten to give it to her. What had doubtless troubled him most (and what astonished Kate) was the return address:

San Francisco Health Clinic
Box 1116

I want you to come here at once and see me. I tried to find
you in Houston but they wouldn't let me. They're curing
me. You'd be surprised at how much progress I've made.
They let me go home on weekends if I want to, but I don't
have any place to go.

I don't live the way I used to. I've been here a month
now and am down to one meal a day. The tumor is definitely
decreasing in size and hardness. They're dissolving it. I need
new shorts, chewing gum (sugarless), a package of Tarot cards

161

and any books you can get on the Old Religion. We're starting a coven here.

Paul

She could make nothing of it. She could not imagine how Paul
could have driven alone to California in the first place, and the tone of
his letter was so far removed from the Paul Ardley she had known that
it terrified her: in such a short time, it seemed to her, Paul had lost
everything which had made his life manageable—his self-respect, the
women he had loved, his mental balance. She was wrenched with guilt;
whatever she might say to rationalize, she was partly responsible. *I am
a part of all that I have met* meant also that one shared in the guilt of
other people's failures. If she had been able to help Paul more, he
might not have gone on needing her love so much. The preempting of
freedom for oneself was ideal in theory; but in fact, one left a wake of
misery and abandonment because "love" was a drowning liquor from
which the weak swimmer could not rescue himself alone. Most people,
probably herself included, were not strong enough to be alone: they
had to build nests, like birds.

Sadly she put away the letter while calculating how she could possibly fly out to San Francisco to see Paul. Perhaps her presence would
shake him back into some kind of reality, if nothing else. But her trip
to San Antonio had exhausted her funds. She had nothing to sell except her watch and Shaddy's ring (which was probably worthless), unless perhaps she could hold some kind of sidewalk auction of all her
drawings. She knew they did such things in New York and San Francisco, but she did not know about Houston: Texas was another world.

On Wednesday, she refused to take any more pills; she did not
want to be groggy again when Caleb arrived. He had every right to expect clear-headed communication from her. By ten o'clock she had
finished breakfast, showered and washed her hair. She had even finished her volume of Proust and had begun on the magazines in the
ward; but Caleb had not come. She was obliged to admit that her pride
was hurt; he had promised to come; then he had not come: it had
doubtless turned out to be too long a ride up from the border. At the
same time she was sorry she had spoken to him so cruelly: she confessed to herself that if he had spoken to *her* in that way, she would
have been bitter and grudging for a long time afterwards. It was a curse
of her nature, she thought harshly, that she did not forgive easily: and
never forgot.

She spent the rest of the day doing pen and ink sketches of the
Mexican women in the ward: they were enchanted, it seemed they had

162

never seen a woman with such artistic talent—certainly never one who spoke of herself seriously as An Artist. When they asked her about herself, her husband and her children, Kate simply said shortly: "I'm married to a man who's presently in Salt Lake City and I don't have any children." They had apparently decided that she was a happy lunatic who was willing to idle away the time while waiting for Caleb doing as many sketches of their lovely profiles as they wanted. But when Kate asked if they would pose in the nude they turned shocked, startled eyes upon her as if she had suddenly metamorphosed into a monster. Kate felt at once the change in their attitude: they distrusted her instincts more than they would have feared an army of pillagers whose violence they would have understood as natural. Had she been a male artist they would have smilingly refused, flattered nevertheless; but for a woman to ask them to pose without clothes seemed to them perverted. They had been so brainwashed into thinking of their bodies as forbidden objects of lust, it seemed not to have occurred to them that the human form could be observed for any other purpose than pornographic. So they whispered between themselves and fell silent.

Kate turned away with a sigh and began, instead, a bitter but vivid sketch of the entire ward: Ward Six she called it after Chekov's story, drawing the beds in cruciform. She drew the bars of the plain white metal beds so that each face was incarcerated behind them. The dark eyes of the Mexican women stared out from behind this prison, their hands resting lifelessly on the metal slats . . . . All the doors and windows of the ward were sketched as open, opening: one wall of the hospital behind them was completely torn down so that a vista of trees, birds, mountaintops, shone with reflected light, making a certain slant of light on the hospital floor. Beneath this cartoon the caption read: *Save me, save me.*

When evening twilight finally came, Kate was restless and bored, annoyed by the dim lights and the sulky women who pressed their transistor radios to their pillows like lovers. The doctors had told Kate that she would have to remain two days more before she would be beyond the risk of reinfection but she decided she would not spend another day in the ward; tomorrow she would put on her clothes and sit all day in the visiting hall, if necessary, a small crescent-shaped room with a bay window where ambulatory patients met their visitors.

By the next day she had forgotten her injured pride at Caleb's failure to show up and had begun to worry about him. It would be like him, torn between two fidelities, the friends he loved and the woman he loved, to delay parting until the decision for departure was out of his hands—determined, say, by the death of a hunting dog or a sprained ankle. But it was not like Caleb to altogether forget that she was scheduled to be discharged from the hospital today, and she would naturally prefer not to ride the bus back to Houston alone.

During the first few hours she gave herself the routine explanations: he was having car trouble on his way back to San Antonio; he had been obliged to return suddenly to Houston and had not gone on the hunt at all but was completely involved in some intercontinental purchase for his Noah's Ark. Or—and this came to seem terrifyingly rational—he had been in an automobile accident: he was perhaps, lying somewhere injured and helpless, waiting for someone to rescue him. This image catapulted her out to the hallway to use the public telephone.

She did not have enough money for calls to both Houston and Brownsville so she gambled her remaining coins on phoning the local police. The San Antonio police were bored and indifferent. What could she expect them to do about a man who had very likely crossed over into Mexico for all they knew: have to leave that to the border patrol, they said. She made another call to the Texas State Highway Patrol. They offered to call her back at the San Antonio hospital if they received word of an accident involving Caleb's car: did she know the license number? She didn't . . . . The voice at the other end sighed its impatience: "Sure would help a lot if you women would just learn the license number of your own husband's car." "He's not my husband," snapped Kate. There was a long silence, then a suggestive chuckle: "Well, whose husband *is* he then, m'am?" This was followed by a whispered exchange with another patrolman, then another silence. At last the voice, somewhere between a sigh and a chuckle, assured her that they would let her know if they heard anything.

She chastised herself for being an "hysterical woman." Caleb could take care of himself; what she ought to be doing was getting herself ready to leave the hospital even if he didn't show up. She needed money for bus fare, needed, also, to be careful this time to take the Express, not the Local. In despair she realized she did not have enough money for bus fare.

There was only one possible source of money: the hospital social worker who after the first day had never again returned to talk to Kate whom she described in her report as "recalcitrant, ill-advised and unrealistic." Whatever the woman's attitude toward her, however, Kate would have to approach her to get enough money to hold off Starvation and Ruin till Caleb returned.

When she had packed her few things, she cleaned her hair, fingernails and teeth and went down to see Mrs. Odum, the social worker. She knew she would have to lie, the only problem was to remember what one had already lied about: the questions were always leading

164

questions, meant to be a cross-reference of one's authenticity. The story this time, Kate thought, would have to be that she wanted to repent, "to give up this way of life," "to turn over a new leaf" (she fingered the clichés like apples, testing them to see if some were not too ripe, even for Mrs. Odum). If she could only get enough money for transportation back to Detroit, her story must go, she would "go back home."

But Kate found the atmosphere of Mrs. Odum's office intimidating. Pictures of Mrs. Odum's sons, both apparently officers in the armed services, dominated the walls like medical degrees; snapshots wreathed the huge brass frames in technicolor poses of grandchildren on tricycles, on bicycles and (abruptly) on the Eiffel tower. A deckle-edged Bible used as a paperweight rested at one corner of the desk. Mrs. Odum herself was naturally hostile and suspicious. Kate had made a very poor impression on her the first day. And the record of her "unrepentant promiscuity," as Mrs. Odum pointed out, was only too well-known; indeed, there were indications that Kate was jeopardizing the health and welfare of other girls who had come to the hospital for *respectable* reasons, Mrs. Odum added, her mouth a corrugated line of restraint.

Kate became desperate. She reined in her anger, explaining as calmly as she could that she needed the money to get back to Houston first. What did they expect her to do in San Antonio? Kate should have thought about all that before she took on herself to behave so rashly, was Mrs. Odum's retort. Kate sat staring at the social worker, trying to understand her. She could only understand that she was dealing with a woman who appeared to be without imagination: it was a void which her own imagination could not leap.

"I've *got* to have at least ten dollars," admitted Kate at last in a strangled voice: she would rather have dug sand in the broiling sun than beg for ten dollars; but she was in no condition to take chances. The doctor had warned her that she was still convalescing: "no sex for at least a month" (with an arch look as if he doubted her capacity to contain her own lust for so long a time), "no lifting of heavy weights; plenty of food, rest, sunshine." The usual blind admonitions, in short, to enjoy life and live a leisurely middle-class existence by those who knew nothing of surviving on the barest subsistence.

A look of shame crossed the grey-white face with its seams of age, futility, boredom and vicarious pain. *No greater bitterness than a man who has lived his life in vain*, (or woman either, thought Kate), and softened her voice to another lie: "I have *almost* enough to get back home for the holidays . . . ." She racked her brain to remember what Jewish holidays might be coming up soon, but her memory flickered and blacked out at the strain. "My mother's having a baby." There was some satisfaction in tacking on this truth, though it seemed—even to Kate—irrelevant and specious.

There was a great sigh from behind the desk. Kate had rung all the changes. There was nothing more to be said, so the woman with an expression of infinite weariness drew an opened checkbook toward her bosom and wrote out a personal check for Kate in the amount of twelve dollars. Why twelve? wondered Kate aloud.

The woman looked at her scornfully. "We can't expect you to *starve*."

"Oh." Kate said softly, then managed to ask: "Couldn't I have it in cash? It's so hard to cash a check when you don't have identification."

"Why don't you have identification?"

"I don't have a driver's license. They don't accept a social security card—and anyway, it doesn't have my married name on it . . . ."

Mrs. Odum stared at Kate with contempt. "No charge cards, anything like that, of course. Or even a birth certificate."

Kate shook her head. *Who carries a birth certificate around?*

"Well, that's your problem," said the woman sullenly. "We're not allowed to give cash. You want the check or not?" Her pen stood poised over the half-written check.

"Yes . . . please," said Kate. *Humbly*, she thought.

When Kate returned to her ward to finish getting her things together, the Mexican women were astonishingly friendly—considering, thought Kate ruefully, that they must have described Kate to the social worker as if they had been exposed to a social disease. She tried to drive the humiliating interview with the social worker out of her mind, but found that her memory kept returning to it with fresh indignation: it was perhaps only that she had been through so much in the past two weeks, but she felt at any moment she would begin to cry. It grew close to noon and still Caleb had not arrived. At one o'clock, after observing with resentment that they had skipped her lunch, preferring to count her as an already discharged patient even though she was still sitting on her bed and watching the others eat—at one o'clock she picked up her bag and waved goodbye to the women in the ward. They were warm, friendly, well-wishing. *Why they like me*, thought Kate sadly: *it's just that they're afraid of the unknown.* It was Kate's first experience with the ambivalence of women who long to be free, envy freedom, but are terrified of it.

At the desk in the receiving room she had some final papers to sign, releasing the hospital from responsibility in the event of complications resulting from the dilatation and curettage. Kate was weary unto death

166

of the place, signed without reading, and prepared to make her escape. But the switchboard operator now informed her. "You'd better wait in the lobby. You had a phone call awhile back and your husband said to wait for him, he'll pick you up in about an hour. He called while you were in to see Mrs. Odum," she added.

Kate groaned with relief; she had had no idea how she was going to cash that preposterous check over the weekend, and she was down to her last dollar. She sat down on one of the hospital's lounging chairs and managed to fall asleep for over an hour. When she awoke she was very hungry and was beginning to feel hurt at Caleb's keeping her waiting so long. But when a car finally drove up to the entrance to the hospital and a man came through the swinging doors, it was not Caleb at all: it was Shaddy.

"Well for God's sake," she couldn't help exclaiming. "What are you doing here?"

Shaddy looked somber. "Weren't expecting me, were you? . . . ." With a hasty glance around him, he added brusquely: "Well, let's get out of this place so's we can talk." Mechanically he picked up her bag.

Shaddy slid her overnight bag into the front seat, beneath her feet.

They were both too overcome by their emotions to trust themselves to speak: it was not an auspicious reunion. She was certain Shaddy knew why she had been hospitalized. Such gossip leaked through the air and besides Shaddy, always suspicious, was the kind of man to guess correctly at such things. Kate felt that any "explanation" would be irrelevant, so she remained silent as they cruised through the summer heat, the endless road ahead spanned by the horizon. It was difficult to associate what she had been through—the germ-laden *barrio,* the filthy dogs dancing around her blood-flecked towels, the threat of death itself—with the milk-white skies extending into a flood of blue light as far as the eye could see. Cattle ranches and cultivated farms lay on either side of them; glossy black Angus dipped their heads into ponds mirroring the sunlight like the eye of God. Kate sighed; it was good to be alive after her skirmish with death and darkness. Whatever Shaddy might say to her she was determined to accept with stoicism: *sticks and stones can break my bones . . . .*

"We'll stop along the highway, get something to eat." Shaddy said. He snapped on the car radio and at once the silence exploded into country western. At the familiar refrains Shaddy relaxed into his seat as into a saddle: they passed road signs offering peaches, pralines, turkeys, hunting privileges, pecans, goats, picnic sites and antiques, but not a single restaurant. Finally they spotted a truck stop, barricaded by gas pumps and with an oil rig in the back yard. Beside the window stood a Coca-Cola cooler full of Dr. Peppers, Frescas, Chocolate Soldiers and

Cokes. An unlit neon sign assured them that the restaurant was air-conditioned, a factor more important than the food: the sun on the seat belts had heated the metal to such intensity that Kate cried out as it slid across her wrist in a quick burn.

"One thing for sure, it's hot down here," said Shaddy with a light-heartedness which was familiar and reassuring. He stretched lazily as he eased his legs to the concrete, calling out to the attendant, "Hi there. Hot enough for you?" The cliché brought a wave of pleasant nostalgia, like an old song. Kate's heart lifted momentarily, feeling she might be able to cope with everything after all. But her body was not as resilient as her mind: she needed the overnight case into which she had carelessly packed all her sanitary napkins; but when she bent over to pick up the bag she discovered her legs were unsteady from having lain in bed nearly a week and there was a sharp pain in her womb. Awkwardly she stood by the door while Shaddy pulled out the small bag from the floor of the car. A worried scowl had settled into Shaddy's forehead. She had never seen him look so depressed and the sight made her feel guiltier than ever: was she responsible for Shaddy's illusions too?

When she came out of the ladies' room, she found two drafts of beer on the table. "You're old enough to drink now, I reckon," he said.

If she had thought she was to be spared an inquisition, she was mistaken. She had hardly sat down at the table when Shaddy said: "So you went and done it. Just like I said. I wasn't hardly out of town before you got in bed with him."

Kate gasped at the suddenness of this attack. She had been beguiled by the peaceful pastoral on the highway into hoping that perhaps Shaddy had come to ask her to come back to Salt Lake City with him, or even to talk about a divorce—but not merely to gratuitously insult her.

He straightened his shoulders against the back of the chair. "Just like I said," he repeated. "The minute my back was turned, you went to bed with the first guy you saw."

She could feel her face grow white with anger; but she was growing hardened to the notion that she could expect to be most insulted for her "freedom" by the people who were most affected by it. "When you left," she said slowly, "we didn't make any promises . . . . I'm sure that you—"

"A man's different," he interrupted. "Look at yourself. Knocked-up first thing." He seemed torn between jealousy and bitter triumph at the fulfillment of his prediction. "And this guy, where is he? What kind of a guy lets a woman go through all this by herself? Are you in love with him?" He asked the question quickly, as if the deliberate *non*

168

sequitur might jar the truth from her.

"If I say 'yes' does that mean anything? And if I say 'no' what does that mean?"

"Well, Christ," he said angrily. "You ought at least to know the answer to a simple question like that. Unless you've gone clean out of your mind."

"It's not a simple question. It's not simple at all . . . . Yes, I do love him—"

His face flushed crimson and his eyes grew suddenly bright. "*There* you go!" he exclaimed. "Whyn't you admit it in the first place? You never did have any respect for me—a dumb hunky from the pits . . . ." His mask of lighthearted cynicism had fallen momentarily away and he sat gloomily staring at his fingernails as if remembering the nights he had tried in vain to remove the coal dust embedded in his flesh.

"That's not true." She put her hand over his, feeling the same comradeship she had felt when he had told her about his life in the mines. "I've always respected you," she said. "But you have no right to tell me what to do."

He gripped her hand till her fingers went white. "I *do* have a right . . . . Listen, Katie, you remember how we done . . . We went into it like a pig in a poke, we didn't know a thing about each other. And we hit the jackpot, just like it was ordered for us. We haven't give it a good chance yet. We never lived a secure life, like normal people—"

"There's no such thing," she interrupted him.

He seemed not to hear her. What preoccupied him was her confession of feeling for Caleb. "So you love this guy, eh?" He lifted his head with his air of precocious, invincible curiosity. She could see he would rather not have asked the question, but was compelled by a curiosity in him stronger than revulsion: "Then whyn't you just *have* the baby, for Christ sake. 'Stead of goin' through all *this*? Was he already married?" he added, as if that were a situation he could have understood.

She shook her head, weary unto death of this question: "I wasn't *ready* to have a baby," she said sullenly.

He stared at her unbelievingly: "Katie, you sure have gone all the way down the drain since I first met you! Who'd have believed a nice girl, like you was, could change so much in a few months."

"Over a year . . . . And I haven't changed. I was 'like this' when you met me. All Paul did was clear up a bit of hypocrisy which stood in my way of understanding things. Then you came along."

"But dammit, that didn't mean you had to go shack up with every dick you came across," he said with disgust. "Just like any old two-bit

169

whore. Christ, you were a good clean girl when I met you," he repeated.

There was an embarrassed silence. It was clear that he had degraded her so much in his own eyes by his words that he no longer knew what role was expected of him. Kate smiled mirthlessly: after Othello has called his wife a "whore," the play is over. When the waitress brought their food they ate it in silence.

When Shaddy had finished the last morsel of food on his plate, he asked: "What you fixin' to do when you get back?"

At this question, unlike the others, she lost command of herself; she could feel the quaver in her voice. "I don't know."

"Well, you'll be seein' *him*, I suppose?"

"I don't know," she repeated. There was a sudden rise of terror in her stomach. "I don't know where he is . . . exactly."

He lapsed into contempt not unmixed with pity: ". . . He's not run off and left you?"

Kate felt he would have been pleased to hear that Caleb had abandoned her. "No . . . he's on a hunting trip. Down by the border."

"You got a job?" he demanded with sudden insight.

She nodded. "I work for . . . Caleb."

He whistled softly. His tone lilted in mournful parody. "Worser and worser. You let yourself get laid by the boss. Boss gets you knocked-up, then hotfoots it out of the country, down Mayheeco way. Sounds like the same old jazz to me."

"For God's sake, shut up!" she snapped. "You don't know a thing about it!"

But he had scented serious trouble and was not ready to surrender this opportunity to badger her. "Leave you any money?"

She was about to lie, but she remembered all too clearly the humiliation she had gone through to get a check for twelve dollars which she probably would not even be able to cash till Monday morning.

She shook her head, dumb with injured pride.

He rubbed his hands over his eyes in a kind of comic despair.

"Why you don't even have the good sense to get any money out of it!" he exclaimed.

Kate bowed her head disconsolately: they were beyond communication on the subject of Caleb.

The waitress brought Shaddy their check. With a studied gesture he opened his wallet, slowly fingered several bills, then tossed one onto the plate for the waitress. "Just keep it," he said, smiling brightly up into the girl's face, his eyes on the satin shimmer of her blouse. Kate thought for a moment of asking Shaddy to change the check the social worker had given her. She knew that if Caleb had not yet come back,

170

she would need the money at once in Houston. But some grip of pride seized her. *I'd rather starve*, she thought; and wondered mirthlessly whether she would have been able to come to the same decision an hour ago, before she had put away that big platterful of food.

While Shaddy was engaged in light patter with the waitress, Kate went to try to phone Caleb. She called the shop, then dialed his house, asking the operator to let it ring another minute or so; but there was no answer. She tried to think of whom she might call to leave a message for Caleb that she was on her way back, but the only place she could think of was the San Antonio hospital itself. She did this, and was left with about thirty-five cents in change.

She walked back to the table where Shaddy was still carrying on a conversation with the girl; he was telling her a story about how hard it had been for him to get beer one night in Salt Lake City. Smiling feebly, Kate waited till he had finished his story while the girl eyed Kate with a faint, guilty smile. When they left Shaddy waved goodbye to the girl as if he had known her for years. Kate could not help wondering whether he had in fact arranged something with the girl and asked herself whether what she felt was sexual jealousy. Mainly it seemed to her what she was experiencing was fear: she was beginning to be definitely frightened. She was not strong enough at the moment to struggle physically to survive on twelve dollars; there had been a kind of insult in Shaddy's intimacy with the waitress at which her self-esteem plummeted. Altogether she was feeling that somehow "they" had contrived to make a punitive, shameful and even murderous thing out of her "freedom." She climbed back into the car feeling timid and compromised.

When they were still about a half hour away from Houston Kate began feeling pains in her back; her legs were trembling as though they had forgotten that their purpose in life was to sustain her in her courageous actions . . . . And in the core of her where they had scraped away the last vestiges of Sin, she felt a pain as though a dry piece of wood were slowly splintering to pieces. Wearily she lay her head back against the seat and was instantly asleep. When she awoke she realized Shaddy had stopped at a motel.

He explained: "I got a gig to go to in Sugarland. Kleig and the boys will be meetin' me there. And this is as good a place for you to wait as any, while I wash up."

It struck her as amusing that they did not look the least bit illicit as they registered; even their names would have checked out if a house detective had come along. Yet Kate felt a vague uneasiness; this was not where she meant to find herself. She wanted to hurry on to Houston, she needed to talk to Caleb. But a sense of gratitude toward

Shaddy kept her from protesting. Shaddy had helped her when she had needed him; it seemed not right to quarrel with him over a brief delay.

He began stripping his clothes almost as soon as they were alone in the motel, dropping them everywhere on his way to the bathroom. She could hear him singing and scrubbing lustily. She lay on top of the neatly-made bed, happy not to be sitting up in the car where even the occasional bumps of the highway pulled at her insides. She would have liked to try to call Caleb again to see if he had come into the shop, but felt Shaddy might come out of the bathroom at any moment and interrupt her. She did not feel herself strong enough for that sort of affront.

Shaddy emerged from the shower and at once threw his naked body across hers. She thought he must be joking, but from the hardness of his sex she knew he meant to have her; indeed, the whole business of the "gig" and the need of a place to wash up had all been a transparent ruse, exactly as if she had been a girl he had picked up and they were both pretending they did not know why they had come to the motel.

"Uh. Uh. It's not allowed," she said, trying to play it lightly.

"Who said?"

"Doctor said. It'd be too soon after."

He frowned his disapproval of her candor. Then, as if his mood had changed mercurially, he explained with a businesslike air: "There's lots you can do besides a straight fuck."

It occurred to her she had never heard Shaddy use this expression before. She rested her eyes on his face thoughtfully, trying to see through the hard ring of the language to where Shaddy's real emotions lay. He placed his hand expertly between her legs, waiting for her response; but there was a certain impatience in his manner as if he had not much time and after all they were two consenting adults who did not need to spend all night at this sort of thing.

"I *do* have this gig to do," Shaddy laughed, as if he expected her to applaud his tactic, ". . . tomorrow."

As she put her arms around him her hands touched the jagged scar which had stirred her compassion so many months before. She touched it lightly: there was always something fragile, something hopelessly insecure about Shaddy which evoked her tenderness. But Shaddy was in no mood for compassion. He had a right to expect pleasure and gratification, she had been his friend, his mistress, his wife; according to the law she was still his wife. Dutifully, as though it were an act of expiation, Kate sought to bring him to a climax. She did not enjoy fellatio; it strained her neck, her back, and above all at the moment, the still-convalescing center of her body. Shaddy's digital manipulations only exacerbated her weariness. She positively was not interested in

172

sexual pleasure at such a time and was relieved when Shaddy, with a gasp of pleasure, ejaculated in a slow bubbling stream across her mouth.

Shaddy lay for a while pretending to sleep. Kate quietly slid out from bed to shower. The jetties of hot water seemed to help the soreness at her back and she stood tranquilly submerged under the water for a long time. While under the shower, she thought she heard Shaddy calling to someone, then the sound of what might have been running or scuffling. She cracked open the small screened window which gave on the highway; but saw only the naked strip of Texas highway which seemed to speed like an electric tape into the setting sun. She carefully washed her underclothes in the washbowl as she did not have many clothes and in the terrific heat of late summer in Texas the taint of menstrual blood could follow one like the odor of murder. As she washed and scrubbed, first with cold water, then with warm, the loud girring sound of the faucets seemed to fling themselves on the tiled room like ricocheting rockets. The echoing jarred on her nerves: she was getting damned claustrophobic, she thought; nervously she set the bathroom door ajar. She peered into the room: where Shaddy's bare feet had lain, there was now only a heavy blanket; her overnight case lay conspicuously on the bed. A kind of nausea gripped her, and barely waiting to wrap herself in the small, white, inadequate towels of the motel, she walked barefoot into the empty room. On the bureau lay two twenty dollar bills and a ten. There was also a note:

You were real good and worth more, especially with all
those new tricks he's taught you. But it's a rule of mine I
never pay a whore more than $50.

Shaddy had found the ultimate weapon.

A Texas highway; the grass breathing lightly though there is no wind; the sun going down so slowly it is like death—an interesting death, beautiful enough to bring tears to one's eyes: a death for other people, not oneself. The black dirt of the farms lies side by side with the clay gullies; one is assailed by colors as rich as fragrance, a bouquet so heady there is nothing to do but stand silent, reeling. Her eyes narrow at the vision. This crescendo will soon reach an all-embracing velvet darkness, poignantly beautiful, but for herself, extremely dangerous: a glint of bare thigh walking alone on the highway may well be interpreted as an obscene invitation.

Kate considered her choices: what she needed was an immediate and safe ride to Houston. She could not stand on the highway waiting for the next bus which might come anytime in the next three hours. Her isolation was doubly dangerous in an area where snakes came out in the cool of evening and where a trooper could come and pick her up for vagrancy: perhaps forcing her to bargain for her freedom in sexual terms, on the premise that no "lady" would be alone on the highway.

With a burst of courage Kate decided to take what seemed to be the least risk: she flagged down a Humble oil trucker who stopped at once at the sight of a lone girl apparently stranded on a Texas highway. The driver, she discovered, was an older man, very kind, but he beseiged her with a thousand questions about how she had got there. Kate invented a story about visiting her aunt at a nearby town (she glanced out the window at a road sign and picked the name of a town five miles south). Her car had refused to start, she said, so she had left the car behind at her aunt's place: she had to be at work first thing in the morning, she said. For her unladylike apparel—shorts and sleeveless blouse—she could think of no explanation. While they rode together she tried to emphasize her Texas speech, a trick she had learned from Caleb who had once assured her that the proper drawl could be the password in a world where at any moment one might be swiftly judged by a kangaroo court and hanged as a spy in an endless and invisible war.

When the Humble truck had come within sight of the Carins Taxidermy Shop, Kate asked to be let out. The driver obligingly stopped and even offered his assistance in getting her home, but she assured him she lived not far from the highway. She waved him on his way, forcing herself to look as innocent and empty-minded as she could: a nice girl who had been on a family visit to see her aunt, a girl whose parents would be worrying and waiting for her return.

She tried not to run toward the Shop, but found that, like a frightened animal, her speed continued to pick up. About fifty yards from Caleb's front porch, however, she came to a dead stop: on the porch were the three hunters who had been with Caleb at the hospital. They were sitting on the porch railing, their rifles between their legs. A Texas Ranger stood beside them, writing into a neat, looseleaf, leatherbound notebook. Caleb was not with them. From behind the screen door, Jessie was screaming at them like an injured cat. Kate stood on the sidewalk staring while the Ranger took each one of the rifles from the hunters in turn, unloaded it, then wrote down their numbers in his book. "You'll have to come down to the Sheriff's," he said. "There's sure to be an inquest. There's been altogether too dammed much of this kind of thing goin' on. Seems like you guys ought to be able to tell what you shootin' at. Now haul those goddammed bloody bucks from out your truck and all of you come along with me. I'll need you to identify Cairns."

A low keening sound came from Kate's throat. She sat down on

174

the sidewalk and began vomiting. She could feel the menstrual blood seeping through, soaking her underclothes as her womb emptied. She was not sobbing at all. The three hunters had no trouble remembering her. They picked her up, gave her time to wash her face, gave her some aspirin, and took her along to help identify the body.

"A good day for a funeral," she heard someone outside the mortuary say. Kate looked out the window. The pallbearers were arriving on time. Seven in the morning, before the heavy heat clung to the sweat of their hands.

She looked out at the red clay path neatly lined with cactus and quartz rocks reflecting the sunlight like human hair. Perhaps there were, after all, good days for funerals. Perhaps there were days when death was unbelievable and the sinking of the earth was like the weaving of nests: tomorrow birds would sing in it.

Caleb lay in his open coffin; the funeral had been delayed until the arrival of his parents from Florida. She knew as she wept for Caleb that she wept for herself: because everything was mutable, because there was no certainty in anything; the man one loved could be dead tomorrow; the children one adored could be wrecked by disease; the world one loved be pillaged and burned. So she wept. Caleb himself had lived his life with all the dignity he could muster; he had lived nearly twice as long as all the beautiful young men lost to the wars of his generation; but he had not lived as long as he needed to. He had not completed his Ark, which was already falling to pieces in the hands of creditors.

Kate had had no idea Caleb was so deeply in debt. His "estate" had been immediately confiscated for back taxes, loan sharks, funeral expenses—even dental bills. Hunters and private collectors had begun at once laying claim to his animals, with scraps of paper Kate could not have imagined existed: it was as if immortality itself could be burned out by the loan sharks. The depredators arrived in pickup trucks, their rifle racks behind the back seats; sometimes a bumper sticker would warn the observer of their true enemies: fluoridated water or the Communists. Mostly, they were apolitical; they just wanted to take away Caleb's magnificent animals and get rich if possible. So even before the inquest, Kate had sat on the front porch of Caleb's house watching with despair as innocent-looking ranch hands with suede chaps and jingling spurs trekked into the Ark. When they came out again, their spurs still jingling, their heads had grown invisible, hidden behind gigantic antlered mounts. It had been like some grotesque Greek tragedy in which the principal players were apparently Gods of the Hunt wearing these magnificent masks; but from the waist down they were human, all too human. Kate did not even cry when they took Jessie away to a zoo.

"Will it be a good zoo?" was all she asked. She knew there were zoos where animals were kept in medieval cages, unable to roam free of their own ordure; but there were also zoos where the animals lived freely in the open air, in their own environment—as free as though they were still in the Peruvian jungles: almost.

"Oh, she'll be all right," had replied the deputy. " 'Soon as she learns she's just an ape like the rest of 'em. Trouble with some of these keepers, they get the idea they're human—get to feedin' 'em out-of-hand, talkin' to 'em and all that. Ain't never heard of a chimp that could talk French neither—have you?" He grinned at Kate conspiratorially. Privately Kate thought Jessie would make her own way: Kate thought she probably had more sense than the deputy who was shoving her into his van as though he were a dogcatcher and Jessie were a mangy dog caught without a license.

Ironically Caleb had wanted to be cremated. Ah, Caleb, Caleb, she chided him gently as she stood by his coffin: you didn't believe in the immortality of your own ark, did you? A bouquet of flowers had been placed in his hands as if he were going a-courting; he was wearing a dark suit (Kate had never seen him in it); and his face was so callously rouged that it was all she could do not to wipe it off with her handkerchief. His hair lay in strands, as though it had never been living hair at all, but a doll's wig in nylon skeins. *They couldn't even do a decent taxidermy job on you. Just covered up the holes with that stupid suit* . . . . The first sight of him had been so shocking that, uncertain whether to laugh or cry, she had simply bowed down over the coffin, torn between tears and horrible laughter. The mortician had stared, scandalized, but piecing the matter together (Kate could see him reverse his order of thinking on Caleb's celibacy), he smoothed out the wrinkles under his eyes with the palms of his hands, as one might smooth the wrinkles from a dollar bill, and said with dignity: "Only Jesus gives Eternal Life," and left her to her strange grief.

When Caleb's parents arrived, Kate stood shyly in the background, uncertain how to behave. They were a curiously identical couple, so alike in manner and movement one would have thought them the sole survivors of an alien race. Their faces were creased in the same manner, their necks cross-hatched with the same deep lines; their eyelids protruded into a slight fleshiness as they crinkled in simultaneous sorrow. Altogether, they looked like a pair of dwarves hired for some grotesque Disneyland performance in the Hall-of-Death.

She tried to introduce herself. "I'm Kate Kalokovich," she said. "I'm so sorry . . . ."

They stared. She realized with embarrassment that they had never heard of her and were puzzled by her presence there. They glanced simultaneously at her left hand to see if their son might have married a woman without letting them know. They exchanged significant glances at the sight of Kate's bare hands. What they seemed to have taken in was the guilty fact that not only was Kate not wearing a ring, but that, unlike Mrs. Cairns whose grief might be expected to be deeper than Kate's, this strange woman was not even wearing suitable clothes: and no gloves at all (Mrs. Cairns was in black with black gloves). Everything had happened so quickly that Kate was wearing the only dark dress she had; a sleeveless brown jersey with a faint rose pattern. It would have been more appropriate for an informal party than for a funeral. As for a hat, she did not even own one, but had looped her tawny hair under a scarf. These details, of which she had not been conscious when she had left her apartment, were suddenly buffeted back to her through Mrs. Cairns' critical eyes; it was as if Caleb's mother were trying to identify her: who was this Kate Kalokovich (whatever in the world sort of name *that* was) and what was she doing at her son's funeral? She seemed to be trying to decide what manner of creature Kate was—whether widow or whore—by certain external cues which would have been familiar to her. Kate gnawed her lip in irritation.

Apparently Mrs. Cairns had decided something, because when she spoke it was in tones of deep bitterness, as if she felt her grief were being compounded by the insult of Kate's presence there. "Was it *you* tried to push the crematin' business?" demanded the woman at last.

Kate gasped. Did they think she was a salesperson for the funeral home? She felt a constriction at her heart almost as intense as grief; it was the familiar sense of frustration at the pitiful ceremonies which people used to make things meaningful.

"I wanted to do what Caleb would have wanted," she said.

"*You* wanted to . . . ." The old man's lips fumbled with the words as though they were obscene. "Well, we come here expressly to see he done the proper thing. We come to make sure that nothing will prevent the Resurrection. How'd you reckon he was goin' to face God, his ashes in an urn?"

Kate would have liked to know how God was going to face *Caleb* after having cheated him out of his life.

"Put them flowers down," Mrs. Cairns ordered her husband. "Lay 'em right down into the coffin near his head."

Mr. Cairns quickly executed her order, then stood looking down at Caleb. "He don't look old enough to be dead."

"Nobody's old enough to be dead," his wife contradicted. "But that ain't what counts."

"You're right. The Lord giveth and the Lord taketh away. We had the blessing of him all our life. Now, Lord, let thy servant depart."

177

The Reverend Cairns looked up at the ceiling. Kate followed his gaze. She noticed for the first time that the ceiling was gilt, intersticed with stars. Along the upper wall, like a frieze in an ancient temple were a few well-known biblical messages laid in mosaic. Kate noticed that several of the words were misspelled, and the inverted Spanish question seemed to add a metaphysical error: ¿HOW ARE THE MIGHTIE FALLEN?

Well might he ask, thought Kate bitterly.

The Cairnses continued in their private expressions of grief, ignoring Kate. They were expert at it; they had clearly attended many funerals and their strophe and antistrophe retained something of the ritual expected by a visible and listening audience. But Kate was not invited to share in it. Her own grief was slowly giving way to a rising anger. She knew it was foolish to take seriously the insult of these two old people, submerged in myth and piety as though it were immortality. Yet she felt herself vulnerable to their contempt; she did not think she could take much more from either of these two strangers. She wanted to scream at them: he was a fine man, an *eagle* of a man. But it would have been of no use. They saw only the stubborn child who had disobeyed them, yet who had never like the prodigal son come home in joy and repentance, and now their only hope was to protect his body from burning, ignore his Jezebel, and pray for his soul. This they did, with an unfaltering dedication. When Kate picked up her handbag and walked slowly away, they did not even look up.

13

What her friends at the art school expected was some sort of nervous breakdown; but instead, Kate showed up at the school every day—pale, silent, hostile, wondering what all the ferment about "Art" was about. She was surprised at all the excitement people attached to trivia. One day she overheard a girl greet her friend with a welcoming: "How *are* you?" "Oh!" the other girl had replied. "Terrible. I'm so depressed!" and ignoring everyone, had continued her work, painting great radiating suns of orange, copper, yellow and green: a psychedelic picture of joy. Later that afternoon the girl had gone swimming with a crowd of laughing young men and women. Kate thought deeply about it: *depressed* was a word people used to describe how they felt when they had a migraine or the flu or had lost their jobs. It signified deprivation of pleasure, from which one could quickly be rescued into delight by the arrival of a fat check in the mail, an unexpected (or expected) telephone call, a capable physician. Since she, Kate, waited for nothing, expected nothing, then perhaps what she had felt since Caleb's death was not "depressed" at all. For her there was no fat check to be hoped for, no *deus ex machina* ringing up by phone, no doctors or healers who would cure her of this ill. It struck her that what her classmate had called "depressed" was merely another form of rage, vibrant with life; it was not even despair. The girl still wanted Everything, whereas she, Kate, felt she wanted nothing. She would have liked to sleep, that was all. A long sleep, filling up one's days and nights with white feathers falling: a cocaine of sleep—white, powdery, un-wanting. Instead she felt obliged to come every day to the classroom. She sat before her drawing paper, looking at the empty space she was supposed to fill, and it seemed to her that the space peopled itself with creatures which were invisible to all but herself—dead and vanishing species of animals and of men.

For one entire day she sketched nothing but eyes—Caleb's eyes. The art teacher was wise enough to say nothing. The other women in the class, who knew all about Caleb, asked her no questions. They were very kind. They lent Kate their art supplies when she arrived at the school empty-handed (she would not be able to recall whether she had left the supplies at her apartment or had lost them on the way to class), they shared their lunches with her, asked her to go shopping with them. Kate was dimly aware that they were trying to help her; but the one problem they could not solve for her was that of survival.

179

As the weeks went by (how many, she was not sure) she became aware of one inescapable fact: she was in need of a job—not merely to pay for the "extras" of paints and brushes, but to pay her rent and buy some food. She was down to eating Mother's Oats cooked twice a day on an electric hot plate (at some time, she didn't recall when, the gas had been turned off). It now came to her as if it had been revealed to her alone for the first time in history that no matter how nice land-ladies are to you, even if they bring you tea and toast in bed after a funeral (as hers had done), sooner or later they tot up the fees, and if you can't pay them, they find a nephew, a grandson, a cousin, who *needs* to occupy the space.

So she had finally worked up her will to answer an ad for a sales-girl at one of the big stores where they seasonally hired and fired girls of all shapes, sizes and colors, as though they were filling a gumball machine. To get the "position" it was required that Kate's intelligence be thoroughly tested; she was then given a lie-detector test to determine whether she was the kind of person who would shoplift from her very own store; and finally she was sent to school for two days to learn to print "legibly" (they did not approve of any of the styles she had mas-tered at art school). Before being allowed on the salesroom floor, she was reminded that she must wear nylon stockings, black or brown shoes with medium heels, a black or brown dress, and a string of (fake) pearls. No other jewelry. Her hair was always to be neat, her nails clean—not too long . . . . Kate listened, shutting her eyes from a boredom as excru-ciating as pain. Could this be real?

It was altogether too real. On the job she was obliged to stand, "erect but graceful" for eight and a half hours (one-half hour for lunch) while women came in to slide dresses, skirts, blouses around the racks, escaping for a few minutes from their own dull jobs as stenographers, filing clerks, salesgirls. Every day there were young mothers in jeans who tried to idle away the afternoon till dinnertime while their children slumped down among the waving pennants of belts and skirts. Kate knew she was a sales*person* (what kind of a person was *that*?), and as such she was supposed to help other women decide what to wear, help them find beauty and a sense of identity from among the worthless syn-thetic baubles which could not even rot decently in a compost pile. Now and then a harried, aging woman would come in, drearily push the small-hipped fashions around on the rack while she looked for some-thing that would pull her back from quick-coming death, if only for a moment. Kate would carefully take in their spotted hands, their pouchy eyes, their tints of orange at the lip and blue at the eye and gray at the scalp, and she would want to shout across to the women in the dressing room as from across Yorick's grave: *Now get you to my* *lady's chamber, and tell her, let her paint an inch thick, to this favour she must come . . . .*

Every day it got worse, she knew she could not keep the job much longer, they were bound to let her go. She hid away in the stock room reading *Lust for Life*: it was her only consolation. When they fired her, she vowed, she'd find something different, some job where she would not have to tell lies every time she opened her mouth: *O what a beautiful waistline. O what beautiful hair. O what beautiful hands. O what beautiful shit.* She herself did not say any of these things but they flew across the dressing rooms from other saleswomen like flies on a barrel of fermenting wine. Kate scanned the want ads every night to see if she could find another job that would keep body and soul alive when they fired her from this one. The only thing she qualified for was a part-time job washing specimen bottles for a urologist: and the guy didn't even own an automatic dishwasher, but informed her in her interview that the bottles must be boiled for twenty minutes on top of the stove. She decided she was dealing with some sort of obsessed maniac and left the laboratory feeling so ground down she forgot to express any surprise or indignation at his closing offer of sixty cents an hour. (She preferred to think perhaps he had said a *dollar* sixty, but later she heard that a Mexican-American girl had taken the job.)

Sixty or a dollar sixty, there had to be something better. As she walked home from the interview, she felt so utterly oppressed and humiliated that (compared to her misery), she felt a positive wave of pleasure at the sight of a letter lying on the floor of her apartment—a letter bearing Yasha's handwriting. The landlady had evidently slipped it under Kate's door instead of leaving it on the table in the hallway downstairs—as if anything so special as a letter for this strange tenant of hers who seemed to have no contact with the outside world, had to be taken into protective custody.

Kate stood leaning against the door reading Yasha's note:

Papa says PLEASE come home. Mama is sick. He says she
needs you to help. She has a new baby.

Inexplicably, the letter brought a sense of relief, a palpable slackening of will. With one heavy stroke Jacob K. could free her from freedom and impose upon her the vegetable peace of necessity. She would not need to struggle. She could go "home," be fed, kept warm, be covered with the warm rot of security: back to the darkness of the womb. But she could not fall into the darkness of such a decision without sleep. What she needed was sleep . . . and only sleep.

Without removing her clothes she lay down on the bed. She did not wake till several hours later, her stomach griping with hunger. She

181

sat up, put some water to boil in a pan and shook the Mother's Oats box. A few soft grains slid around its empty sides, making a *whishing* sound gentle as sleep. No more Mother's Oats. Mother, mother, why hast thou forsaken me? With a groan of impotence, rage, and hunger Kate fell back into bed to sleep again.

But she was too hungry to sleep long, and awoke this time as with a ringing of matins in her brain: PAPA says PLEASE. PAPA says PLEASE. Yet: if Jacob K. had indeed felt obliged to express such (for him) desperate politeness, then Channa must be very ill . . . . Alarmed and decisive, Kate sat up in bed: what a secret relief to have one's decision forced upon one by "duty." Tossing the empty Oats box into a garbage bag, Kate began to pack her suitcases. She was already figuring out how to sneak past the landlady's covetous eye, her smaller canvases tied to her luggage. She would have to jump the rent: she couldn't possibly pay the rent and get back to Detroit too.

At the last moment, in an act of contrition and gratitude for the tea and toast, Kate left the landlady two large canvases. "Someday they'll be worth a million," she murmured to the empty, echoing room which, now that her paintings were stripped from the walls, looked as if it had just been burglarized.

Discreetly, she locked the door.

With some trepidation she laid out her last dollars for the ticket to Detroit. The cost of shipping her paintings would have kept her in food and lodging for a month, it was sheer robbery: she felt some special dispensation should be allowed Starving-Artists-in-America. It was ridiculous to have the wood on her frames weighed in as if they were horns of cheese, sold by the pound. But once on the plane she relaxed long enough to enjoy the ride. It was her first flight and it was surprisingly uneventful; the physical arrangements offered the same lack of privacy as the Greyhound bus station in Houston. People in pastel plastic seats sat staring at the heads and arms of people in similar plastic seats. She thought it was hopelessly dull and wished she had taken the bus to St. Louis, then the train. At least on a bus one had the exciting option of ignoring one's neighbor who sat rubbing knees with you: one could look out the window. Here, there was nothing to see but oily clouds, and as they came down to Detroit, the vapors of white ice on the field seemed to toss her bones into a basket. They landed at nightfall, the airfield was black as a mineshaft, except for the streaks of ice; the freezing winds hit her fingers like a toothache. Were there any artists out on the rooftops tonight; she asked herself lugubriously. The abrupt transition from Houston's semitropical humidity to these bitter winds coming down from Canada exhausted her courage: she spent most of her last two dollars for a limousine ride to the downtown hotel.

Since Jacob K. did not drive, she still had to pay her bus fare from the inner city to the north side, where the Kalokoviches had lately moved, so that by the time she arrived at her parents' new home her purse was as empty as an itinerant monk's. She was rather surprised that in spite of their "poverty," Jacob K. and Channa had bought this decent-looking home on the North Side. It was not quite out of reach of the *schwartzes*, as Jacob K. ruefully admitted almost the moment she set foot in the door, but they had hoped it would be close enough for Yasha to go to a good Hebrew school and still be home slightly before dark. Ah, so that was it, thought Kate with a faint twinge of jealousy. For their *son* they were even willing to try to buy the Right Neighborhood.

"Mama's in bed with the baby," interrupted Yasha, sensing that Kate was annoyed. "You should see her, Katie, she sucks her whole fist and has reddish hair like yours." Yasha had always been an admirer of Kate's hair, his own was a predictable mass of black curls which (though Kate would not have told him) gave his face the delicate bone structure of a girl.

Evidently there had been an agreement not to ask her any questions; it was understood that she was here to be of assistance—a family hand was cheaper than a hired hand any day, thought Kate grimly—and so part of the implicit bargain was that Jacob K. remain silent on the subject of her marriage to Shaddy. That it was considered a scandal was clear from the way Jacob K. hushed visitors at the door; and when one or two old friends phoned to find out whether Kate had in fact returned to Detroit to stay or visit or study, or whatever rebels like Kate finally turned to in their rational moments, Papa merely cradled the phone along his arm as if to hush any sounds coming from the house and explained that Kate was home to help Channa with the new baby.

Yasha pulled her into their mother's bedroom. The baby, still asleep, lay in a wicker crib beside the bed. Her mother oddly dressed (as it struck Kate) in a button-down sweater and grey pajama bottoms, sat up to embrace her. Channa cried a few moments, whether with joy or disappointment in her eldest, Kate could not be certain.

Kate was so shocked at Channa's appearance she could barely speak. Her mother had seemed shrunken when she had last seen her at the Sanatorium over a year ago, but she now appeared grotesquely inflated at the breast and stomach, as though filled with dropsy. At the same time her face was stripped down to the bone; her eye-sockets were ringed with purple as though the blood were drying out as she lay there. Ribbony scars lay above her lips, and for the first time Kate noticed that her mother's teeth were not her own . . . . Her hands, especially, had thinned and aged, as though someone had taken a piece of tinfoil, carelessly crushed it to be rid of it, then on second thought unfolded it into these wrinkled parodies of hands. The breasts were swollen so that when Channa sat up they shifted of their own weight like sacks of meal; the muscles of the belly which had sealed in the baby all those months now hung like dead lung-meat, soft and airless.

Kate began to talk nervously about her plane ride, her experiences at the airport, about the trouble and expense of weighing in her paintings (here Channa gave her a long troubled look as if she had hoped Kate had outgrown this obsession), and then switched suddenly to her surprise at finding the Kalokoviches in this fine house.

"You think it's fine?" Mama observed with a shrug. "You like it? It's the same old *tsoris*. You buy a new house in a nice neighborhood and they change the neighborhood right under your eyes. Yasha had here a *cheder*, he could walk to it and be home before supper, now they're moving it farther north. Pretty soon there won't be a Jewish family in the block."

Kate made no comment on the apparently irreversible flight to the suburbs; she only felt that ironically Jacob K. would always be at the tail end of a new lily-white neighborhood in which the blacks would be coming up hard behind him. She found herself distracted by a sudden idea for a cartoon which struck her: Jacob K. triumphantly shaking his fist into the face of the advancing ghetto which lay just on the other side of the street from him. Between them—a single fire hydrant; the fire alarm ringing, the firemen approaching. Even as she thoughtfully bent over the crib, she had already begun editing out the firemen as unnecessary: she awkwardly kissed her baby sister on the brow. She tried to think of all sorts of questions one might ask about a new baby. Mama seemed happy with it, it seemed cruel to be thinking it was only another baby. In Channa's altogether overcrowded life, what good would they be for each other? At Kate's kiss the baby began at once stretching her arms and legs, unfolding herself with soundless grace like an underwater plant.

"It's all right. She should be up," said Channa wearily. "It's time she should eat again. Usually she doesn't sleep so good. For your homecoming, maybe, she's acting so good. I slept a whole night last night for the first time. Five hours . . . Yasha, go out. I'm feeding the baby. Anna sit down. Tell me how's this place you've been living? It's nice down there? Yasha said they have cowboys."

Kate sat down beside her mother. She felt a certain reluctance to be watching her mother nurse the infant, but Channa herself seemed to feel it not only fitting but necessary (she's instructing me in the maternal arts, thought Kate, and felt a sinking guilt about Caleb and his child).

While Channa was preparing to nurse, Jacob K. came to the door; he had closed the store for a couple of hours until Kate's arrival; but the flood of supper-time customers must now be dealt with. To Kate's astonishment (she had never seen him perform any service for her mother), he brought in a glass of tea with two lumps of sugar and placed them beside Channa's bed. "Tea makes milk," he said approvingly. "If there's something else, Anna will get it for you."

Kate tried not to feel childishly annoyed. While she did not feel either hungry or tired she would have appreciated a word of kindness from Jacob K. But obviously he preferred to act as if she had not been away. Having crossed his threshold again, she was expected to do whatever was necessary: that was her role in life as it had been Channa's. Kate tried not to sound ironic as she said: "Of course I will. Have you had your dinner, Mama? Shall I fix us something while you feed the baby?"

"No. No. Sit, we'll have a talk in a minute. Yasha, you go with your father to the store, help him. Don't forget to lock the doors. Two women alone . . . . It's not now like it used to be in this neighborhood, you could leave your doors open."

"*Three* women," corrected Yasha with a roguish laugh and dashed out the door. During her absence Yasha had grown from a child into a sensitive young man. He was still at that pleasant age when knowledge of his perceptions did not embarrass him, so they did not embarrass others. Kate realized with a shock that Yasha had noticed Jacob's rudeness to her and understood the reasons for it.

"Can I stop by the Vittores on my way over?" he asked politely. It struck Kate that her brother could have stopped off at his friends' house without permission, Channa would not have known the difference: some uncompromising honesty kept him from exploiting Channa's illness for his own ends. She felt a wave of comradeship for her brother. Perhaps her coming home would be of some use after all: Jacob K. was as immovable as stone; but Channa needed her desperately and she had somehow overlooked the fact that her brother would some day present (along with herself) a solid front against the older generation. For a moment her spirits revived as she sensed that she was not alone in her struggle.

When Yasha had gone, Channa slipped out of the bedcovers into a rocking chair. The baby who had seemed so serene in the sheer exercise of her limbs a few minutes ago must have sensed the presence of food. At once her small face became contorted, turned red; a few experimental coughs of frustration followed. But within seconds the

185

irrational cries had become hoarse and angry. As Channa hurriedly collected her nursing equipment—the baby's complicated paraphernalia of survival—she looked exasperated. Kate watched, amazed at how complex it all was: the sterilization of the nipples, the wiping off of soured milk left by the brassiere, the settling of the infant into a perfect position so that the baby's head rested with maximum efficiency just within sucking reach of the nipple. Channa was a veritable general of infant logistics, thought Kate with surprise.

Channa then unbuttoned the grey-white sweater. The nipples were already drizzling milk into the unhooked maternity brassiere. Patiently Channa took swabs of cotton and laid it into her brassiere to soak up the milk. When she had carefully cleaned the nipple she beckoned Kate to hand her the baby. Rather clumsily now, because the baby was turning red with protest or hunger (or perhaps merely her first experience of helplessness, thought Kate), Kate bent over the wicker basket. At the pressure of awkward hands under her the baby's screams grew louder. Kate paused timidly. What had she done?

"Just pick her up. Pick her up. She won't break," commanded her mother.

Kate was not sure. The small being struggled in her two hands as though she understood well enough her own precarious grip on life.

"Put one hand under her head," instructed Channa sharply, who had been watching Kate's awkwardness with something like self-reproach (it must have seemed to her she had done something wrong that her own daughter knew nothing of these things: what business had a Jewish bride being so ignorant of babies?). "Put her head this way, across my left arm," added Channa.

The baby fell with a famished clutch of breath upon the nipple which Channa placed into her mouth like an expert pool player. The baby herself was too small to find the nipple: without Channa it perhaps would not have survived at all. "Oh," said Channa dismally, "I forgot to weigh her. *Nu* let it go. We'll see now if she stays awake. Where's the clock?" Since she had forgotten to weigh the baby Channa now seemed to be trying to estimate the baby's intake of milk by her nursing time. Her mother explained that the baby had just missed being an incubator baby, she was so small, and that made everything more difficult . . . .

Kate had been one of those who believed that a mystic peace settled over the faces of mothers as they nursed; but Channa now sat with a worried frown staring at the clock. "I can't tell: is she just sucking or is she taking milk? I'll have to weigh her after all." She now instructed Kate to bring the baby-scales down from the rickety chiffonier which Kate realized with humble shock had been in their family as long as she could remember. *Poverty, thy name is familiarity*. "Lay this blanket in it, she shouldn't bump her head," instructed Channa. "How much does the blanket weigh? Yes, I remember it now, it's the same blanket I used last night. So what does she? . . . Take away the ounces for the blanket—that's how much she weighs . . . ."

It seemed minutes before the arrow of the scale ceased its slight tremor. The baby, having been deprived of the comforting breast, was screaming with helpless rage. The whole process was an endless round of frustration, thought Kate, and wondered if she could possibly have endured it for Caleb's child.

"Write it down," her mother instructed, "we shouldn't forget. That mixes me up." Dutifully, as though in a trance, Kate wrote it down. "O.K. Give me her back now," said Channa, and again Kate lay the bawling child in her mother's lap. This time: peace. The baby suckled for about six or seven minutes; then, exhausted from her crying, fell asleep.

"No, no. No sleeping," said Channa in a weary, wheedling voice.

Kate would have thought sleep a necessity for infants, but Channa complained that if she allowed the baby to sleep she would waken in a half hour or so and be hungrier than ever. The infant was too small to suckle without tiring quickly and falling asleep; yet she must be *forced* to suckle in order to grow big enough to suckle *without* fatigue. If the baby did not take enough milk, Channa's breasts would swell painfully and she would have to express the milk by hand, a slow irritating process, or with a mechanical expressor, which was painful. And besides all that, her mother went on with a sigh, as if relieved, at least, to have a woman confidante in the house, there was the ever-present danger of mastitis.

"It's fever. A fever. It's like the breasts get infected. I don't know exactly. I had it with Yasha, they gave me pills to dry up the milk. So what good did it do me, God blessed me with so much milk? They wrapped me tight with towels the milk shouldn't come out. For two nights I couldn't sleep. *Then* I had all the trouble to get him to drink from a bottle. *Oi*, he didn't like a bottle. So this one, I have to get her started right. I *got* to keep her awake to make her nurse."

What followed was the most grotesque performance Kate had ever seen her mother partake in. A hollow-cheeked woman, whose own exhausted body was dangerously losing weight except at the breasts and belly, sat fiercely fighting to inject a few ounces of milk manufactured by herself into a sleeping indifferent homunculus who seemed as yet neither brain nor body but only a sucking mouth whose mouth refused to suck. Channa tapped the baby's nose, tweaked its cheeks, tickled its feet, blew its hair, called to it in a voice hoarse with fatigue; but the baby slept—indifferent to this battle for survival: mother vs. child. The longer the struggle endured the less likely Channa would be to regain her strength.

"I'm supposed to take three thousand calories a day," complained Channa with a look of disgust. "But never in my life could I eat so much—and especially now, when I'm so tired. And anyway, Jacob, he never knew to lift a finger in the kitchen . . . ."

"I'll cook dinner!" cried Kate in desperation, feeling Channa's total psychic energy drained by this passionate struggle to keep alive and feed this one small mouth so that it would grow to be a real Human Being. Kate looked at the baby with hostile curiosity: was it worth it? Didn't Channa see it was a kind of suicide? Her mother couldn't possibly have the strength to keep up this struggle for months.

"How long will you . . . nurse her?"

"Oh a year, maybe. Some do longer, but I haven't the patience."

Kate felt she herself could not have endured for a week this struggle in which the weak won all and the strong died out. Small wonder the early settlers wore out three or four wives.

"You rest a while," she said. "I'll go fix something for you. What do you like?"

Her mother looked at her sadly. "A nice homecoming for you, I wanted to take you some place, we could do something nice together. There's a play, even, from New York, with Yiddish actors. Mrs. Halpern told me about it, she cried like a baby."

"Oh God, Mama, who needs to cry like . . . a baby!" She thought she herself would begin to cry in a moment. She swept out into the other rooms, calling to Channa through the open door. "If you need me for anything, call me. I'm going to fix dinner!"

Kate whirled into the kitchen, wracked with guilt. This then, was the way it was. Her mother had been through it for her, then for Yasha, and now for the new baby. None of these trials could have been predictable ordeals; each one in turn must have been fought over, resigned to, and finally succumbed to: in Mama's case sickness and retreat to the Sanatorium. For other women, perhaps nervous breakdowns, alcoholism, drugs. The burden was such that no one talked about it: there had been a time when to multiply on the earth gave one the power God had commanded to our first parents; therefore, to be childless was to disobey God.

First Kate fixed dinner from what she could find. Jacob K.'s idea of the necessities of life was limited to jars of gefilte fish and plenty of milk. But she discovered a pickled tongue shoved away in the ice cube tray, which she quickly defrosted and set to boiling. While the meat percolated, steaming up the small kitchen, Kate attacked the dirt. Although the Kalokoviches had been in the new house only since Channa's last release from the Sanatorium, the dirt was already ingrown. Jacob K. had obviously never hired anyone to assist Mama in getting settled. Even the pots and pans were piled up on each other as if taken from boxes and tossed into the pantry pell-mell. The stove looked as if it had never been cleaned (well, she would tackle that tomorrow). Zealously, and at the same time with rage that she should be fulfilling precisely Jacob K.'s expectations (but she was doing it for Mama who couldn't do it for herself, she repeated over and over), she swept, scrubbed, put to order the catastrophic confusion. By the time Jacob K. and Yasha returned from the store, dinner was ready. Channa had had a sparing taste of spinach and boiled tongue, and there was a clean tablecloth on the dining room table which Kate had rooted out of one of her mother's never-touched cedar chests: she felt she had a perfect right to ransack the house—the whole city if necessary—for some decency and order.

Jacob K. expressed his pleasure at the orderliness of the table by taking a sip of wine before dinner (when he was displeased he would affect to be too exhausted to enjoy these pleasures, and even deny himself the cold fish he loved). Kate had evidently taken a great burden from his mind and his way of showing his appreciation was to ask her for things; his way of showing displeasure was to ignore her: one ceased utterly to exist before Jacob K.'s icy disintegration of Self. But to be asked to wait on him he considered a sign of favor. He now permitted himself a rare flush of pleasure as he finished off his glass then asked Kate for his usual cold fish and horse radish. Kate wondered if the sky would have fallen down if she had asked him to get it himself. But momentarily caught in the spell of childhood obedience, she rose from her own dinner, as if all her pleasures derived from the fulfillment of his and hunted around in the refrigerator for some beet-flavored horseradish (she remembered he did not like it plain) and served it to him as submissively (she thought) as if she had never left Egypt.

Promptly after supper everyone went to bed exhausted. There was no conversation, no social exchange, no radio or television or telephone call or even any washing up. They fell into bed like peasants sleeping in their own sweat in the fields. Twice during the night the baby howled; each time she heard Channa move creakingly from her bed to quiet the child: whether the baby ever got enough to eat or whether Channa ever got back to sleep that night, she never figured out: she slept through several bad dreams, shaped like movie frames. The people in them stood in arrested motion, hungry and supplicatory; masses of dark people standing under a balcony, each one with a rice cup, demanding food. Two dead white cows lay on their swollen bellies, starved to death.

189

The days passed, the baby did not get perceptibly bigger, and it turned out as Channa had feared. By the end of the month, the milk around the nipples was repeatedly caking up, the liquid in Channa's breasts swelled to tremendous udders. The painful process of expression by hand began, but Channa was too tired to sit for an hour at a time, slowly dripping milk into a cup . . . . One afternoon, Channa, her eyes bright as a beetle's asked Kate to send for the doctor, the pain in her breasts was excruciating. Then she lay silent and defeated, not even lifting the baby. It was as if Channa had desperately fought upstream, against her own survival, yielding to some instinct which was also to be her last act: having reached the point where every effort was useless, she was content to do nothing. She now lay glassy-eyed, a fine white film drying around her lips which she wiped away with a swaddling cloth. She coughed nervously, expectantly, as if she anticipated the final siege of coughing which would, at last, free her forever from this terrific combat: she had no desire to survive. And why should she? Kate asked herself bitterly.

Kate phoned the doctor who complained to her that he couldn't leave his patients every time somebody's temperature shot up. He instructed Kate to bind Channa's breasts tightly and to withhold all liquids until he could come later in the day. In the meantime he would phone in a prescription to the nearest drug store. Kate didn't know where their nearest drug store was. The doctor gave an audible sigh of impatience, had his secretary check it out for Kate. "Thanks a lot," said Kate ironically and crashed the phone down. "They'd take better care of a milk-giving goat," she thought furiously and went to repeat the instructions to Channa.

Channa nodded impassively. She knew it all by heart, she had been through it with Yasha (And with me *too*? Kate wanted to ask but did not dare: perhaps she was fearful of tapping that depth of resentment which she imagined *must* lie buried somewhere in Channa's psyche).

After the doctor had gone, Channa—spent with exhaustion and a sense of her repeated "failures"—lay weeping. Tears rolled unchecked down the cheeks which were now colorless as stone, wetting Channa's straggling grey hair. "Mama, let me comb your hair for you," begged Kate, close to tears herself at the terrific physical effort which had resulted in nothing but this nameless despair. But Mama could not bring herself to care.

Now that she did not have to get up to feed the baby any longer, Channa turned from the child in a wave of reaction. It was as if in turning the child over to others to care for, she felt they had also taken it away from her; as if now that she could not perform the function which she believed was expected of her, she did not feel it necessary to concern herself at all. Others could sterilize bottles, wash diapers, boil canned milk, find the right bathing temperature: only she had been able to nurse the baby, and she had done all she could to "succeed" at that and had "failed." It was absurd, but it was as if Channa sensed in some way that she had already laid down her life for the baby, there was no more she could do. The rest was up to the world.

After lying in despair for about three weeks, Channa suddenly gave up eating altogether. They coaxed, they wheedled, Kate cooked delicacies which would have tempted a Czar, as she told her mother jocularly, trying to communicate, but Channa shook her head. She sipped her tea, she ate her toast, but the rest disgusted her. She would, above all, never touch milk. Finally Kate and Jacob K. persuaded her to put on her clothes, to go out for a breath of fresh air, the weather was brisk but there was a fine splurge of sunshine on the front porch. Obediently, as if she had grown accustomed to taking orders, Channa slowly dressed in layers of outdated clothing and went for a walk.

She returned from her walk with two high spots of color in her face, the first Kate had seen in weeks, but also with a slight cold. That evening the cold had turned out to be flu: the raw air had been too much for her after weeks of living like a mole.

The flu lingered for weeks, sometimes with fever, sometimes without; nothing much could be done about it, especially if Channa would not eat. Kate fixed her puddings and delicately colored dishes of rennet in an effort to get Channa to take milk again in any disguised form; but it was as if she had learned to sniff out the treacherous stuff which Jacob K. placed so much faith in and which, in fact seemed to protect him; she wanted no more of it. What she liked was a bit of coffee cake or a pickled tomato: but there wasn't much nourishment in these.

After about a month of this, the doctor suddenly ordered Channa back into the sanatorium. And at once everybody in the Kalokovich household was rounded up and taken to an emergency ward for an X-ray, as if cholera had broken out in the neighborhood. Even the baby, screaming at being roused from a nap (the call came during the afternoon to appear at the emergency room for an X-ray *at once*), was taken in her blankets, without bothering to change her (Kate experienced her first maternal responsibility at the realization that the baby's diapers were sopping wet: and whose fault was that but hers now that Channa was ill?). Jacob K. received a call at the store and was told to shut down the store for forty-eight hours until his lungs were O.K.'d by the Department of Health. Altogether it was a frightening experience. Jacob K. kept repeating as he changed into his best dark suit as if he were going to the synagogue: "She wouldn't take nothing to eat. She's stubborn. She didn't want to take nothing." As if to ward off the

191

symptoms from his own delicate lungs he drank two glasses of milk standing in the kitchen, shaking his head like a doomed man. "She don't take care of herself. Anybody wants to live, he has to take care."

Frightened and chastened Kate felt forced to agree. She had seen Channa's look of triumph as they took the baby away from her and she was left at last to lie alone in the bed, despairing and indifferent.

At the emergency room it was determined within a matter of hours that everyone was in good health in spite of their exposure. For some reason they made no attempt to X-ray the baby, though her examination in some ways was more complicated than anyone's. Kate sat beside the doctor while he made the child scream again and again as he pressed his cold instruments to her chest and back and listened with great care. "Sounds O.K. to me," he said angrily. "But to leave a baby around a woman who's been a *known* tubercular is downright criminal if you ask me." He sounded as if Channa were some kind of drug addict. Kate flushed with shame, without knowing why: perhaps it was a sense of the flagrant waste involved, of having watched Channa throw away her life like a gambler. They all took a taxi home in silence. Only Yasha leaned his head a little against Kate's shoulder, as if sensing that his fate lay now in her hands, not Channa's.

With Channa gone the management of the house fell entirely to Kate. There were days when she felt bitterly angry with her mother for having escaped all this responsibility into the world of illness and death. She's no better than an alcoholic with her damned "illness," Kate found herself thinking with rage as the days passed in sterilizing bottles, doing diapers, in walking the baby through the icy slush so she could get some sunshine and air (what about *my* getting some sunshine and air, thought Kate irrationally, as though she were somehow being deprived of these benefits because they were being inflicted on her). It had been weeks since she had done anything except care for the Kalokovich household. Self-pity rose in her gorge: she had scarcely touched her paints and easel since returning home. She was being exploited by Jacob K. who would never get hired help to do for him what he could extort from his children. The months were passing and she was learning only to fulfill a role which she had, at least for the time being, so decisively rejected when she refused to bear Caleb's child. So that she could learn to paint! The irony tasted like blood in her mouth: as she shoved the carriage angrily down a curbstone her sister's head was given such a jolt that she began crying loudly. There was nothing to do but pick her up and try to comfort her. She found herself in the impossible position of trying to push a carriage with one hand and carry Zhenia in the other. She could not keep the path of the carriage stabilized and it continually veered off to the left (there was, in addition, something wrong with the front wheels of the carriage, something for which she could compensate when both arms were free). It was all so vexing and frustrating she began crying herself. It was ridiculous. With the tears streaming down her face she slowly pushed the carriage back to the Kalokovich front porch and sat on the step, blowing her nose, and rocking the baby back to sleep.

When she had stopped crying she decided that what she needed was to get back to her painting. Since Zhenia was asleep, she decided she would run back into the house and unpack some of her art materials which had lain under the bed all these weeks. Then a peculiar sensation came over her; it was a combination of fear, of outrage and terrible clarity; she understood quite suddenly the wretched anomaly of women: she did not feel free to leave the baby alone, even long enough to fetch a few pencils and her drawing pad. Her imagination, so luxuriant in sketching, was caught up in the human possibilities which bloodied the daily papers: baby stolen from front porch; baby's carriage goes plunging; baby strangles to death in crib blanket; baby wakes hungry and terrified; baby sits up alone, falls from carriage; baby chokes on pacifier while sister paints . . . . Appalled at the monstrous possibilities dredged up by her imagination, she sat shaking with impotence. Absurd: she dared not leave the baby alone long enough to fetch a drawing pencil. With a kind of fierce determination she checked the brakes on the carriage, set four large stones in its tracks, removed the pacifier from the sleeping mouth (now she'll wake! thought Kate in exasperation, but the baby's mouth only twitched, sucked air for a moment, and continued sleeping); set the hood of the carriage so that if a cloudburst should come (though the skies were absolutely clear) the baby would not get wet. *And what else, what else?* thought Kate torn between laughing and crying: then she literally dashed into the house, tore the brown wrapping paper from off her art materials and returned, her heart pounding with apprehension, to the front porch where Zhenia lay sleeping. With a sigh, Kate sat down on the doorstep. She had been so tense at the thought that something might happen to Zhenia while she was hunting her materials that her hand was still clenched; it took minutes to still the faint tremor in her fingers until—with a surge of delight—she could begin drawing. Pictures flew in her mind as though she were on a roaring train: she would never have time to draw them all. She sketched for more than an hour, her hand moving ceaselessly across the pad. Scenes from those days in San Antonio, memories of Caleb, the funeral, the grotesque and pitiable Mr. and Mrs. Cairns. Tears spilled on her pad, her emotion filled the plain black and white sketches like color. She thought fiercely, I've never drawn better. She could have gone on making sketches for hours, gone on long after twilight, correcting, adding, straightening a line, a limb. As her pencil flew over her sketchbook a bitter cartoon grew under her eyes: a cartoon of hunters killing off whitetails to "keep 'em from starving." Caleb and the three hunters (of the Apocalypse) stood in the foreground. And the deer . . . . At this moment an angry wail came from the carriage and the deer fled from her vision as though he had vanished into a thicket. She tried to ignore it, perhaps the child would go back to sleep. Kate understood that it was late, the sun was already waning, it was time to take the child in to feed her, bathe her, hush her so that Jacob K. could eat his supper in peace. Tears of frustration filled her eyes. She felt some sacred right was being denied her; she had not even begun her own life, was she already to be called upon to sacrifice it for others? She was sitting as if hypnotized by the wailing sounds of the baby when she became aware that she was also being watched. Their neighbor, Gio Vittore, had paused near their front porch when he heard the baby crying. Yasha often played with his younger sister, Angelina, and Kate knew the young man had just graduated from high school.

"Anything the matter with the baby?" he asked, as if he were familiar with crises in the Kalokovich family.

"*Nothing*," Kate retorted with heat. "Just hungry."

"Maybe you ought to pick her up. Maybe she needs patting on the back or something. My mother—"

"Oh, now *you're* going to tell me what I should be doing! I certainly get plenty of instruction, but no help at all." What she wanted was five minutes more of privacy so that she could finish, at least, the main outlines of her sketch. If the boy went away, maybe Zhenia would settle herself into a short doze. She could then put in a few details of the hunters' faces as she now recalled them: the cruel streak of *voyeurism* as they had stared at the Mexican girls in their beds, the sensual loll of their rifles across their arms, their regulation caps like army uniforms. Tears of frustration filled her eyes.

The boy stood attentively, trying to understand her. "I'm sorry your mother's sick again," he said with a kind of controlled compassion. "We've been wondering how you had managed so long. My mother and Angie wondered, that is. I'll send my sister Angelina over to help you. She's good at that sort of thing." He faltered, perhaps fearing he had insulted her. Obviously in his home "that kind of thing" was the ultimate preoccupation of women. "What I mean is, Angie knows all about kids. She practically raised my brother Pietro. And he's blind . . . . Born blind."

"Oh," said Kate, ashamed of her tears. The thought of what Mrs.

194

Vittore's life must have been during those years before Pietro's hold on life was assured gripped her heart with fear. It could happen to any woman—worse things than had overtaken Channa.

She tried to smile. The boy was being thoughtful, generous, friendly. His unexpected kindness had the impact of shock; it had been so long since anyone had offered to do anything for her without trying to exploit her that she began to cry. Tears of loneliness, despair, self-pity drenched her. It had been a terrible year, a decade of a year, and this sensitive alien boy who stood beside her, baffled by the intensity of her tears, seemed to her a child though he was probably her own age.

At the sight of her face which must have been wretched in its cumulative despair, the Vittore boy stood stiff as a soldier; then with a slow decisive movement he came over and sat down beside her on the steps. Without affectation or playfulness he put his arm around her shoulder. "There now. Go ahead and cry," he said. And she did—great wrenching upheavals such as one cries at funerals, at divorces, at weddings. She remembered now that she had laughed like a madwoman at the ceremony in Toledo; that she had stood still with shock beside the dead body of Caleb and that Shaddy's denunciation had turned her cold with hatred. Nothing had elicited from her this electric shock of tears.

She began looking for a handkerchief. "I ne—ver have a handkerchief," she wailed, and broke into short hiccuping sobs of despair. The baby had begun crying too, as if tears were a contagion about to sweep the city. At first it was only a plaintive pathetic cry (like mourning doves, thought Kate, and the tears welled up from a source so deep she was sure they would never stop); then the cries became puzzled, whining, questioning (the baby was accustomed to immediate attention); then anger; and finally (Kate shuddered at the sound), a long outraged cry of impotence.

"I'll take her," said Gio. He handed her a handkerchief. She accepted it with surprise: it was a rough blue and white calico handkerchief such as she had seen the black laborers and factory workers in her father's store carry with them. Like theirs, Gio's handkerchief was streaked with oil.

"I work at Ford's," he said. "Spot-welding."

Kate stared. She wanted to cry, "But you're only a child!" But it occurred to her suddenly that people like herself and Gio Vittore had probably never been children at all. With a sudden clear grasp of what this young man's life must be like—a younger sister, a blind brother, Italian parents overwhelmed by old traditions and new poverty—she looked at him with the intense comradeship of shared suffering.

"You have—a nice face," she said solemnly. "I'd like to paint your face."

195

He smiled sadly. "You have a nice face too. I'd like to take your face to the movies."

It struck her with astonishment that he was asking her for a date. She found herself smiling at the realization that although she had had affairs with three men she had never been on a date. Gio seemed to sense something of the irony of this, or perhaps he felt that a date with *him* for a woman-of-her-experience might not be much of an attraction, because he added: "I mean it's really a very good film. Bogart." He looked at her inquiringly.

She nodded. "Should be. Should be a good film."

"You're an artist," he said abruptly as he helped her carry Zhenia to the bedroom. He laid the baby down in her crib and stood rocking it.

Kate noted the quiet way he had stated that she was an artist; there had been no implication that this made her different from the women he knew. He stated it as though it were her job, like being a teacher or a spot-welder.

"Yasha told me. He talks about you a lot. He really admires you."

Kate wondered what else Yasha might have told this strangely self-possessed young man blessed with the calm of ignorance or wisdom.

She opened a can of strained chicken and a jar of peaches and put some of each on Zhenia's heavy plastic plate. From the refrigerator she poured out six ounces of formula into a baby bottle and set it beside the high chair.

"Shall I get the baby for you? She needs changing," announced Gio. "She's sopping wet."

Kate stood watching, humbled by Gio's expertise as, without the least embarrassment, he stripped the baby of her diaper, powdered and repinned her into a fresh diaper and had her sitting in her high chair a few minutes later—all without a single protest from the baby who now sat staring at him with wide, contemplative eyes.

While the baby swallowed teaspoonfuls of strained chicken, Gio talked—easily, comfortably. He had known the Kalokoviches for about a year, since they moved into this neighborhood. He thought Yasha some kind of genius, maybe in mathematics or something; he said there were times when he really didn't understand the boy. Kate smiled and accepted the praise as if it were meant to be a form of indirect flattery. Gio added that he knew Jacob K. very well—that he had worked for him one *very long* weekend as a delivery boy. "That was one Sunday too many," he said shyly, glancing at her out of the corner of his eye.

They smiled conspiratorially. She knew he was too polite to speak out against Jacob K. but they were in obvious agreement about her father. She felt she had found another comrade to help her survive the buffetings of Jacob K.

While Gio talked of his high school days Kate fed the baby. Her sister was delighted with Gio's presence; she chortled, babbled, sucked in her cheeks and when (without interrupting his conversation), Gio waggled a playful finger at her she took it as a game. The two at once set up a game of Catch-the-finger which Zhenia won every time. Kate sat marveling at his calm, which permitted him to go on talking while wiping peaches from his fingers with his blue handkerchief. Then there was a sudden lull as Zhenia took the bottle herself; she snuggled down against the side of the high chair and looked peacefully up at Gio, her eyes opening and closing with contentment while she drank her milk.

Kate picked up her pad and began sketching them together: the baby and Gio. Gio seemed pleased that she had found them to be a worthwhile subject and sat quietly watching her. Kate hurried into the bedroom to fetch her oil paints, her easel and brushes which were hidden under the bed. Within minutes she had put together one of the best paintings (she thought) that she had ever done: Zhenia's white arm rose from the center of the canvas as though it were carved into space. Gio's denim work clothes (like Caleb's, she thought, the recollection pouring into her colors like hot yellow light), Gio's already aging face, and his blue calico handkerchief settled over the canvas in a soft grey dust. At the point where their fingers met—Gio's and the baby's—the canvas glowed with a soft nimbus, a mist of luring light like the scent of honeysuckle. Then quite abruptly Kate realized what was happening. She had fallen face-first into a puddle of Sentimentality. She was painting the so-called simple joys of Home, Family, and Property. She had been tempted into the ultimate trap, The Tenderness Trap.

At once Kate changed her subject in mid-canvas. First she inflicted a thick wide wedding band on Gio's left hand. She softened and lined the face, making it older and dulled by the long days in the factory and nights of vigil; the fingers were thickened—gentle and tender with children but, like an old man's, awkward in the turning of pages. In the background Kate added another figure: the mother. She painted the mother as though she were standing at the entrance to the kitchen, her legs truncated by shadow; across her waist Kate placed an apron as thick as skin. The toys of cookery hung on the walls in the background—a skewer, a sieve, a pan. She placed the mother's left hand gently in mid-air—a benediction or a curse. On her left hand too lay the holy yellow band testifying that this was a lawful union, with all its rites and rituals, its rewards and punishments. It was on the eyes of the mother that Kate devoted her utmost care (as Caleb had taught her!). She painted them a glowing yellow, the color of sun-streaked sand—proud, fierce, loving, tender, and possessive: translucent as a

197

tiger's. And the child, the beautiful child who had struck awe into Kate herself when her arm had lifted from the canvas like Excalibur, a mystery of supernatural grace—Kate now prepared to sacrifice the child. She must free herself from the love trap even if she had to gnaw off her own foot to do it. She transformed the baby's golden locks into hard wiry strands; she left one eye open like a wary cat's, the other eye winked shut with obscene coquetry. Instead of a game in which the two fingers playfully tapped and clung, she placed the baby's hand at the suspender near Gio's heart: one could see that the power of that small but determined hand would soon rip apart the threadbare cloth. Gio-as-Parent sat submissively. Kate painted first white, then black circles around his eyes, like a clown; the slats of the baby's high chair were rendered as bars separating the three framed figures from the world. The painting which had been one of any family in the world had become transmogrified into a Daumier-portrait of the Damned. She called it *The Trap*.

When she had finished she dropped her brushes into a mason jar (Jacob K. would not like that—mason jars cost money. But so be it, she reflected, everything costs something). Then she went to clean her hands. The canvas gave off a smell of paint as strong as blood; Kate felt unexpectedly faint as if she had in fact gnawed off her own foot.

Gio stood up to go. Politely he glanced at her painting. He had seen the beginning of it, but not the end. He seemed perturbed at what she had done. He didn't exactly say she had ruined it, but she could see that he was disappointed: he had expected something he could take home to his mother. His mother would never approve of a painting in which Mother and Child looked like tigers. "*Madonna mia!*" exclaimed Gio Vittore. "What've you done to your picture?"

"Changed it," said Kate succinctly.

"You did. I see that." He looked embarrassed. He obviously wanted to say something admiring, but his innate honesty forced him to be silent. Finally he said, "It's scary."

She smiled her gratitude. "Good!" she said, and went to wash her hands.

"You *want* to scare people?"

She was very happy; she could not explain it to him, nor perhaps to anybody, but she was very happy. "Oh yes," she said blithely. "Scare 'em to death!"

He was silent a long time. A soft, plaintive sound emerged from his throat. He said with dignity: "You're laughing at me. That's not *right*."

She looked into his eyes which were a rich hazel. When he flushed anxiously the color suffused his skin like the throats of pigeons in the sunlight. Kate shook her head in denial: *no, no, she was not laughing, it was no laughing matter.*

He rose to go. He waved goodbye to the baby who only looked at him, her eyes luminous with satisfaction.

Kate walked her new neighbor to the door. She stood and watched him as he went, a frail manly boy in working clothes, his hands in his pockets, his shoulders curved slightly against the wind. She felt again the desire to cry: instead she went back into the house to prepare dinner; there was a lot to do before she would have time to paint again. But she did not put away her easel and paints or hide the brushes flowering in the mason jar before Yasha and Jacob K. came home. She left it all out for them to see.

Photo by Steve Hennings

Natalie Petesch was born in Detroit and attended public schools. She attended Wayne State University, eventually received her B.S. from Boston University, an M.A. from Brandeis, and Ph.D. from the University of Texas at Austin.

In 1974 her short story collection, AFTER THE FIRST DEATH, THERE IS NO OTHER, won the University of Iowa School of Letters Award for Short Fiction. She received the 1976 *Kansas Quarterly* Fiction Award and in 1978 First Prize in *The Louisville Review* Competition. Among her anthologized short stories, several have been cited for Honorable Mention in Martha Foley collections of BEST AMERICAN SHORT STORIES. Her story, "Main Street Morning" was in Solotaroff's BEST AMERICAN SHORT STORIES OF 1978. In 1978 *New Letters* published her novels, *The Leprosarium* and *The Long Hot Summers of Yasha K.* as *A New Letters Summer Prize Book*, soon to be released in hardback by Swallow Press as SEASONS SUCH AS THESE. In 1979-80 Les Editions des Autres (Paris) will publish a French translation of her novel, THE GRIEVANCE ADJUSTER. She recently completed a novel about the Vietnam era and is working on a new collection of short stories.

Ms Petesch taught English in universities in Texas and California. She now resides in Pittsburgh, Pa. and was recently appointed Consultant in Literature to the Pennsylvania Council on the Arts.